SHADES
of US

SHADES
of US

D.L. SIMS

wattpad books **W**

wattpad books **W**

An imprint of Wattpad WEBTOON Book Group

Copyright© 2024 D. L. Sims

All rights reserved.

No portion of this publication may be reproduced or transmitted, in any form or by any means, without the express written permission of the copyright holders.

Published in Canada by Wattpad WEBTOON Book Group, a division of Wattpad WEBTOON Studios, Inc.

36 Wellington Street E., Suite 200, Toronto, ON M5E 1C7 Canada

www.wattpad.com

First Wattpad Books edition: December 2024

ISBN 978-1-99834-153-5 (Trade Paper original)
ISBN 978-1-99885-459-2 (eBook edition)

Names, characters, places, and incidents featured in this publication are either the product of the author's imagination or are used fictitiously. Any resemblance to actual persons (living or dead), events, institutions, or locales, without satiric intent, is coincidental.

Wattpad Books, Wattpad WEBTOON Book Group, and associated logos are trademarks and/or registered trademarks of Wattpad WEBTOON Studios, Inc. and/or its affiliates. Wattpad and associated logos are trademarks and/or registered trademarks of Wattpad Corp.

Library and Archives Canada Cataloguing in Publication information is available upon request.

151302999

Cover design by Amelia Schiffer
Images © lfH via Shutterstock

This book is for every cake-loving ace person who has always wished to see a little bit of themselves in a story like I have.

Chapter 1

I stand in the middle of the common room of my new home, Jupiter Hall. Around me, families bustle in and out of the dorm with boxes or kiss each other goodbye. To my left, a resident advisor gives a family instructions in Spanish. On my right, students are sitting on the large sectional and getting to know each other. An air hockey table stands at an angle to the couch, and two small children are playing with the puck; their parents seem to be nowhere in sight.

This is *not* how I was supposed to start the new chapter of my life. My high school boyfriend, enji, was supposed to be here. My parents are supposed to be crying about how I'm a man now. Nana couldn't get the time off to drive two and a half hours to the college. And after a huge fight with my best friend, Alan, I've felt like I have been on my own since the middle of April. Being this alone makes me very confused, pissed off, and sad.

God, I'm so fucking sad.

The building is newly built and was donated by a former Westbrook star student, Marcos Jupiter, Pittsburgh's resident Bruce Wayne. The dorm is a modern marvel made of glass, stone, and steel that doesn't fit in with the ivy-covered bricks and columns that adorn the rest of the campus. The building is minimalist and sleek, or as I like to call it, sterile.

A buzzing comes from my right. I turn and see a girl my age with light-brown skin and curly hair that's been pulled into a ponytail. She's wearing retro cat's-eye sunglasses, ripped jeans, and a BTS shirt. I pull my headphones from my ears. The sounds of Coldplay fade, and the person's voice intrudes.

"—Westbrook alone?"

"I'm sorry? I missed the beginning of that."

"Did you come to Westbrook alone?" she asks again.

How do I tell her?

How am I supposed to tell her that in just four and a half months I have lost everything? How do I tell this complete stranger that my boyfriend abandoned me to attend college on the other side of the country, my parents are gone, and my best friend thinks I'm a complete asshole? The only person I have now is my nana; she's the only person who has stuck by my side through all of the bullshit. How do I tell this girl that the reason I chose to go to this school is to escape the hell that I've had to endure since April?

"My parents went here."

The girl pulls her sunglasses off, revealing dark-brown eyes. "A legacy. Cool."

"I don't know about that. My parents weren't exactly the type of people their professors would remember. They listened to music and smoked pot in their dorms while barely scraping by."

"Sounds like my kind of people. I'm Amy, by the way."

"Jesse."

"Where are you from, Jesse?"

"Plainsburg. It's about two hours to the west."

"No way! Me too! Don't tell me you're a Lincoln Lion!"

"Cut me and I bleed yellow and black." I cringe at my own joke and tug on the long sleeves that I've started wearing even in the dead of summer, making sure they hide my scars. "I take it you went to Ford."

Amy fist pumps the air. "Blue and green, baby!"

I make a mock disgusted face. "Our sworn enemies."

"Move, nerds," comes a gruff voice, cutting off her retort. Behind Amy is a solid wall of muscle carrying a box labeled AMY'S SHIT.

"Don't mind my brother. Too much testosterone has shrunk his brain cells."

Amy's brother balances the box in one hand to flip her off with the other as he heads to the elevator. As I watch him leave, my gaze catches on a bulletin board listing clubs and events happening around campus. Taking over a large chunk of the bulletin board is a poster for the photography club; I make a mental note to check it out before I head upstairs to find my room.

"Well, I should probably go before Geoffery gives me more shit." Amy punches my arm lightly. "Nice to meet you, Lincoln."

As she leaves, I pull out the paper with my room assignment. Room 205. Roommate: Tobias Washington. The paper should say Benjamin Caine. A ping tweaks in my chest. Does Benji miss me as much as I miss him?

I can't take care of you anymore. Will those words ever stop hurting?

Once I dig out my phone from my pocket, I check the message thread I have with Alan and type out a quick text.

Made it 2 WU.

I can see Alan read the message and wait for another minute to see if there's a reply, but nothing. I sigh, sliding my phone back into my pocket.

I was the one who caused this rift, so I can't blame Alan for the silent treatment. The sadness and anger created a monster inside of me that turned me into something ugly and unrecognizable, and that monster pushed Alan away. The only time I heard from Alan after our falling-out was when he told Nana about becoming prom king and told her to relay the news to me. Alan couldn't even be bothered to share something as big as being voted prom king with the person who had been his best friend for eight years, and that hurt more than I will ever admit. I thought that we would have worked things out by now. We've fought plenty of times over the course of our friendship, but we always made up. This time feels different, and that's what scares me, but I still have hope that we can reconcile.

The breakup with Benji is my fault too, but I refuse to go down that road. There's no hope for mending that wound, so why even think about it? It's better to shut the lid on that can of worms, padlock it, and store it in a cupboard in my mind.

After stopping by the bulletin board to look at the clubs and getting distracted by a poster advertising a band called Poisonous Winter, I finally head to the elevator to meet my new roommate.

When I step out of the elevator, the second floor already smells like ramen noodles and weed. The door to Room 205 is open, with a family of eight crammed inside the small space. A set of twins are jumping on a bed that is made up with blue sheets and an orange comforter. Three more children jump on a plain white mattress on the other side of the room. A girl in her early teens sits at a desk, clutching an alien plushie and watching the oldest sibling hook up a PS5. The mother organizes books on one of the small shelves above the desk across from the orange-and-blue bed.

"Court, I can do that," the oldest says.

"Don't be silly, Toby."

Toby shakes his head at the woman and ties up his long dreads using a hair tie from around his wrist. "If you insist."

"Y'all better stop jumping on the beds. I'm going to count to three." The mother turns and sees me in the doorway. She pauses with a copy of *Moby Dick* in her hands. "Hello!" She greets me in a heavy Southern accent.

All seven children turn. The five youngest stop jumping on the beds, and Toby stands, crossing the room.

"What's up? I'm Toby." He has freckles that dot the bridge of his nose and his cheeks. His light-brown eyes twinkle with something that I can't quite put my finger on—a sort of charm that makes him seem mischievous.

"Jesse."

"Hi, Jesse." Toby's mom puts the book away and stands behind her son. "I'm Courtney." Courtney has beauty marks all over her dark face, and her head is buzzed. "I made Toby cookies before coming; please help yourself." She gestures to a tin next to the elbow of the teenage girl, who is munching on one.

"Mommy, I have to pee," one of the younger siblings says.

"All right, come on, Arina."

"Your mom seems nice," I say as Courtney leaves with the child. I begin unloading my backpack on the empty bed.

"Stepmom," Toby corrects. "That's my mom." He gestures to the corkboard on his side of the room, where pictures of his family have been pinned up with star-shaped thumbtacks. In the left corner is a picture of a Filipina woman holding her pregnant belly. She's smiling up at whoever is taking the photo. "She left when I was seven."

I can't believe how casual Toby sounds about his mom leaving him when he was a child. Will there ever be a time when I'll sound the same when talking about my parents? Right now it seems impossible. The loss of them is still too new.

"Tobias." A warm voice comes from the doorway.

A tall, broad man stands in the hallway. His shiny bald head reflects the hall's lights. His suit seems expensive. He's a bit darker than Toby but has the same light-brown eyes.

"Daddy!" The other children jump up and hug the man. Toby squeezes in last, informing his father that Courtney has taken Arina to the bathroom. Their father looks over his children's heads at me.

"Hello, I'm Lee."

"Nice to meet you, sir. I'm Jesse."

Lee turns his attention back to his children, greeting them fondly as they all talk over one another. The love the family has is so palpable. My lungs begin to constrict, making me feel like I can't breathe. My hand flies to my chest, and I sink onto my mattress. My eyes squeeze shut as I try hard to catch my breath.

A hand lands on my shoulder. "You okay, dude?" Toby asks.

"I'm fine," I lie.

Breathe, Jesse. Breathe. In. Out.

Squeezing my eyes tighter, I turn my whole body from Toby's family. I don't want to see their concern, their pity. But I can feel it. One of the children asks their parents what's wrong with me.

The answer: everything.

"Do you need anything, Jesse? Water?" Courtney asks.

I shake my head.

"Do you want me to call one of the RAs?" Toby asks.

"No. Please. Just . . ." *Just leave me alone.*

There's a pause, and then Lee speaks again. "Toby, we'll be at the car. Come say goodbye. Call us if you two need anything."

It's not until I hear the door click closed that I open my eyes again. It's just me and Toby. Toby's hand is still on my shoulder; he's bent down in front of me, looking up at me with patience.

I reach for the headphones that I discarded on the bed, turning on my playlist but keeping it low so I can still hear Toby. The music begins to soothe me.

"Are you sure you're okay?"

Dumping all my problems on Toby doesn't sound like a great way to start off our new roommate-ship, so I simply nod and shake off whatever the hell feelings and anxiety just happened. I nod toward the PlayStation. "What games did you bring?"

Toby heads to the stack of boxes on his side of the room. He flings the lid off of one and digs through it, contents spilling over the rim: collectible figures, headphones, framed pictures of his family, a small bi pride flag. He pulls out four games.

"Courtney said I couldn't bring them all. My collection wouldn't fit in here." Toby throws the games on my bed, and I pick them up to look through them. *Mortal Kombat*, *God of War*, *Grand Theft Auto*, and *Call of Duty*. The essentials.

Toby notices the bi flag that has fallen out of the box. "Courtney must have put that in there. You don't mind if I hang it, do you?"

"Considering I'm part of the community as well, I'm going to say probably not."

"You're a bit of a smart-ass, huh?"

"You can blame my mom for that."

"Good. We'll get along just fine." Toby tells me that he's going to say goodbye to his family. "We can play something when I get back."

"Sounds good."

"Are you sure you're okay?"

I brush off Toby's concern with a nod. As the door shuts behind him, I crank up my playlist, find my favorite song, lie back on my bare mattress, and close my eyes. Maybe coming to college right after leaving SunnySide was a mistake, but it's too late now. Not only that, but I need this change. Since leaving SunnySide, I have done nothing but watch TV, attend therapy, and hang out with Nana. I was rotting away in Plainsburg. I just want to feel alive again.

Chapter 2

After two hours of playing *Mortal Kombat*, Toby and I leave our room to explore the campus. Westbrook University has large, lush grounds that are filled with trees, grass, and flowers. The brick buildings are historic, some dating back to the early 1900s. The beauty of the campus is inspiring, and since I left my camera in the dorm, I pull out my phone to take pictures. The campus isn't large, so it only takes about ten minutes to walk from our dorm to the center of campus. We stop at the edge of the large duck pond in the middle of the grounds; we find a bench and sink down onto it, watching as kids, college students, and parents feed the birds and fish.

"You're from Austin?" I ask, picking up our earlier conversation.

"Born and raised." Toby pulls out his phone, showing me pictures of the city. I have only been to three states in my entire life: New York, Pennsylvania, and New Jersey. The idea of traveling anywhere that isn't on the East Coast is appealing, but based on the pictures Toby is showing me, Austin seems colorful and vibrant and not like the type of place I would like to visit.

Toby pauses when he gets to a picture of himself standing next to a blond girl with large brown eyes. They're wearing cowboy hats, and she's snuggling into the face of a horse. "This is Madison. My girlfriend."

"She stayed in Texas?"

"She's in California for school. She and my friend Chaz got scholarships there, so at least she knows someone, you know?"

California. That's where Alan went to study filmmaking. Shaking off thoughts of my best friend, I ask, "Why didn't you go with her?"

Toby shrugs. "Westbrook has the best creative writing program in the country. This is where Malcolm Parks, Charlotte Mulroney, and Brett Cables went to school."

"Am I supposed to know who those people are?"

Toby shoves my shoulder, causing me to laugh. "They're great American authors. Think modern-day Austen, Wilde, or Stevenson."

"And I'm supposed to know who they are, right?"

"You really are a smart-ass." Toby pulls out a small baggie of Courtney's cookies from his pocket. They're crushed, but he doesn't seem to mind. "What are you here for?"

"I came to Freemont because I grew up hearing stories about Westbrook from my parents. They loved it here." Tears begin to burn in my eyes. I look away from Toby and out at the pond. Across the water, there's a familiar-looking oak. My parents have several photographs of them sitting under that tree when they were students here. "You see that tree?"

"Yeah."

"My parents had their first kiss there. My dad proposed to my mom under that tree."

"They died," Toby guesses.

A tear slides down my cheek, and I roughly brush it away. "Drunk driver."

"How long ago?"

The sun suddenly feels too bright, and I squeeze my eyes shut.

The world seems too big and too small all at once. More tears flow down my cheeks, and I let them. What's the point of trying to stop them now? The silence stretches. Toby reaches out, squeezing my arm in an attempt to comfort me.

"You don't have to tell me about it," Toby says.

"I'm . . . I'm not ready."

"No pressure. If you ever feel like talking about it, just know I'm here."

The chains clipped to my belt loops jingle as I pull my knees up and hug them to my chest, crying and wishing I brought my headphones. Music is the only thing that calms my mind when it's fuzzy and too full of thoughts.

Toby rests a hand on my elbow, and I distract myself by looking at his fingernails. They're short and jagged as if he chews on them. Mine are painted black, expect for the pinkies, which are purple—Mom's favorite color.

We sit in silence for a long time, looking out at the water.

"Fuck, I need coffee," I say when the tears stop flowing and I feel human enough to move.

Toby stands, brushing off the butt of his black basketball shorts. "Come on. There's a café in Rosenberg Hall."

Toby offers me cookie crumbs, and we munch on them as we walk to the building.

The café is on the third floor of the building and has several tables in front of a small checkout counter. There are a few more tables out on a balcony that overlooks the campus. We order our drinks: black coffee with sugar and a hazelnut latte.

After we claim a table on the balcony, Toby leans forward, tipping his chair back on two legs to look over the railing. "How far up do you think we are?"

On instinct I reach out, trying to pull Toby back by his bicep. "Far enough that if you fell right now you could seriously injure yourself."

He looks at me with a smirk. His honey eyes spark with mischief before he settles back on the four legs of his chair. He sips his latte, looking out at the tall brick buildings.

"We should explore the town tomorrow."

"I have to check in with my new boss at Wendell's Donuts, but maybe after."

Toby tips his head, resting it against his hand. "You really like taking pictures, huh?"

"I want to be a photographer."

"Of hot models?" Toby wiggles his eyebrows.

"Of nature, smarty. My dream is to one day have my pictures in a magazine like *National Geographic*."

"Does anyone still read that?"

"Maybe not, but it's still my dream."

"That's awesome."

The song on the speakers ends, and a DJ comes on. "You're listening to WU Radio. We just played 'Forever You' by Poisonous Winter. If you have a song request, text the Westbrook Radio cell phone or go to the radio's website. Now let's do a throwback with Blink-182."

Toby stands. "Come on."

"Where are we going?"

"Bookstore." Toby throws his cup in the trash and heads back inside, holding the door open for me.

"Why are we going to the bookstore? Classes don't start until Monday."

"The announcement on the radio reminded me of when I

toured the campus last spring." Toby reaches the elevator before me and pushes the button. "The tour guide kept going on and on about this local band called Poisonous Winter. Apparently they have a bunch of merch in the bookstore, and I'm curious to see what all the hype is about."

Chasing a band is *not* what I had in mind for my first semester at college, but to be fair, who would have thought this was something that would happen? I'm not going to protest too much. I love discovering new music. What else would I be doing on a Friday afternoon? Plus, I promised my nana I would make friends, and Toby seems cool.

The bookstore is predictably empty when we arrive. Everyone has either already bought books online or is waiting for class to start before buying them. There is one bookstore associate, with bright pink hair and a crescent moon tattooed on their temple. They barely look up from their copy of *The Hobbit* when we enter.

The store is laid out with school merchandise taking up most of the front and a huge display of Poisonous Winter items to the left near the windows. All the bookshelves are in the back and categorized by subject. The store is brightly lit with wooden floors that creak when someone walks over them.

"The band members are students here," Toby explains as we walk toward the display. "The lead singer and the bassist are the dean of students' kids."

I bump my shoulder against Toby's teasingly. "You seem to know a lot about them. Are you sure you're not a fan already?"

"Shut up, man."

Toby heads to the shirts while I peer into a bin of posters. A plaque next to the bin says that all the money from sales goes back into helping the community of Freemont. There are five band members in total, and their names are stamped below their faces on one of the posters: Sebastian and Shelby Winter, Mahara Adabi, Zack Cameron, and Abel Ryan. They all look way too cool and intimidating to be playing bars and gigs in Freemont, Pennsylvania.

"You gonna buy anything?"

Expecting to see the associate who was reading *The Hobbit*, I turn with a polite smile, but instead it's Shelby Winter. Her hair is long and blond and shaved on one side with the buzzed part dyed pink. Her eyes are vivid blue and rimmed in eyeliner, and her lips are dark and glossy. She's wearing beat-up combat boots and a simple black dress with a jean jacket covered in patches and studs.

"I don't know," I reply, putting the poster I was holding back in the bin.

"You don't like giving back to the community?" Shelby tilts her head. It's hard to gauge whether she's joking or serious.

"Of course I do, but I've never heard you play."

"Newbie?" Shelby finally smiles. "Come to the party at Beta Kappa Zeta tonight. You can decide for yourself if our merch is worth buying."

Shelby looks at me in a way that feels like she's studying me. What does she see? Probably a short, unimpressive guy who hides beneath beanies and hoodies and has no idea who he is. That's what I see when I look in the mirror anyway.

"What's your name?"

"Jesse Lancaster."

"Well, Jesse Lancaster, I hope to see you tonight." Shelby looks over his shoulder, waves her fingers at Toby, and exits.

Toby rushes over. "What the hell just happened?"

"I think we were just invited to a party."

"Oh, hell yeah!"

"No. Not hell yeah." The idea of being in a room full of people I don't know is not my idea of a good time. "The thought of it is already giving me hives."

Toby squeezes my shoulder lightly. "We don't have to go if you don't want to."

Toby really wants to go. The excitement is written all over his face. This is what people come to college for, right? Partying? Making friends? Experiencing new things? I promised Nana I wouldn't be a recluse this semester, and I'm taking pills for my anxiety. Everything should be fine.

You can do this, Lancaster.

"If we go, do you promise not to leave my side?"

Toby crosses his heart. "Scout's honor."

"You did that wrong." Toby's blunder releases the last of the tension in my chest.

"How do you know?"

"I was in the Scouts."

"Of course you were." Concern furrows Toby's eyebrows. "Are you sure you're going to be okay?"

"I'll be good. Just promise you won't leave."

Toby places a hand on my other shoulder and gives me the most serious look he can muster. "I promise, dude. You and I are going to be stuck together like glue." He takes his hands from my shoulders and presses his palms together, pretending he can't get them apart. "You and me. We're gonna be *tight*."

I shove him away with a laugh. "God, with you as my roommate this is going to be a long semester."

Chapter 3

"I'm going to throw up." I bend forward, hands on my knees. I took a pill to help the anxiety, but either it hasn't kicked in yet or I needed to take more. I'm freaking the fuck out, and my fight-or-flight response is telling me to run for the hills.

Toby's hand comes down on my back, causing me to jerk slightly as he starts rubbing between my shoulder blades. He squats down next to me so I can see him. I focus on looking into Toby's honey-brown irises, at the way one of his dreads hangs in his face, the smattering of freckles and the small scar on his cheek, distracting myself from my jumbled thoughts.

"We can go back to the dorm if you don't want to do this."

Ahead, the frat house looms like a huge Colonial-style beast. Greek letters hang above the door, and the Westbrook flag swings in the breeze. People spill out onto the porch and front lawn. Nana's voice pushes inside my head, telling me that meeting new people is good for the soul.

Nausea churns my stomach again.

"I didn't used to be like this," I explain to Toby with my head still between my knees. My beanie is askew, and bits of brown hair are poking out from beneath the navy blue. I itch to fix it, but I can't until I get this wave of nausea under control. Dealing with social anxiety is nothing new to me, but since my parents died, my mental illnesses have amplified by ten. The static in my brain seems to constantly be there, and I can't figure out how to turn it off. "I'm sorry. I have depression and anxiety, and it's hard for me to be a functional human sometimes."

"No harm, Jess. I'll do whatever you want to do." Toby continues to stroke my back.

"Give me a moment." I breathe. In. Out. In. Out. After several moments, I inhale one last lungful of air and stand, steeling my nerves and fixing my beanie. The queasy feeling is still in the pit of my stomach, but it's more manageable. "Let's go."

"I knew you could do it!" Toby loops an arm over my shoulder as we walk up the lawn. Music echoes throughout the night, like a beacon calling all Westbrook coeds.

Upon entering the house, we're met with raucous laughter from a game of beer pong being played in the dining room. Bodies grind against one another in every room of the house. People make out in dark corners, hands slipping down pants or up shirts. We pass a line of glass doors that lead out to the backyard, where the pool has been filled with bubbles and people are splashing around in the soapy water. A stage is set up on the grass for Poisonous Winter to play, but at the moment a DJ is playing music.

This was a bad idea. I want so badly to tell Toby that we should leave, but I stay quiet. Toby wants to be here, and being here sounds a hell of a lot better than being alone with my thoughts.

"Let's get drinks!" Toby yells over the speakers that are blaring a Kid Cudi song. Toby leads me to a counter where different snacks and drinks have been set up. I grab a soda since I'm not supposed to drink with my meds. Besides, after everything that happened at the funeral, I've sworn off liquor. Being here reminds me of the only party I attended with Alan and Benji while in high school. Sometimes I swear I can still smell the puke in Alan's Camry.

The memories of Alan and Benji sour my mood slightly, but they're not going to ruin my night. Toby is talking about sports with some frat boys, and I have no interest in that conversation, so I decide to leave the kitchen before someone asks me who my favorite football team is. Amy's sitting on a couch in the living room. Her whole body is melted into the cushions like she's molded into the fabric. Her short skirt is riding up, dangerously close to revealing everything underneath. She rolls her head along the back as I approach. A slow smile creeps across her face upon seeing me.

"Lincoln."

"Ford." I pull off my flannel and drape it over her thighs to cover her. My arms are exposed in public for the first time in a long time, but hopefully everyone is too drunk to notice the scars. On the coffee table is a tray of brownies; I put two and two together as I sit down. "We a little high, Ford?"

"Very much so." Amy adjusts herself, leaning against my shoulder. She looks up as a shadow falls over us. "Who are you?"

"Toby," he says. "And you?"

"Amy Benson." She giggles. "You're hot."

"Thank you." Toby sits on my other side. "Ooh, brownies."

"Careful, Toby. They're pot brownies."

Toby pats my knee in a way that makes me feel like a small, innocent puppy. "I would expect nothing less." He picks up the middle piece and takes a huge bite.

I welcome the fact that my night will now consist of taking care of these two. Playing mother hen sounds better than aimlessly floating around an unknown place with unknown people. Having tasks is oddly comforting. When my mind is focused on something, it gives my thoughts less of a chance to wander.

"You made it!" Shelby sees us and beelines toward the couch. "I didn't think you guys would come! We go on soon. Make sure you get front-row seats, Jesse Lancaster," she snarks. "I want to make sure we blow your mind."

"You're not going to let me forget about this afternoon, are you?"

"Nope!"

"Shelbs!" someone calls. "Hurry up!"

Amy gives my flannel back as we stand to go to the backyard. I hurry to put it back on. Having my arms bare left me feeling too exposed.

A large crowd has already gathered around the stage in anticipation of Poisonous Winter's set when the three of us make it outside. Every other person seems to be wearing a Poisonous Winter shirt. Some girls are fawning over the drummer as he warms up on his drum kit.

From far away, it's hard to make out the details of the drummer's face, but there is an intense focus about him that is hard to look away from. He is zoned in on his task, his long black hair falling into his face as he taps on his snare.

Shit. The drummer has many, many tattoos, which just happen to be my biggest weakness.

We move toward the stage, quickly getting lost in the crowd that has amassed before the band.

"Hello, Westbrook! If you're new to campus or have been living under a rock for the past three years, we are Poisonous Winter!" the lead singer yells into the mic. He looks like Shelby with his blond hair but has a more laid-back style.

As soon as the singer finishes speaking, a guitar riff wails, echoing through the night sky. The keyboardist on the left of the stage plays with such intense ferocity that he reminds me a little of how Benji would get lost when practicing Bach or Chopin for his recitals. He would hate this band. He only ever listened to classical music (because of his parents) or pop, nothing in between. Benji was rigid about most things including never branching out music-wise. He and I were total opposites in that way: while Benji had just one or two artists he listened to, I'm interested in any genre and love discovering new music.

Across the stage from the keyboardist is Shelby. She's plucking her bass, standing back to back with a girl wearing a hijab who strums her guitar with her fingers flying over the strings. Sebastian's inviting voice carries over the crowd. The style of music Poisonous Winter plays reminds me of two early-2000s bands that Alan's older brother listened to: Panic! At the Disco and Paramore. The emotional lyrics of the song draw everyone in. They begin to invoke something inside me that feels too personal to be experiencing in a backyard full of strangers. The song is about a love lost—something I've had a lot of experience with.

Memories flash. Benji. The first boy I truly loved. The first breakup that left a scar on my heart that probably will never truly heal. Alan, my best friend of eight years who was just gone one day. My parents and their inability to see me graduate, to see me start college. The spiral of booze and a razor that led to SunnySide. Every single bad thing that has happened since the middle of April fills me up to the brim until it pours out and I can't breathe. But I don't want it to stop. Sebastian keeps singing, and when Shelby joins in, that's the final straw that makes the tears spill over. Her voice cuts me open, unleashing all the emotion I have been carrying.

Oddly, despite the lyrics, the song itself is upbeat. All around, people are jumping and dancing. I'm the only one standing still, crying in the middle of the backyard.

"Are you all right?" Amy asks.

I wipe my tears, flashing her a watery smile. "I'm fine. They're pretty good, huh?"

Toby and Amy share a look of concern but say nothing. People continue to scream and jump, and although I still feel cut open by the lyrics of the song, I join in on dancing too.

Chapter 4

After Poisonous Winter's set, I look for Shelby while still riding the high of their music and performance. One day, they're going to make it *big*. Anyone can tell they have passion for what they're doing, and they've worked hard to get where they are. It is also clear how loved they are by the students at Westbrook; all I've heard since arriving at the party is how wonderful of a band they are.

Shelby's standing at the drink table in the backyard when I find her. Her face is still sweaty from performing, and she's pouring herself a Jack and Coke.

"You've converted me!" I yell over the dance music that is blaring through the speakers once again. "I'm officially a Poisonous Winter stan!"

Shelby's eyes still sparkle with the adrenaline of playing a great show as she turns to me. "Told you! We're irresistible. Come and meet the others."

Shelby leads me through the mass of grinding coeds to a backyard set surrounding an empty fire pit. The band members are surrounded by fans, and they look very much like a famous rock group that has just stumbled upon a random college party. They all look at me quizzically as Shelby and I approach.

"You picked up another stray?" her brother asks, popping a handful of popcorn into his mouth. "Where did you find this one?"

"Bookstore! This is Jesse. We've made a PW believer out of him."

The attention from the band members causes me to blush. Where the hell are Toby and Amy? I don't want to endure this alone.

"How did you like the set?" Sebastian asks, placing a hand on Mahara's knee.

"It was so good." Ugh. *Really? You couldn't come up with something more interesting to say than, "It was so good"?*

Shelby nudges me playfully. "He's the president of our fan club now."

"Here, here!" Abel raises his cup in a playful cheers.

Up close, I can make out more details of his face, like the slight crookedness of his nose, as if it was broken at some point, and the way that one eyebrow is scarred. His long black hair falls to his shoulders, and he has the most *incredible* cheekbone structure and jawline I have ever seen. No wonder everyone was fawning over him while the band was playing. The man is fucking beautiful.

"That drumming was unreal!" Millions of questions for Abel flow through my mind: *How did you get into drumming? Do you want to be a musician after college? How long have you been drumming? Can you play other instruments?* But every single one of those questions leaves my brain as Abel's eyes meet mine. It's hard to look away from his beauty. A crush is quickly building, and for a moment I consider asking Abel for his number, but then the voice of reason intrudes.

We're not dating anyone this year, remember?

Right. The promise I made to myself when I left SunnySide and decided to attend Westbrook was to spend the year focusing on myself and my studies, not on romance.

Something over my shoulder catches Abel's attention before I can tear my gaze away from him to focus on the lemon soda in my hand.

"Thanks, man." Abel stands, clapping me on the shoulder. "See you around."

Behind me is a woman with bright purple hair. Abel kisses her cheek and hugs her tightly before taking her hand and leading her inside.

Figures.

"You're drooling," Shelby whispers in my ear.

"I am not!"

She laughs. "Abel's beyond hot, so I don't blame you."

"I wasn't even staring."

"Sure, buddy. Don't pout, at least you still have me to look at."

"Um . . . You're beautiful, but I'm gay."

"Cool. Me too."

At that moment, Toby and Amy reappear with drinks in hand. Toby's wobbling on his feet, and Amy's fighting to keep him vertical. I jump up to help her steady Toby.

"The frat boys made him do a keg stand and another round of beer pong," Amy explains. "I found him inside dancing and trying to take his shirt off."

"I was bullied!" Toby slurs.

"He participated willingly."

"I did not!"

Toby tries to down his drink, but I take the cup and hand it to Shelby.

"Time to go home, Toby."

"Yes, Dad." Toby tries to salute, but it's very sloppy.

"Do you have this?" Amy asks. "There's a very cute anime dude I was chatting up inside."

"Go. I got it."

Adjusting Toby so I have a better grip on him, I begin leading him through the party and out to the front lawn. Toby protests the entire way, claiming he's fine. The cool air feels refreshing as we begin walking down the sidewalk. Ahead is a group that is arguing about where they should eat.

"Did you have a good time?" Toby slurs, stumbling as they walk.

"You had enough fun for the both of us."

"I really did, huh?" Toby replies. He hums a Queen song for a few moments before coming to an abrupt stop and yelling, "I should call Madison!" His shouting causes the group ahead to turn back and stare. "I miss her!" He fumbles with his phone, but I snatch it before he can get it unlocked. "Hey! Give it back!"

"Maybe drunk-dialing your girlfriend at two in the morning isn't smart, so I'm going to hold on to this." I slip the phone into my pocket.

"Fucking rude." Toby pouts, sticking his tongue out. "Thanks for coming out. It was nice having my buddy with me."

Technically we're not buddies, considering we met less than twenty-four hours ago. I would call Toby an acquaintance if I had to pick a word other than *roommate*.

But since losing Alan and Benji, I've been so fucking lonely, and having a new friend sounds kind of nice.

Chapter 5

"Coffee!" Toby singsongs on Saturday morning.

This is not the way I would like to have woken up after a night of loud music and listening to Toby vomit into his trash can.

"Too loud," I grumble, rolling over in my small twin bed to face the wall.

The dorm is dark; the only light comes from a slit in the black-out curtains over the windows that I hung up before unpacking anything else. Sleep is now out of the question since Toby is being way too fucking chipper. I turn over again, glaring at him in the semi-darkness. He's sitting up in bed, stretching his neck and humming. I can *feel* him smiling.

"Coffee!"

He's the one that got drunk last night; why is he so fucking cheerful this morning?

"Of course they stuck me with a morning person." I sit up and head to the sink in the room to wash my face. "It's like the universe is playing a joke on me."

A pillow hits me square in the back as I bend over to turn on the water. The attack is followed by laughter. I flip Toby off.

We joke around as we get dressed and then head out to the café we visited yesterday. Toby bounces around, singing a song he made up about his love for "bean juice."

"You're ridiculous." I shake my head at him and keep walking.

"You love me."

"I don't even know you."

Toby stops. He tips his head to one side and then the other, studying me. He nods and says, "We're going to be besties, just wait."

Alan's face pops into my mind. Eight years of friendship down the drain because I couldn't handle the pity in his eyes when he visited me at SunnySide. Completely cutting him off was the only option my angry, grieving mind could think of at the time.

Yes, I'm an asshole. And I miss him every damn day.

I've lost count of how many times I've reached for my phone to call Alan. Our text thread is filled with my one-sided conversation, telling him about Westbrook, about the party and Abel Ryan's cheekbones. He's read every single message but has never replied. I'm longing to apologize for the black hole I spiraled into after my parents died, for the things I did and said when I was drunk and off my meds, for almost taking my life, and for my anger and my impulsive decision to tell Alan to fuck off. More than anything, I want to apologize for causing Alan so much pain.

"You okay, Jess?"

"Yeah, man."

Toby purses his lips as if he doesn't believe me, but he doesn't say anything. His silent presence makes me feel a little bit better, but I'm missing the piece of my heart that Alan once filled. It's right next to the hole that Benji occupied.

Don't think about Benji.

The coffee shop is packed when we arrive. People we met the night before at the party greet us with half-hearted, hungover nods and listless waves. Toby orders a latte, and I order a green tea and a water. The barista gives me a flirty smile, saying he likes my eyebrow and septum rings. He asks for my number, but I decline, explaining that I'm not really dating now. He looks dejected but shrugs off the rejection.

After we get our drinks, Toby and I find some overstuffed chairs on the first floor of Rosenberg Hall, just outside of the cafeteria. Toby kicks his feet up on the coffee table, blatantly ignoring the NO FEET ON THE TABLE sign.

"So," Toby says, taking a sip of his drink, "Shelby told me something interesting this morning."

"When did you and Shelby have time to talk?"

"She said she got my number from Amy. We exchanged numbers last night while you were flirting with Abel Ryan."

"I was not flirting."

"Anyway, Shelby and I talked for like twenty minutes before I gently woke you up this morning."

"Aggressively."

"Gently."

I pull out my tin of pills and motion for Toby to continue.

"Do you want to know what she said?"

"I'm on pins and needles."

Toby rolls his eyes. "She told me that Abel was asking about you."

I toss my pills in my mouth, washing them down with water. "Cool." Did that sound nonchalant enough? But my heartbeat ticks up, causing me to scowl into my tea. *No attachments, you dumbass organ.*

"Oh, come on! You were practically drooling over him last night."

"He's good-looking." I throw in a shrug for good measure, hopefully selling that I'm not like the other men and women drooling over Poisonous Winter's hot drummer.

"That he is. We're in college, now's the time to sow some wild oats. You should make a move."

Yes, making out with Abel Ryan would be a grand time, but I made a promise to myself, and I'm going to stick to it. Losing everything in such a short span of time has left me feeling like I'm floundering in the world. I went to group therapy when I was in SunnySide, and it helped to curb some of the anger and let me think a bit clearer, but there are still moments when I feel like I don't know who I am anymore. This year is about rediscovering myself, which led to the no-dating rule. Aside from all that—and the biggest reason for the rule—I already have one gaping hole in my chest from a romantic encounter. I don't need another one.

"Dating isn't on the table right now."

"Why not?"

"Benji." Just saying his name out loud hurts so fucking much. It's like a punch in the gut. "We were supposed to start college together." Toby's gaze is too focused on me; it makes me squirm. "We'd been dating since sophomore year. I loved him very much. He accepted a lot of the dark, weird parts of me that other people didn't understand, like my depression and anxiety. He was never upset when I had to cancel plans because my brain was being too much. He would hold my hand and calm me when the world was too loud."

Benji accepted and understood these parts of me, but he couldn't deal with the one part that was the hardest for me to figure out. That hurt more than anything. How could someone accept the raw, most terrible parts of me but not accept me being asexual? Why could Benji understand the buzzing in my brain but not that I had no desire to engage in penetrative sex? His inability to love me despite this made me feel more broken than I've ever felt.

I tug at the sleeves of my flannel, a nervous habit I picked up in SunnySide. "After my parents died, I—I wasn't in a good place. I pulled away from everyone, and I guess Benji couldn't take it anymore."

I expect to see pity in Toby's eyes, but it's not there. I'm not sure what to call Toby's expression, but he is really *listening* to my story. It's such a relief to know I can talk to my roommate like this and not feel judged. Toby listens to as I work through all the words jumbled inside my brain, giving me a platform to really let go and process.

"He came over a few months ago, right before I—" I shake my head. "He came over and said that he was moving to Oregon for school. He had been planning it for a while but could never bring himself to tell me. He told me that he had felt like my caregiver throughout our entire relationship. I never knew he felt like that, ya know?"

No one else should have to go through the shit I put Benji through.

"I'm an anxious, depressed mess, and I had been going through shit. Of course, he felt like my nurse or something." I pull off my beanie to run my hands through my chestnut hair. "It's a lot for someone to handle."

"He should have talked to you," Toby says. He pauses, considering his words. "What you went through would be rough on anyone, but you have depression and anxiety on top of that. I can see why and how those things would take over at the darkest time of your life. No one can blame you for that. He should have tried harder to understand you while you were grieving the loss of your parents." Toby shrugs, looking away as if he's embarrassed. "You seem like you're worth the effort, Jesse."

Heat creeps up my cheeks. *Am I worth the effort?* I don't think so, but the words are nice to hear. "Thanks, man." Silence falls between us; neither of us knows how to proceed. "This is awkward. Let's go check out the town."

Chapter 6

"That's all you have to do," Wendell of Wendell's Donuts explains as he shows me the proper way to work the ancient cash register. The 3 button gets stuck if the person operating it doesn't jam their finger into it hard enough to break a bone.

The shop is decorated in a 1950s diner style with shelves that encircle the top of the entire sitting area. Along the walls are red plastic booths that a person's legs stick to if they wear shorts. The floors are checkerboard with blue and white squares. There's 1950s and '60s music playing on the ancient jukebox in the corner.

Wendell himself is a grouchy seventy-year-old with a short gray beard and a handlebar mustache. He's been my grandfather's friend since their time in the navy. He lost his wife twenty years ago to breast cancer, and he opened Wendell's shortly after to keep himself busy. I'm used to Wendell's grouchiness, since the man was such a big part of my grandparents' lives and visited often while I was growing up. It's slightly refreshing that the old man hasn't softened since I last saw him two years ago at my grandfather's funeral.

"Got it, Scout?" Wendell asks, calling me by the nickname he gave me when I was five.

"I got it, Dell. Thanks."

The next three hours of my shift pass in a blur. Ringing people up and serving donuts and coffee makes time move quickly, since Wendell's is popular not only with the college students but with the rest of the townsfolk as well. There's no time to rest, and when it's time for a break, I welcome it.

Working at Wendell's isn't my first job, but it's more fast-paced than filing folders at Dad's car repair shop. Working at the garage, I was able to goof off with Dad's employees and watch TV on the small, ancient television set in the staff room for most of the afternoon.

"Grab a donut," Wendell tells me when he taps my shoulder to go on break. "You have twenty minutes."

I open the nearly empty case for a jelly filled, grab the second to last one, and then head back to the small cubbyhole next to the kitchen that Wendell calls the break room. Roger and Fran are bustling around in the kitchen, hurrying to fry more donuts to replace those that have been sold.

I sit on a rickety folding chair that is barely held together by sheer will and duct tape and tear into my donut, staining the sleeve of my gray sweatshirt with jelly. As I'm cleaning my sleeve, my phone vibrates in my pocket. My heart jumps to my throat as I pull it out to look at the screen. The incoming message is from Alan.

IDK if u care.

My video thing is 2wks frm now.

Let me no if u can make it.

After two months of talking to myself in our message thread, Alan has finally sent something. Elation buzzes through me like a live wire. There are so many things I want to talk to him about. I want to tell him all about being at Westbrook and meeting Amy and Toby, to send him Poisonous Winter songs to listen to, to ask if he has watched anything good recently. How does he like his new school? His classes started last week, and I want to know how they are going. Has he made any new friends?

Though there's so much I want to say, all I type back is:

Thank u. I'll B there.

About a week before my parents were killed by a drunk driver, Alan won the Plainsburg New Voices Award. His short movie—which Alan, Benji, I, and some of Alan's other friends had shot the summer before senior year—is being featured at Movie in the Park. His picture and a short article about his accomplishment were published in the *Plainsburg Gazette*—the same issue that carried my parents' obituaries. I still haven't read the article. I couldn't bring myself to buy a paper that day.

I was so proud of Alan when he got the letter saying that he had won. We celebrated with Benji at our favorite burger place and did everything Alan wanted to do, which consisted of skateboarding down Main Street, yelling to anyone who would listen about Alan's achievements, and asking his crush, Natalie, out. It's the last *good* memory I have of Alan and Benji. After that night, everything changed. Everything involving Alan and Benji after that became a thick, black, angry fog.

The phone buzzes again. Only one word fills the text box from Alan.

Cool.

Annoyed and sad that Alan didn't ask how things are going

at Westbrook, I scroll up to the first text I sent him after leaving SunnySide, informing him that I had left the center. I didn't apologize for my behavior when he'd visited me until a week later, and then all I said was "I'm sorry" and nothing more. As friends for eight years, we have never needed more than that in order to make up. Usually all we had to say when we fought was "I'm sorry" with no explanation and everything would be forgiven.

Maybe I should tell him I didn't mean all that shit I said. I should tell him I miss him.

Instead of saying any of that, I simply put my phone into my pocket and finish eating my donut.

Chapter 7

When I get back to the dorm after my shift, Shelby, Toby, and Amy are hanging out in the room. Toby and Amy are on his bed with a box of cheese and sausage pizza between them. Amy's lying on her stomach, kicking her fuzzy sock–clad feet lightly against the wall.

On the TV, a horror movie is playing, but Amy seems to be the only one invested. She jumps when one of the characters gets killed. Toby's playing on his phone, probably texting Madison. They talk constantly, and they were on the phone until four this morning, which kept me awake.

Shelby's on my bed, wrapped in my forest-green comforter. She's flipping through my copy of *The Picture of Dorian Gray*, one of my favorite books. I don't read much and only have three favorite books. They're the only books I brought to college with me.

"Sure. Make yourself at home, Shelby."

"I am. Thanks."

Apparently, Shelby was Amy's tour guide before school started, and they hit it off, bonding over BTS and their love for fashion. Shelby showed up an hour before I left for my shift at two, asking Toby and me if we wanted to get food at the cafeteria with her and Amy. It seems they have been hanging out for the four hours that I was gone.

"How was your first day of work, Lincoln?" Amy asks.

SHADES OF US

"Oh, great." I lift a purple box of donuts that didn't sell today. "I was gonna give you guys these, but you all have pizza, so . . ."

"Gimme!" Shelby swipes the box. She's wrestled the top open and has a cruller in her mouth all within the span of five seconds. "Are you going to bring donuts home every day? 'Cause if you are, you are my new best friend."

Toby and Amy scramble from his bed to dig in to the donuts while I change into sweats. Since there is no room on my own bed, I climb onto Toby's and bite into a slice of pizza. The smell of Toby's soap wafts up from the orange comforter and surrounds me, filling my nose with a soft, light, citrusy scent.

We're quiet for a few moments as we eat. Eventually, we turn off the horror movie and switch on YouTube videos.

Hours later, when the clock reads midnight, I turn to Toby and Shelby, who are sitting on my bed; Amy has moved to the floor, where she's leaning against a bed post and hugging her knees.

"Hey, Tobe?"

He looks over, still semi-distracted by the video playing.

I swallow and stall by sipping the soda Amy got for me from the vending machine on the first floor when she went to throw the pizza and donut boxes away.

Why is this so hard?

Toby turns his full attention to me. He waits patiently for me to untangle my thoughts. Amy and Shelby pause the video and turn toward me too.

"Would you maybe come with me to Plainsburg for Labor Day weekend?" *God, this is so stupid.* "There's this . . . thing I have to go to, and I don't want to go alone."

Toby's face falls. "I would, man, but Madison is coming that weekend."

"Oh. Okay." My heart hammers in my chest. I expected Toby to say no, but hearing it out loud is such a disappointment. "No worries."

"We'll go with you, Jess," Shelby offers. "Amy was just saying that her parents are already missing her."

"Really? Thank you."

Despite my even tone, I'm disheartened. Having Amy and Shelby come with me to Alan's movie premiere is great, but I realize that the person I really wanted to come with me was Toby.

Chapter 8

The first morning of classes is overcast with the smell of rain on the horizon. Summer doesn't officially end for another month, but the weather seems to agree that it's time for a break from the heat wave.

I itch to take my phone out of my pocket and call my mom as I walk the tree-lined paths to my first class. I want to tell her about Toby, Shelby, and Amy, about the party and seeing Poisonous Winter perform; she would have liked their music. When they were in school, Mom and Dad vandalized a wall with their names; I wish I could ask her where exactly they did it so I could find it. Mostly, I just want to tell her that I love and miss her.

College is hopefully going to be the something new after all the grief and heartbreak of the last few months. But my parents always linger in my memory, even when I'm doing the smallest tasks like playing video games or watching a movie. There really isn't a way to start anew when you've lost the most important people in your life.

My mood turns melancholic, causing me to pause. I tighten my grip on the strap of my backpack, mentally steeling myself, bricking up the wall in my mind so I can try to make it through the day. I focus on the music playing through my headphones; I've been listening to an EP by Poisonous Winter to learn more about their music. Let's not talk about how I pay particularly close attention to the drumming.

Inhale.

Exhale.

I'm a few minutes late to American literature, my first class of the day. Whoever decided this class should start at eight in the morning hates people, but the class is mandatory, and all the later slots were full. At least I've already read some of the books on the syllabus in high school and in SunnySide. There wasn't anything to do in there besides read and stare at the walls. I find a seat in the second row from the back. It's where I have sat in every class since ninth grade. If a student picks the last row, then teachers think you're lazy and will always pick on you, even if you don't raise your hand. If you pick the front row, then you look too eager, and teachers will assume you know everything. Always pick the middle. The second to last row is best; it says, "I'm willing to put in a mediocre amount of work. You can expect some Bs but mostly Cs from me, Teach." Being an average student is the most anyone should expect out of me; I've never been good at school.

As I slide into the empty seat and remove my headphones, my wallet chain scrapes against the plastic chair, disrupting the silence in the quiet room. The rest of the class turns to look at the person who dared to break the hushed atmosphere it seems they've all agreed upon. My ears immediately turn red.

"Sorry."

The girl next to me shoots a judgmental glare and pushes up her glasses. Ignoring her, I pull my laptop from my camo-print backpack. One of the stickers on my laptop is beginning to peel up, and I resist the urge to peel it off, even though the unglued corner is bugging me beyond belief. It's like an itch that won't go away until the problem is solved.

"Morning," says a familiar voice at the front of the room.

I look up from the offending sticker to see Abel Ryan settling in at the front desk. He sets his black backpack, with its sloppily drawn Poisonous Winter logo on the front, on the chair. "Professor Connelly is running a little late, so I will be going over the syllabus with you all."

My gut constricts at the sight of him. "What the fuck?" I didn't mean for that to actually come out of my mouth; I sink further into my chair.

The girl next to me cuts me another dirty look and sits up straighter as Abel begins walking around to pass out the syllabus.

She seems like a front-row sitter who has lost her way. This girl is going to be raising her hand a lot throughout the semester, bringing unwanted attention to my row and disrupting my precious system. Next class, I plan to sit as far away from her as possible.

"Are you our TA?" a guy in the front of the class asks.

"I'm not. Professor C is my mentor and asked me to do this favor for her. She'll be here soon."

It's hard to miss the reactions from the other students as Abel makes his way around the room. I hate that I'm also one of the ones gushing over the drummer. Abel's hair is up in a ponytail, but a few strands hang in front, dancing around his face as he walks. Despite the gloomy weather, he's wearing a white shirt that is thin enough that the colors of the tattoos on his torso and back peek through the fabric. His black jeans are ripped at the knees, showing off more tattoos on his legs. He has studs in his nose, lip, and eyebrow. As he gets closer, my cheeks heat, and I begin to fidget.

What the hell is wrong with me?

When he reaches my table, our eyes clash briefly. Abel smiles in a way that makes my stomach flip and my breath hitch. His eyes are so dark, I can't help but lose myself in them for a moment.

"Nice to see you again, Jesse."

I just nod. What are words? I don't know what those are anymore.

Abel hands me the syllabus and makes his way back to the front of the room, talking about what the class can expect from Professor Connelly. I hear only 25 percent of what Abel says; every time the guy comes near me, my brain begins to malfunction.

Error. Error. Cannot compute.

Professor Connelly arrives halfway through class. She's a tall, thin woman with a gray streak in her black hair. She reminds me of a lady from a clothing makeover show Nana would watch when I was younger.

"Sorry I'm late. My daughter threw up all over the back seat on the way to daycare this morning." She waves at Abel to finish whatever he was saying before she addresses the class. Once he finishes, she introduces herself.

Abel settles into a seat in the front row.

Professor Connelly pauses in telling us about how much she loves skiing to address him. "You can go now, Mr. Ryan."

"It's cool. I have nothing better to do until eleven anyway."

"Suit yourself."

Professor Connelly begins introducing the first book of the semester, *The Grapes of Wrath*. Since I read the book junior year of high school, I zone out during her summary of the novel. My eye catches on the sticker on my laptop again. The itch to peel it off is overwhelming, but I have to get a new sticker before I can, because the stickerless hole will bug me more than the slightly raised corner of this one.

Class ends with Professor Connelly telling us to read the first four chapters of *The Grapes of Wrath* by next class. Everyone gathers their notebooks and laptops. I stuff mine in my backpack and rush toward the door. Abel's at the front of the room talking to the professor. He smiles as I pass.

Sweet Jesus, he has dimples.

Reminding myself of the promise I made, I hurry out of the room.

No romance. No messy breakups. This year is for focusing on myself, friends, and school.

Yeah. Tell that to my fucking hormones.

Chapter 9

After my other classes, I return to my room long enough to drop off my backpack and grab a donut from the box I brought back from work yesterday. Toby has eaten all the good ones, and only chocolate is left.

Fucking yuck.

Twenty minutes later, I'm sitting in a chemistry lab, but not for chemistry (I'm trying to avoid that subject as much as possible). Westbrook University has several student-led clubs on campus, one of them being the Aro/Ace Alliance. It's held once a month in chem lab 104.

Before coming to college, I promised Nana that I would join one other club besides the photography club. Apparently, joining the photography club was, for me, "a fish going to water." The Aro/Ace Alliance is the only other club that piques my interest. Who knew a small-ass college like this would have a club dedicated to those who fall on the asexuality spectrum? One point for Westbrook.

There are only five people in the room besides me, and one of them is Zack Cameron, Poisonous Winter's quiet keyboard player. When I make eye contact with him, I have the urge to run. The only available seat is right next to him—the rest of the chairs are on top of the tables—so I make my way over to it. Zack brushes his brown hair out of his face and smiles at me shyly.

"Never seen anyone I know in here," Zack says, stretching his tall, lanky frame out under the table.

"To be fair, we only met on Friday night, so technically we're still strangers."

"That is fair. Have you met everyone?"

"Literally just walked in."

Zack ignores my sarcasm and begins pointing people out. He starts with a jock-looking guy and a brown-haired girl on his left. "That's Paxton and Marla. They're dating. She's ace, and Paxton is allo." He points to a guy with deep-brown skin and black hair. "That's Ali. He's aro like me, but also ace. I still bone from time to time."

My face scrunches at the word *bone*.

Last, he points to a woman with blond hair and freckles. "That's Holly. She's our president. She's demi."

They all greet me with a collective, "Hey."

My skin begins to crawl with the familiar *there are too many people looking at me* feeling. I kind of wish I brought my headphones. My hands are clammy, so I stick them under my thighs and smile nervously, hoping they turn their attention elsewhere, but they don't.

"I'm Jesse. I'm a freshman."

"Hi, Jesse," Holly says. "Welcome to Aro/Ace Alliance."

"Now we just shoot the shit for an hour," Zack says. One of his front teeth is crooked and overlaps the others. "Tell us about yourself."

"What do you want to know?"

"Where are you from?" Ali asks.

"I was born and raised in Plainsburg."

"Are you ace, aro, both, neither?" Zack asks.

"Asexual." I swallow. "I knew I was gay when I was like ten, but figuring out where I fall on the asexuality spectrum was a struggle. All my friends were having their first sexual experiences while we were in high school, but I never had that desire, and I started to think there was something wrong with me. I experimented with an ex and found that I do like some sensual and sexual things, but for the most part sex wasn't something that was important to me. It wasn't until about October of last year that I learned the term *asexual*. I read up on everything I could about being on the ace spectrum, found ace social media influencers and listened to their stories, and I finally felt something that clicked with what I was feeling."

"That's very similar to my journey," Marla says. "I was a freshman here when I finally realized who I was."

"What year are you in now?" I ask.

"I'm graduating in December."

We spend the next hour playing icebreaker games, and at the end I even exchange numbers with the members of the club and promise to meet up for ice cream over the weekend.

Nana would be proud that I'm not holing up in my dorm room watching reruns of *Dragon Ball Z*. I actually met people.

When I get back to my room, Toby is sitting at his desk working on the short story he has been writing for a year.

"How was your club meeting?" Toby asks, not looking up from his computer screen.

Toby doesn't know which club I joined. Three clubs met up today, so it's not like he could guess. I'm not sure why I didn't tell Toby about joining A/AA; it's not like he gives a shit about me enough to judge me for not finding sex fun, and after I changed the subject when he asked, he hasn't brought it up again.

"Good. They all seem cool."

"Do they? I'm still your best friend though, right?"

"We've only known each other for like three days."

"Best, fast friends."

"You're so weird. I'm going to take a shower."

Grabbing my towel and basket of shower stuff, I head to the bathroom that we share with the room next door. The neighbors keep leaving pee stains on the toilet, and I have half a mind to leave a note on their door telling them to be more considerate. If I can wipe up my drips then so can they.

I catch a glimpse of the mirror. It's still hard to look at myself; I'm afraid of what I will see in the reflection. My wavy brown hair is matted to my forehead from my beanie, my blue eyes have bags underneath, and the lone beauty mark on my cheek stands out starkly against my pale white skin. It's a healthier image than what appeared four months ago, but mirrors still make me uncomfortable. I turn away as quickly as I can.

As I strip out of my clothes, I look at the vertical three-inch lines that mar the skin of my arms. They were so deep that they needed stitches. Sometimes, when I close my eyes, I can still see the bloodstained tiles of Nana's bathroom, the razor I had bought from the hardware store the day before lying on the edge of the bathtub. Oddly, the dozens of horizontal scars on my thighs don't bother me as much as the two on my arms. Cutting my thighs was to either temporarily shut off the static in my brain or feel something — anything — other than numbing apathy. The scars on my arms are different. Weirdly, I don't feel shame when I look at them, I just don't want the reminder of the lowest point of my life, of the angry monster I was when I was off my meds and full of alcohol, seeing my parents in their caskets. I don't want to be reminded of Nana's face when she found me bleeding out on the bathroom floor.

I just wanted it to end, but Nana found me before that could happen.

If I keep thinking about this, then the darkness is going to settle in and take hold.

My phone vibrates on the back of the toilet. It's a message from Zack.

Abel asked me for your number.

Would you be cool with me giving it to him?

Unsure of what to say, I leave Zack on read and get into the shower. I really should tell him to not give Abel my number, but damn, when someone that attractive is equally interested, it makes it very tempting to tell the keyboardist yes.

Chapter 10

As I stroll across campus on Wednesday evening with my headphones blaring Queen and drowning out the world, I think about how proud Nana would be to learn that even though I have been living on campus for less than a week, I have already joined two clubs.

Once inside the art building, I find the room where the photography club is being held and settle into a chair at the back as the other students around me greet one another as if they have known each other since middle school. There's only one other freshman in the classroom, and the only reason I know her is because we have photography class together on Tuesdays and Thursdays. After ten minutes of mindless chit-chat, two guys stand up at the front of the room and introduce themselves as the president and vice president of the club, Craig and Greg.

"Welcome!" says Greg. "We meet every other week, work on projects, and talk about what we've been working on. You can ask each other for advice and help if needed."

Craig chimes in, informing everyone that our faculty advisor is Professor Hale, aka Wimbley. She is my favorite teacher so far. She's eccentric and blunt, and the class I had with her yesterday flew by.

We go around the room introducing ourselves. Excitement buzzes through me because I'm in a place where people share the same dreams and hobbies as me. In the last twenty minutes of the meeting, we are broken up into groups to begin discussing our first project. There are four groups of three, and I'm paired with a senior named Val and a sophomore name Kat.

The three of us decide to take pictures around the town of different historical buildings. Kat wants to use her graphic design skills to add fantastical elements to the buildings. It's something I've never done before, and the idea sounds interesting. Since the projects aren't graded, it seems like the perfect time to play with elements that I'm usually not comfortable with — all my photographs are rooted in real places and people in their everyday lives and settings.

At the end of the meeting, Craig and Greg dismiss us, and a girl with bright-blue hair runs up to my group. She's waiting for Kat. Apparently they're friends and have a class after the meeting.

"Hi!" The girl beams, turning her attention to me as Kat packs. "You're new, right?"

"Yeah. I'm Jesse."

"I'm Lenora. This is my second year. I hope you enjoy it! You're Shelb's new friend, huh? I saw you talking to her at the party on Friday night."

"You know Shelby?"

"She's my girlfriend! I'm sure we'll be seeing a lot of each other."

Kat finishes packing up her bag, and as they leave Lenora waves her fingers at me. "See you around, new friend."

After the meeting, I walk to one of the benches at the edge of the duck pond. The night is humid with a full moon. There are a lot of people out, most heading to the cafeteria for dinner. I pull out my phone to text Shelby.

Jesse: Guess who I just met

Shelby: There are 8 billion people on the planet. Just tell me.

Jesse: Cutie w/ blue hair goes by Lenora

Shelby: My gf?! Did you like her?

Jesse: She seems bubbly

Shelby: She's the best! I have to go, but I'm glad you met Lenora!

After texting Shelby, I text Nana, telling her about my night at photography club. She replies with two thumbs up. I really regret teaching her how to use emojis. The woman has stopped replying to my texts with actual words ever since.

Chapter 11

Even though I've been in therapy since I was twelve, and Doctor Hartland will be my third therapist, meeting a new doctor ramps up my anxiety. Even sitting in the back of the rideshare on the way to her office makes me all jittery and itchy, like I've had too much coffee or there're ants crawling all over my skin under my clothes.

Doctor Hartland's office is a small building on the other side of the city that shares a parking lot with a vet clinic. After I check in with the receptionist, who is a bit too jovial and smiley, I make my way to the sage-green chairs in the beige waiting room. The colors are supposed to be calming, but at the moment I feel like I'm going to vomit. After fifteen minutes, a voice calls my name from the other side of the room.

A red-haired woman stands in the doorway to the office. She's wearing a sensible pantsuit but has on a cactus-print button-up underneath the navy jacket. The cacti make me feel a bit better, like Doctor Hartland may not be as stuffy and analytical as I pictured her to be.

Her office is painted a soft cream with plants taking over one wall and books taking over another. In front of the bookcase sits a wooden desk with two plush chairs in front of it. Along the third wall is a love seat and another chair. The fourth wall is floor to ceiling windows that look out to the park across the street.

"I'm Doctor Hartland, but you can call me Morgan if that makes you feel more comfortable." Doctor Hartland sits in the velvet office chair behind her desk, while I stand in the middle of her office, feeling unsure of myself. "Please, sit wherever you like."

"What if I choose the floor?"

She laughs softly. "Then we can sit on the floor. It may take me a few tries to get down there, though."

I choose one of the chairs before her desk instead and nod to the picture of Doctor Hartlandwith a blond woman and a child. "Is that your family?"

"My wife and son, but let's talk about you."

"What do you want to know?"

"How have things been since leaving SunnySide?"

My fingers mindlessly play with my wallet chain, a soft tinkling sound filling the quiet room. "Tough, but not like *tough* tough, you know? Like it's hard, but I've been through worse. I started college last week."

"And how has that been?"

"It's been okay. I've made some new friends."

"That's good, Jesse!" She jots something down in a notebook in front of her. "And how was your first week of classes?"

"They're good. I really like my photography class."

"Yes, Doctor Herrera mentioned you liked taking pictures."

"You've been talking to Doctor Herrera?" It's then that I notice that my file is at her elbow. I can see my name in big, bold letters on the tab. "What did he say about me?"

"That you're a bright kid who has a lot to offer the world."

That's bullshit. I'm a fuckup. An orphan, a loser, a person who never excels at anything. How anyone could think I have a lot to offer the world is beyond me. I say none of this out loud. "You asked me how going back to school is. Honestly, it's fucking hard. Who the hell starts school three weeks after leaving an institution? Most times I think I made a mistake coming here, and other times I think it's what is best for me. I just need something new after what happened in April."

"College is supposed to be hard, Jesse. It's a time where you are truly on your own, trying to figure out who you are as a person and who you want to be as an adult. But it can also be a wonderful time in many people's lives. They make lifelong friends, fall in love—"

"I highly doubt I'm going to fall in love. I plan to study and graduate. I don't want to deal with anything complicated."

"Love doesn't always have to be complicated."

It is when you're asexual.

I shrug at her.

"You've made wonderful strides this week with making new friends, but don't be afraid to open yourself up to new experiences. New experiences are the ones that could possibly help you in your journey of healing and starting over, and that may even include falling in love."

"Sure, Doc." Sounds like a crock of shit to me.

We spend the rest of the time talking about college, my clubs, and my last phone call with Nana.

After the session, I have to hightail it to Wendell's. My bus is late, and by the time I make it back to the north side, I'm ten minutes late for my shift.

"Sorry!" I call out, swinging around the counter and hastily tying my red-and-white-striped apron around my waist. Luckily, the shop isn't that busy when I arrive.

"Don't let it happen again," Wendell says, handing over a plate with a chocolate glazed donut and a cup of coffee. "Take this to your friend over there. He's been waiting for you."

"Jess!" Toby yells from across the shop. "I came to say hi on my way to play basketball at the park, but Wendell said you weren't here yet."

A smile forms at seeing Toby. After the session with Doctor Hartland, seeing my roommate's bright, eager face makes me feel a bit lighter. "Should you be eating sugar and coffee before playing basketball?"

"There's always time for donuts and coffee, Jess." Toby takes a huge bite of his donut as if to prove a point. "Besides, it's not a game, just keeping my skills up until the season starts. Did I tell you I was recruited to come here because of my wicked talent?"

"Twice, actually. I'm sure you'll tell me a hundred more times before the year is over."

"A hundred and one."

"Of course you will."

"Jesse!" Wendell hisses. "Get your ass back behind the register, we got customers."

"Enjoy your donut, Tobe. Try not to get sick all over the field."

"You know it's called a court, Lancaster."

I shrug and walk away, laughing.

About an hour after Toby leaves, Abel walks in. My heart goes up into my throat. I'm trying hard to concentrate on the customer in front of me, but my eyes keep getting drawn to Abel. He's wearing an oversized black jacket with baggy black pants and a distressed black shirt. His hair is up in a ponytail, which just makes his cheekbones and jaw appear sharper.

"Welcome to Wendell's," I choke out when he gets up to the counter.

His dimples peek out. "Hi, Jesse."

"H-hi." *He's too fucking close. I can't breathe. Why the fuck does he look like that?*

"Shelby told me you worked here."

"Oh."

"I was wondering if you would like to go to breakfast tomorrow?"

Yes. Yes! I curse out my mind. It seems to have forgotten that going on dates with hot guys is not on the agenda.

"Oh . . . um . . . sorry, I can't. I have to read a bunch of chapters of *The Grapes of Wrath*. I'm already behind since I didn't read the first chapters assigned."

Lies. I've been keeping up with the reading no problem. In fact, I'm actually enjoying reading the book for a second time. I even answered a question Professor Connelly asked on Friday.

"Oh, shit. Maybe another time?"

"Maybe."

It's shocking how I can stand strong against Abel and his cheekbones. I have a weakness for attractive guys and would usually say yes when asked out, but somehow I managed to keep up my defenses against the hot drummer. Pretty sure that won't last long, though. If Abel keeps hanging around, it will only be a matter of time before I fold.

Chapter 12

Amy, Shelby, and I decide to take Amy's Sentra to Plainsburg, since it has more room than Shelby's Fiat. But I'm regretting that decision as Amy speeds twenty miles over the limit and cuts through traffic like we're in an action movie. With her behind the wheel, I'm going to either get whiplash or die.

"At this rate, we'll cut our time in half," Shelby jokes, playing with the dials on the radio.

Amy is a firm believer in the idea that whoever sits in the passenger seat remains in charge of road trip music, which means the last hour has been filled with America's Top 40 and Shelby turning the dial every thirty seconds.

I lie in the back seat with my head resting against my backpack while flipping through my battered copy of *One Flew Over the Cuckoo's Nest*, one of the three books I brought to Westbrook with me. When I'm feeling particularly good about myself, I like to pretend that I'm like Chief at the end of the book, breaking free and running across fields I haven't seen for a very long time. But most of the time I feel like McMurphy. Trapped and too aware of the world around me.

As Amy and Shelby agree on a station that's playing one of Benji's favorite songs, I pull my headphones from the side pocket of my backpack. Early in our relationship, I made Benji a playlist. The playlist had over twenty hours of music on it, but Benji found only a handful of songs he liked, and this was one of them. I still have it saved in my music library. The name of the playlist remains the same: *<3 BENJI <3.*

Scrolling through my music, I find The Cure, crank up the volume to drown out what's playing on the car's speakers, and then open *One Flew Over the Cuckoo's Nest* to a random page to begin reading. I've read the book so many times that my favorite passages are highlighted and tabbed.

Somewhere between reading and listening to The Cure, I fall asleep. "Boys Don't Cry" has always been a sort of lullaby; Mom used to play it during my nap times as a child.

"Yo, Lancaster," Shelby says, shaking my leg to wake me up. "We're here."

Pulling off my headphones, I sit up to look out the car window to see the city where I spent the first eighteen years of my life. I'm not sure why I expected Plainsburg to look different when I returned, but it's still the same. Everything is still small and simple. Though Freemont is also a small city, home feels even smaller.

"If I see anyone from high school, I'm going to get so much shit for hanging out with someone who went to Lincoln," Amy jokes as we pass by C+W's Burgers.

Benji, Alan, and I spent a lot of time at C+W's. We would always pick the back booth and then bullshit late into the night on Fridays and Saturdays. That was where Alan and I met for the first time when we were in fifth grade, and it was where we made up after our first big fight in ninth grade. Alan had discovered the self-inflicted cuts on my thighs and then told my parents. I had been so mad I hadn't talked to him for two weeks. We both cried and hugged in the booth by the restrooms until Clark kicked us out because they were closing. C+W's was where Benji and I had our first kiss.

I have to look away from the burger place. My chest feels too tight to breathe.

"You okay?" Shelby asks, glancing at me in the rearview mirror.

"Fine. Lots of memories." I close my eyes, focusing on the sound of the engine, the tapping of Shelby's nails on the dashboard, and Amy humming to the song playing softly on the radio.

Minutes later, we pull into the parking lot of Nana's condo. When we round the corner to the front of her building, Nana is jumping up and down, waving like a five-year-old with a huge smile on her face. She's made a sign with glitter that says: WELCOME HOME, BUG!!!

"That's your grandma?" Amy asks as she pulls into a spot. "I already love her."

We pile out of the car, and Nana is running across the crunchy, sun-scorched grass to smother me in a hug before I can even grab my backpack. "My Jess-bug!" She's crying. Her face is streaked with blue mascara. She pulls up the neck of her purple sweater to wipe her nose. "Oh, I'm so happy you're home!"

A small twinge of guilt churns in my gut seeing how excited Nana is to see me. She has always been so loving and gracious, especially after Mom and Dad died. She put her own grief aside to care for me, but I didn't allow her to visit me for the first month I was at SunnySide. She called every day while I was in there. For five weeks, she asked, "Can I see you this week?" and the answer was always no. It wasn't until I began to feel less angry that I was able to handle seeing anyone I loved, but by that time the only person around to visit me was Nana.

"Hi, Nana." My voice is so quiet that I'm not even sure she'll hear it.

Nana used to tell me that I was too mellow, but I would argue that she has enough excitement to power a whole city. She throws her arms around me, squeezing me in one of her signature bear hugs.

When Nana releases me, she turns her attention to Shelby and Amy. "You must be Amy!" She pulls Amy into a hug that is sure to crack a few ribs. "I'm so happy my Jess-bug has made friends so quickly." She pulls back to hug Shelby, never pausing in her words. "He's always been a shy boy, only really ever had Alan and Benji." She freezes at the mention of their names and glances at me. Their names cause my stomach to churn and my heart to squeeze, but I pretend I don't care. Maybe one day I won't feel a sharp pain in my chest when they're mentioned. When I don't immediately say anything, she prattles on. "Sweet boy, that Alan! He brought me seashells from California."

"He was here?" It hurts knowing that Alan has no problem visiting Nana but has not once texted since reminding me about Movie in the Park.

"Of course!" Nana takes my backpack and herds Amy, Shelby, and me into the building. "He was here last night. I'm sure he misses you."

I miss him so much that some days it's all I can think about. Why does no one tell you that having a falling-out with your best friend is actually more painful than a breakup?

Despite our telling her that we already ate before leaving Freemont, Nana forces us to eat chicken and dumplings. She regales us with all the gossip of our small city, and it turns out that she plays poker with Amy's grandfather on Friday nights.

It's after ten when Nana finally lets Amy and Shelby leave with their arms piled high with leftovers. They're staying at Amy's parents' place for the weekend, and her parents called twice to ask what their ETA is.

Nana's sitting in her chair when I come back from walking Amy and Shelby to the car. She smiles sleepily. "I'm so happy you're making friends at college, Jess-bug. I don't want you to be lonely."

"I'm never lonely, Nana. You know I tend to prefer my own company over that of others."

"You get that from your father. He was a bit of a lone wolf too." She points to the brown couch where I spent many days curled up in a ball and crying after the death of my parents. "Tell me about your classes, and I want to know more about this roommate. All you said was that he's nice. I want more details."

I sigh, sit on the couch, and indulge her curiosity about college and Toby.

It isn't until one in the morning that Nana stops asking questions and releases me to go to bed. The room I lived in after my parents passed has remained pretty unchanged. The picture of my parents still hangs on the wall near the closet, which is overflowing with my belongings from my bedroom at my old house. Mom is smiling at the camera while Dad is looking down at her like she's the most beautiful thing he has ever seen.

That's how I remember them—so in love that their worlds revolved solely around each other. Many people told me that their relationship was one that seemed to have come from storybooks.

"I miss you," I say to the photograph. "I miss you so much."

The rest of the walls are bare minus a video game poster that hangs over the bed. On one side of the room are tubs and boxes of my belongings that were never unpacked, and under a wall-mounted TV, my vinyl collection is bending the shelves. My PS4 and Switch sit on the shelves as well, collecting dust. I should take the Switch back with me so I can kick Toby's ass in *Mario Kart*.

I take a picture of the game to send to Toby.

Ready 4 Rainbow Rd?

After sending the message, I strip off my flannel and gray T-shirt, making a point to not look at my forearms, and go to the small dresser under the window to pull out some Batman pajama bottoms that I didn't take to Westbrook.

It's nearly two in the morning when I climb into my twin-sized bed. I don't expect Toby to text back until the next morning, but as I'm closing my eyes to sleep, my phone beeps.

You're so fucking on!

Chapter 13

After eating a breakfast of pancakes and coffee, I head to the bathroom to shower. The tiles were once white with small pink speckles, but after my *incident*—as Nana calls it—the white tiles have been replaced with green ones. The mint is kind of ugly, but I'm glad the white ones were removed while I was in SunnySide. I don't need the reminder of the night I tried to take my life. The scars on my arms are enough. Besides, Nana doesn't need to be reminded of that. She's the one who has to see this room every day. I wonder if it still affects her even though the bathroom doesn't look the same.

Once dressed in my hoodie and ripped jeans, I head out into the early morning and cut through the small park behind Nana's condo building that leads to the main part of town.

Being back in Plainsburg brings up too many memories. Everywhere I look, I see my parents. I see my life before everything went to shit. On Main Street are Dad's favorite bookstore and Mom's favorite boutique. Two streets over is the apartment where Benji's family lives, and fifteen minutes away is the lake where we spent spring break, our last big date before he ended things. Every weekend, Alan and I went to the movie theater, where we would let Nigel, one of the employees, decide what movie we would be seeing that day. Sometimes the movie would be so bad that the theater would be empty, allowing us to mess around and talk. Part of me wishes that I stayed in Freemont so I could avoid the trips down memory lane, but I want to support Alan even if things are still strained between us.

Besides, Doctor Hartland believes visiting Plainsburg could be healing in a way. She gave me homework: to write down the feelings I have about being home, which we are going to unpack in our next session. But I don't know what to write; everything is so jumbled with good and bad memories that I don't even know what to feel about this place anymore.

I should be taking a more active approach to trying to heal the cracks in my heart instead of hiding from the pain. A major part of healing is releasing some of the things I have lost in the last five months, but I'm terrified. I'm broken, and sometimes it feels like the trauma has become my whole identity. Getting rid of that pain feels like I would be letting go of myself — without this trauma, who would I be?

I've taken this same route to and from my parents' house so many times over the years I could navigate the path with my eyes closed. Even after their deaths, I would get drunk and go sit on the lawn of our house. The last time I was there, I fell asleep on the grass, and one of the neighbors called Nana to come get me. I haven't been to visit the house since leaving SunnySide. I can't bear to see the empty shell of my childhood when I'm sober—it's too much. I'm supposed to decide what to do with it, but I can't bring myself to think about that. With my permission, Nana sold all the furniture and other stuff that belonged to my parents. She put the money into an account for me to use after I graduate college. I plan to give it all to charity since I can't bring myself to spend it. Better to put it toward something good. Selling the house feels too final, like erasing my parents. For now, the house is staying in my possession, even though I have no plans to live in it. Ever.

I clear the park and come to a small alley behind a strip of stores. I head around the front and stop inside a coffee shop to order two lattes and an iced coffee. After getting the drinks, I pull my hood up and keep my head down, trying not to look at anything or anyone as I walk to the bus stop to get to Amy's house.

Amy's parents live in what Plainies call the Rich Hills. Most of Plainsburg is a flat strip of land that takes up thirty square miles, but one part of the city consists of several large hills where a development company built a dozen vast cookie-cutter houses that the upper-middle-class Plainies swept up before outsiders could claim the lots.

Amy's house is the smallest, at the base of one of the hills, but it is still a lot bigger than the house I grew up in. Just like every other house in the area, it's a mix of Colonial and American Craftsman. There's a willow tree in the front yard with a swing attached to one of its strong branches. It's all boringly quintessential.

A teenager in a orange shirt opens the door after I knock on it. He takes a bite of peanut butter sandwich before addressing me.

"I remember you. I almost ran you over with a box, right?"

"You did. I'm Jesse."

"Jeffrey. Amy's brother."

Behind him, Amy comes barreling out from somewhere. She pushes her brother out of the way. "You brought coffee! Bless you. My parents are tea drinkers, so there isn't a coffee maker anywhere in this house."

Amy leads me inside, where her family and Shelby are finishing up brunch. They all smile at me from around bites of eggs Benedict and fruit. Jeffrey sits on a stool at the island, and even though there is a spread of food on the dining room table, he slaps peanut butter between two more pieces of bread while he finishes his first sandwich.

"You must be Jesse." Amy's mom is short and plump with curly hair and green eyes that look even brighter against her dark skin. "We've heard so much about you."

"You too. Thank you so much for inviting me."

"Please," her father says, waving his hand at an empty chair. He's white with graying brown hair and dark eyes. His smile is easy and broad, an exact match to Amy's. "Sit. Grab a scone."

"Thank you." Despite having already eaten, I take a scone and a small portion of fruit. My father taught me to never turn down free food.

After brunch, Amy and I take Shelby around town. We visit some abandoned buildings on the outskirts of Plainsburg that I photographed for a project senior year. Amy takes us to her high school and shows us where she had her first kiss. We get burgers at C+W's and eat them on the sidewalk in front of the grocery store.

Amy and I spot people we grew up with and classmates that haven't left Plainsburg. Some people look at me with sympathy and what I believe is pity, even though it has been five months since my parents passed and my attempted suicide. That's one thing I hate about living in a small town: everyone knows everyone's business. I wish I could live somewhere like New York or LA. No one would know my name, and I could be just another face in the crowd.

At sunset, we head to Washington Park, which is packed for the screening of Alan's project. We find a small empty patch of grass to spread out the blanket. And this is the thing I love about small towns: when one of our own achieves something big, everyone turns up to celebrate and be supportive.

The town has gone all out—as they always do—for Movie in the Park. There are booths for food and carnival games lining the streets, and music is playing over speakers.

"This is amazing!" Shelby says, eyes wide and bright. "I want a churro!"

Once we find the churro tent, we also find Alan. I'm not surprised to see Alan in line here; churros are his favorite food.

"Al?" My voice wavers.

Alan turns, and I stifle my shock at how unfamiliar yet familiar he appears. Alan's blond hair is shorter. He used to keep his hair to his ears, but now it's styled with short, messy spikes. He's wearing glasses and has grown out his facial hair. Even though that has changed, there's familiarity in Alan's strong, athletic build, his Superman tee, and his steady blue eyes.

His returning smile is sheepish and unsure. "Jess."

Alan's arms are around me before I can blink. I hug him back so tight, fearing I'll collapse if we let go.

"I missed you," I whisper. It's not what I meant to say, but it's the only thing that comes out. "I'm so sorry."

Alan pulls back. In the multicolored lights of the food booth, tears glisten in his eyes. "Walk with me."

Alan leads me through the park, sidestepping people who are running around and laughing. Alan's quiet, and I'm beyond nervous. Neither of us knows where to begin.

"You look good, Jess. Better than the last time I saw you."

The last time Alan saw me, I had been at SunnySide for a week. There were still bandages on my arms, and I was just a shell of myself. Thinking about that time will send me into darkness, so I focus on the smell of fried food and the sound of music playing over the speakers while everyone waits for Alan's movie to start.

"I'm so sorry," I say again.

Just like that, the memories come. The constant drinking, going off my meds, ruining my parents' funeral, the darkness and the static in my brain that became too much to handle. The anger and lashing out at anyone who was nearby. Alan took on a lot at that time because he was always around, trying his hardest to help me in any way he could. After entering SunnySide, I just couldn't handle Alan's visit. I felt guilty for putting him in that position. I was so angry at myself for who I had become. Why the hell should Alan have had to sit through all that?

It was Alan's words—*Jess, what the hell did you do to yourself?*—that really set me off.

Get the fuck out of here, Alan! No one asked you to be here! GET OUT!

The nurses had to pull me out of the room, then I was confined to my own room until I calmed down. After that day, I took everyone off my visitors sheet. I couldn't bear the look in their eyes, the sad tone of their voices. At the time, I didn't think I deserved to be loved. I'm glad Benji didn't see me in that state. He had jumped ship a week before my parents died. He probably thinks he dodged a bullet by breaking up with me.

Alan tried to call me every day for a week after I lashed out at him, but I never took the calls. After a while, the only person who called was Nana. Alan gave up on me.

"I'm so fucking sorry, Alan."

"I'm sorry too. I should have replied to your messages sooner, but I was so mad. I was pissed that you pushed me away. It felt like eight years of friendship meant nothing to you."

"I was going through shit."

"I know how scary that must have been for you, but I was hurt, and part of me wanted you to hurt as bad as I did."

"Trust me. I was devastated." Tears burn my eyes.

"I'm sorry."

"I tried to get in contact with you again, but you always left me on read."

"I didn't want to say anything that would set you off again." Alan rubs the back of his neck. "I was afraid that if I said something wrong then I would lose you for good."

"You'll never *lose* me." I pull Alan into a hug, and we softly cry on each other's shoulders. "I'm glad you invited me here tonight."

"I wanted to see you."

"Are we good again?"

Alan sniffs and nods.

We continue walking in silence until Alan says, "Tell me about you. You seem *better.*"

"Most days are good, yeah, but I'm never going to be better."

Alan glances down at my long sleeves. The words that he said when he saw me in the hospital after getting stitched up run through my head.

Are you fucking kidding me, Jess? Suicide?

I just wanted the pain to stop. I don't want to feel anymore.

"I know," Alan says. "My mom explained it to me when you were diagnosed with depression in the eighth grade."

"Can we talk about something else? How's California?"

Alan wants to continue our talk, but he shifts topics, telling me about his life in LA. He's learning how to surf, and his classes are amazing. He has been talking to one of the girls in his scriptwriting class.

We fall back into the familiar groove of Alan rambling while I listen. Everything is still not completely resolved between us, but I have hope that we are on course for mending our broken friendship. The Alan-sized hole in my heart doesn't feel as big as it once did.

Chapter 14

On Labor Day morning, Shelby, Amy, and I have breakfast with Alan before he heads to the airport. Alan seems different than the last time we really hung out. He seems more driven and ambitious, like the rest of his family. The only time I saw him focus on something in high school was when he was filming short movies. Now that he's working toward his dream, Alan seems to have that intense determination all the time even when he's not working on his movies.

At breakfast, he mainly talks about his classes and a movie he has been writing to hopefully turn in as his final project at the end of the semester. He barely says anything to Shelby and Amy aside from asking what they are majoring in. People find that rude, but that's Alan. He has always been the talker in our group. I'm naturally quiet and don't mind when Alan rambles on and on about something. He tends to be a bit self-centered. It's never bothered me. The more we focus on him, the less we focus on me. It's part of the reason that our friendship works.

Shelby and Amy exchange a look as Alan goes on about himself.

What? I mouth at Amy.

She shakes her head, bending over her eggs and shoveling them in her mouth. Shelby is uncharacteristically quiet.

"Tell me about this Abel Ryan," Alan says around a mouthful of yogurt parfait.

After apologizing to each other, we spent the remaining time before the premiere of Alan's movie catching each other up as much as we could on our lives. Alan told me about his new friends, his classes, and the girl he's crushing on, who is named Heather. I was able to tell him about school, meeting Doctor Hartland, and how I'm hopelessly attracted to Abel Ryan. But before I could say anything else, the movie started, and Alan had to return to his family.

The rest of the weekend has been so busy for Alan that this is the only time for us to hang out again before we both leave the city.

"Well, he's in a band with Shelby."

Alan looks at her. Shelby sits with her elbows on the table and stares out the window of the restaurant. "You're in a band?"

"Yeah," she says, snapping back to the conversation. "Poisonous Winter. You should check us out. We have a YouTube channel."

"Definitely."

Shelby goes back to staring out the window. She has been weirdly quiet all morning, and it's starting to worry me.

"They're really good! Abel's the drummer."

For the next ten minutes, I tell Alan all about Abel Ryan and his cheekbones, with Amy and Shelby chiming in here and there to confirm that Abel is also interested in me.

I still don't believe it's true. I'm no one. The school is brimming with more interesting and better looking people than me. People literally line up to get with him . . . he could have his pick of any person in school, so why the fuck is he interested in me?

Shortly after, Alan has to leave to go back to California. He bids us goodbye and leaves money on the table to pay for his breakfast.

Once he's gone, I nudge Shelby with my shoe. "What's up with you? You're not as loud as usual."

Shelby sighs. "Lenora and I got in a big fight last night." Tears began building in her eyes. "She's mad that I don't have time for her because of PW."

I reach across the table to take her hand. Amy hugs her. "Talk to her when we get back. You'll work it out."

"Hopefully. I really like her."

Shelby's phone rings, and she slides out of the booth to answer. It's Lenora.

As she walks away, I turn to Amy. "What did you think of Alan?"

"Hmm. You guys seem really different. You hate sports, and he talked about football for twenty minutes while we waited for our table."

"Everyone has always said that." Even I sometimes wonder: if we hadn't met when we were kids, would Alan and I even be friends? "I don't know. He's just always been there for me."

"I'm glad you guys worked things out."

Making up with Alan feels like a huge step toward becoming this new version of myself. I needed to apologize to Alan so I could start healing. It's one of the things that caused the most turmoil, even more than the breakup with Benji.

Shelby returns, letting us know that she and Lenora plan to talk when we get back to Freemont. We pay and head out of the packed restaurant to Amy's car to drive the two and a half hours back to the dorms.

On the way back, I listen to Breaking Benjamin. Alan and I used to scream the lyrics at the top of our lungs while we drove around Plainsburg looking for something to do.

When we arrive back at Westbrook, I text Alan saying we've arrived safely. I don't expect Alan to reply right away, but he does. His flight to California has been delayed due to severe thunderstorms in Oklahoma, where he was supposed to catch his connecting flight.

Glad U made it.

Call U later.

It's been so long since I've gotten a reply from Alan, my heart jumps in my chest at the message. A sort of peace settles over me, like a large piece of a puzzle has been slotted back into my life.

>> <<

Toby and Madison exit the elevator as I enter the dorm. Toby introduces her to me, but they're in a rush, so I can't get anything out beyond a quick hello. Madison looks exactly how she does in the pictures on Toby's phone.

"Nice to meet you, Jesse!" she says in a heavy Texan accent.

Toby clasps my shoulder as they start to walk away. There's a hickey on his neck, and his smile is on full blast, nearly blinding me. It's evident how in love with Madison he is.

"I want to hear all about your weekend when I get back."

"Sure." I bid them goodbye and head up to my room.

Once inside, I set my backpack on my stained desk chair and sit on my bed. I should unpack, but that seems like a nonissue. There's a jittery feeling in my bones that I need to expel. Usually, after being around so many people for long periods of time I need to take a nap to recharge, but now I have this overwhelming urge to *move*. My leg is bouncing with this energy that is begging me to go, go, go.

I stand and turn on my laptop, finding the playlist of club and EDM music I made for one of Alan's parties. Most of the tracks are Steve Aoki because the girl Alan liked at the time was really into him.

I start jumping around the dorm room to the beat, throwing my hands and head around like I don't have a care in the world. The steady *thump thump* of the music drowns out everything I've had on my shoulders since April. It's only temporary. It will all come rushing back the second I'm alone with my thoughts.

The song switches, and I decide to unpack while I dance.

I keep expecting Toby to come back and find me jumping around the room, but hours pass, and he doesn't return. Eventually, I get too worn out to dance anymore and switch the music to Bon Iver. Despite it still being early, I change into my pajamas, climb into bed, and am asleep within ten minutes.

When I wake again, the room is black. My laptop is closed, and everything is quiet. Toby is snoring in his bed, and for some reason disappointment settles in my chest that I won't be able to talk to my roommate until the sun rises.

Chapter 15

The week passes in a blur; I feel like I blinked and it's Friday once again. Currently, I'm typing out a paper for European history that is due at midnight, but despite the tight deadline, Shelby has talked me into having dinner at the Poisonous Winter apartment.

Behind me, Toby's bouncing up and down on his knees on my bed, chanting, "Let's go! Let's go!"

Surprisingly, Shelby is sitting quietly on Toby's bed killing zombies in *Call of Duty*. She and Lenora broke up on Wednesday, and Shelby's been upset. It's part of the reason I even agreed to go to dinner. Hopefully being surrounded by all her friends will make her feel better.

She dies in the game again and huffs, "Are you ready yet?"

"No."

To drown out Toby and Shelby while I write, I turn up my playlist until I can no longer hear their voices. Two hours later, I send the paper off to my professor and turn to my friends. Toby's sitting on the floor with a can of Dr. Pepper balanced on his bony knee, and he's showing Shelby how to get past a difficult level in *The Evil Within*.

"I'm ready now."

They shush me.

"You guys were bugging me, and now you're telling me to shut up? Really?"

They ignore me.

Since they're obviously so engrossed in their game that we're not leaving anytime soon, I grab Toby's copy of *The Shining* from his shelf and begin reading where I left off. It's one of Toby's favorite books, and he was appalled to learn that I've never read it before. His head almost spun when I told him that outside of school, I've only read three books. It was hilarious.

After twenty minutes, Toby plucks the book out of my hand and tosses it on the desk. His big, goofy smile is fixed firmly in place.

"Ready?"

"Have been."

"What are you waiting for then?"

I punch his shoulder as Shelby leads us out to the hallway.

The evening air is crisp as we walk outside; autumn is definitely on the way. The seasons need to hurry up and change: I hate summer. Toby zips up his jacket and pulls his bucket hat even more over his ears, complaining about how it never gets cold in Texas.

"Just wait until winter comes," Shelby says. "You're going to be freezing your ass off."

"Great."

The band lives about fifteen minutes away in a historic building that has been converted into apartments. The walls are beautiful brick with white columns framing a blue front door. I pull out my phone and takes a picture, sending it to my photography club group so they can consider the location for our project.

The interior is simple: white walls with dark wood floors and an antique chandelier in the foyer where mailboxes line the wall.

"How the hell does a group of college kids afford a place like this?" Toby asks, his voice an octave higher than usual.

"Zack's dad owns the building."

My stomach begins to tighten with the slightly uncomfortable feeling of being in an unfamiliar place as we climb the stairs. Shelby looks back at me.

"Are you okay?"

Since I went back inside the dorm to get my headphones just in case being in the band's apartment got too overwhelming, Shelby keeps checking on me periodically. She's asked me at least ten times since we left the campus how I'm doing.

I nod stiffly. "It's not that bad."

Toby looks concerned. That look is the worst, especially when it's coming from him. "Are you sure?"

"I'm fine. Just keep going."

I pretend I don't see the look Shelby and Toby share. They don't need to babysit me, but they're asking because they care. It's still annoying. Not them caring but the fact that I need to be taken care of.

Why do I have to be so broken?

You're not broken, my mother's voice reminds me.

I scratch at an itch on my arm as we come to a stop in front of a door marked 3D. Toby stops my scratching by placing his hand over my fingers.

"Are you sure you're okay?" my roommate asks.

"I'm okay. It helps that I already kind of know everyone."

Shelby's leaning against a wall, watching me. "Can I ask . . . how do you handle restaurants and school? Sorry. That was rude. Forget I asked."

"When walking in public, crowded places, I use my headphones, and it helps if someone is there to hold my hand or something. Skin contact gives me something to ground myself to. There are other coping mechanisms for when I don't have music or someone with me."

I fixate on a splotch on the wall that looks like a top hat. I hate explaining how my mind works to people, especially those who don't have to deal with the same issues. They don't really *get* it.

"Going into people's homes for the first time is hard for me; it always has been. I used to cry when I was a kid and my mom would take me to a friend's house. I feel like I'm intruding on their space or disturbing the placement and flow of their personal items."

"I hope you come to feel welcomed in our apartment. You are not an intruder, and if you need *anything* just let us know."

"Thank you."

Inside the apartment, the walls are painted a soft yellow with movie and music posters that cover almost every inch of the living room. Near the front door is a corkboard filled with pictures of Poisonous Winter and their friends. In the middle of the board are ticket stubs from shows they've played up and down the East Coast. The TV isn't large, but next to it is a giant mishmash of different movies—an obvious collection of five different people.

Zack is sitting in a plush but clearly well-loved armchair. Mahara and Sebastian are on the couch watching *The Rocky Horror Picture Show*.

"Hey!" Abel exclaims as he walks down the hall. There's a chameleon resting on his shoulder. "You made it."

Toby surges forward, dragging me behind him as he stares adoringly at the reptile. "What's this little guy's name?"

Abel swings his long hair over the opposite shoulder to take the chameleon from its perch. "Napoleon. I've had him for about a year now. Present from an ex-girlfriend." His dark eyes cut to me. "How are you, Jesse?"

My throat suddenly feels like the Sahara. "I'm good. Great. Awesome."

I'm not usually the type to be drawn to people based off looks alone, but dammit did Abel Ryan alter something about my brain chemistry. I'm infatuated with the way Abel's hair falls around his face, the way his mouth tilts up on only one side when he smiles, the way his fingers look as he lets Napoleon walk along his hands.

The whole *being* of Abel Ryan piques my interest. Not in a "I want to have sex with him" way but in an "I want to know everything about him" way.

In the kitchen, an alarm goes off. Mahara gets up from the couch to check on dinner. Shelby follows her.

"Do you guys want a tour?" Abel asks, placing Napoleon back on his shoulder.

Toby shoots me a smirk. "Nope. I'm going to go watch the movie with Sebastian. I'm sure Jesse would love one, though."

Shelby watches me from the kitchen. It's then I realize this whole dinner was a way to trick me into being in the presence of Abel Ryan. Make new friends, they said . . .

"Tobias." I shoot my roommate a deadly glare.

"You got this."

"I hate you," I whisper.

Toby just shrugs and joins Sebastian on the couch.

"Lead the way." Hopefully Abel can't see how nervous I am to be left alone with him.

Abel leads me down the hall to the bedrooms. He tells me whose room is whose as we pass, but all the doors are closed.

"Of course, Shelby has her own," he says with a laugh.

"Hey! You guys don't call me a princess for nothing!" she yells from the kitchen.

When we get to the last room, Abel opens the door and gestures for me to go inside. "This is my and Zack's room."

All of Abel's confidence has slipped from his face. He suddenly looks shy and vulnerable. Unfortunately, his ears turning pink is adorable as hell.

Abel's side of the room is painted black and gray. The flag of New Mexico hangs over his bed like a yellow beacon in the darkness. On a paper in stylized lettering are the words *Hello* and *Goodbye*.

"Why hello and goodbye?" I ask.

"I was obsessed with Ouija boards when I was in high school." I cut him a look. Abel laughs. "They're the titles of two songs I wrote for the band."

"Can you sing them for me?"

"Maybe."

"Maybe?"

"I will if you give me your number."

My stomach flutters. For some reason, my brain is abnormally quiet and not reminding me about the rules I set for the semester. Against my better judgment, I say, "Sure."

Abel sits on the bed, leaving room on the mattress in an invitation for me to join him, but I remain standing. He hands me his phone to put in my contact info. When I hand the phone back, Abel sends me a message. He's sent me an emoji wearing sunglasses.

"Make sure you save my name so you don't forget who it is."

I won't forget.

Without answering, I continue my perusal of Abel's room. There's a signed K-pop poster on one wall above Napoleon's tank; next to it is a poster of Ghost. Near some shelves of books and knick-knacks is a black flag with Poisonous Winter's logo.

Zack's side of the room is painted gray and covered in posters as well. On the dresser is a cage holding a rat.

"That's Atticus," Abel says. "I don't think he likes Napoleon."

I shiver. "What's wrong with cats and dogs?"

"Mahara's allergic."

We're quiet for several moments. Abel's looking at me, but I'm making it a point not to look at the bed. My heart jumps in my chest at the closeness of him. I wonder if the drummer's hair is as soft as it looks.

I clear my throat. "Should we go see if the movie is over?"

"Sure."

Out in the living room, everyone's gathered around the coffee table. Shelby is sitting on the floor dealing out a game of Cards Against Humanity.

"Come on. We just started!"

I hurry toward Toby on the couch. "I freaking hate you."

Toby snorts. "You love me, Jay."

Jay? Though I'm startled by the new nickname, a smile forms. *Jay.*

I don't know why, but I like the sound of it.

After dinner, Toby and I head to Wendell's for late-night coffee and donuts. It's after seven-thirty, so the shop isn't busy. Fern, a single mother of twins, mans the register while Wendell is in the back.

Toby leans against the booth, completely relaxed. I envy his ability to be calm and comfortable in any situation.

My fingers are wrapped tightly around the handle of a chipped mug. Toby doesn't know that I gave my number to Abel, and I don't know if I should tell him about it yet. Toby will tease me for sure.

Besides, it won't be long until our whole friend group knows anyway. Abel told Zack about it at dinner.

"How was your *tour*?" Toby asks, curling his fingers into air quotes when he says "tour."

"That's all it was, Tobe. A tour."

He studies me, trying to gauge if I'm lying or not. I can't blame him for thinking I'm holding out. Toby's had to pry the smallest bits of information out of me for the past three weeks.

I would never admit this to his face, but Toby is my best friend right now. The friendship so far as been easy and uncomplicated. I'm more comfortable opening up to Toby than Doctor Hartland sometimes.

"Why didn't you guys do the no pants dance? I gave you the perfect opportunity."

There's one thing Toby still doesn't know about me; he still doesn't know that I'm on the ace spectrum. How do you explain that to someone when it's been only a year since you realized it yourself?

"Don't say 'no pants dance,'" I deflect.

"The horizontal tango." He pops a piece of donut in his mouth. "Doing two-person push-ups." He claps then rubs his hands together like he's smooshing something between them.

"Gross." I laugh. "Shut up."

"But seriously. He likes you, and you like him. What's the problem?"

"I don't want to date anyone right now."

I can't take care of you anymore. No matter how many times the words play in my head, they still hurt.

"Who said anything about dating? Just sleep with him. Do a friends with benefits situation."

I sigh and grip the mug tighter. "I'm asexual. Like, making out and some other stuff like hand jobs are cool or whatever, but I don't actually want to, like . . . do *it*."

As I wait for a bombardment of questions, I cringe. It took Benji months to realize that I wasn't faking the fact that I didn't want to have sex. Even after coming out, Benji would still try to get me to sleep with him. Benji never fully accepted me, even though he said he had.

Toby thinks for a long moment before saying, "Why don't you just give him a hand job then?"

Behind the counter, Fern snorts. Luckily, we're the only ones in the building, but it's allowing Toby's voice to carry in the empty space.

"I have a rule, Toby. This year I will not date or hook up with anyone. Just studying and friendship."

"That's the stupidest rule ever."

"Maybe, but it's what I told myself."

Toby narrows his eyes at me. "I see the way you look at Abel and the way he looks at you. If you can keep that promise, I will pay you fifty dollars at the end of the year. If you can't, you owe me fifty."

"You're so on." I feel oddly confident despite having exchanged numbers with the person who could make me lose this bet. "That fifty dollars is going to be mine."

Chapter 16

In the elevator after class, my phone dings with an incoming message from Abel. We've been talking since the night I left the PW apartment. The messages are innocent, friendly, but each one makes my heart jump to my throat. I reply to Abel's message asking how classes were, ask what he's doing that evening, and then return to listening to Peter Murphy.

The room is dark when I enter and smells like chocolate. Toby must have devoured another chocolate Pop-Tart before leaving. He's been obsessed with them lately. There's even an illegal toaster hidden under Toby's bed that he uses to warm them up when he's watching anime so he doesn't have to go down and use the community kitchenette.

I turn on the light and drop my backpack on the floor near my bed. There's a mint-green mug on my desk with a note leaning against it. The chocolate smell is coming from the cup: Toby made me a chocolate mug cake with cream cheese frosting.

"Freaking nerd," I whisper to the empty room.

Next to the mug is a small asexual flag pin and a note. I pick up the note and try to decipher Toby's messy scrawl.

I heard aces like cake.

So, here's one to remind you that you're valid.

Hope you like chocolate.

A dumb smile quickly spreads across my face. He seriously made me a fucking cake? Who does that? I fold the note and stick it in the drawer where I keep my pens, then I settle on the bed with my cake and boot up my Switch.

For some reason, my heart flutters at the gesture. I'm not going to think too much about what that means.

An hour later, Toby comes back from class. He's humming the theme song to Tokyo Ghoul as he drops his backpack on his bed. I give Toby a nod without looking up from my math homework. When the hell will I ever use any of this anyway?

"You got my cake." Toby hops on to my bed next to me.

I welcome the excuse to not look at equations anymore. Toby's playing with the pin, which I've added to my backpack. It means so much that Toby went out of his way for me like this.

"You're such a dork," I say. Toby turns on the TV and begins scrolling for something to watch. "Seriously, Tobe, thank you." I pause, searching for the words to express my gratitude while playing with a hole in the knee of my black jeans. "When I came out to Alan, he didn't really get what being ace means. He tried to be supportive, but he thought it was because I hadn't found the right guy."

"What did Benji say?"

"He thought I was lying and just didn't want to have sex with him."

Toby turns, tucking one leg under the other. He places a hand on my knee. I can feel the warmth of his touch through my jeans.

"Listen to me, Jay. You are fucking valid, okay?"

These are the same words I have been trying to tell myself for nearly nine months, but for some reason it doesn't connect in my brain.

I'm valid.

I'm valid.

When does it start to feel true?

"I fucking love you, man," Toby says.

I'm caught off guard by his words. "I love you too?"

"When I came out as bi in tenth grade, everyone gave me so much shit. They all thought I was gay but too scared to come out fully. I can't tell you how lost I felt. I was too gay for the cishet guys at my school but too straight for the out kids. It was especially hard since I played basketball. The guys on my team bullied me until they got chewed out by the coach, and even then they just hid what they were doing. People kept telling Madison to break up with me because it wouldn't be long until I cheated on her with a guy. It was awful. Trust me, I know how it feels to be an outsider."

"I didn't know that happened to you."

Toby shrugs. "It is what it is."

There's a sadness in his voice. Those days still affect him. I remember there was some trepidation the first day when Toby asked if hanging up his flag was okay, as if he was scared of what my response would be.

I take Toby's hand, which is still on my knee, and squeeze his fingers. "I'm going to tell you what you told me: you're fucking valid, Toby. Anyone who makes you doubt yourself is a fucking idiot."

Why is it easier to say, "You're valid" to someone else than it is to accept yourself? I'll admit, I'm little angry at myself for being this way. A part of me still blames my sexuality for Benji breaking up with me. Maybe if I had just kept it to myself and had sex with

Benji, we would still be together. Maybe if I wasn't ace I wouldn't feel so alone. I would feel less broken.

Toby blows out a puff of air. "This is too heavy after trying to stay awake in biology." He turns back toward the TV and resumes the video he was watching. "I say we spend the rest of the evening losing brain cells and watch something or play games."

"Yes, please." I hand him the half-eaten mug cake.

As Toby takes the cake, my phone dings with another incoming message from Abel. It's a picture of a lizard with a tiny hat. Underneath, Abel wrote:

Should I get one for Napoleon?

He wants to up his fashion game.

I snort and type back that Abel should get one in every color. Toby reads the messages over my shoulder.

"You may as well just give me that fifty dollars now," he says.

I nudge him. "Shut up. We're just friends."

"Mm-hmm."

Chapter 17

Amy hangs on my arm as we walk to the duck pond. It's finally officially fall, and clouds have rolled in to reflect the change in the season. Since everyone else is busy, Amy and I decided to do an impromptu photo shoot for my photography class.

Amy's dressed in a maroon skirt and a green velvet shirt. Her chunky boots have gold stars printed on them, and she keeps gushing over how cute they are. She borrowed them from Shelby for her date last night.

Thankfully, there aren't many people around even though it's Saturday. I can take Amy's pictures without having to skirt around a bunch of people or cutting people out when it's time to edit the photos. I place my beat-up camera bag on a bench and begin setting up my tripod while Amy buys duck food from the feeder.

"Tell me about the guy from last night," I say, putting my telephoto lens on my camera.

Amy finishes feeding the ducks and skips over to me with excitement. "He's *soooo* nice, like *too* nice. Have you ever dated a guy that was too nice?" She doesn't wait for a response before plowing on. "He took me to Bodie's, you know, the seafood place. Then we went back to his apartment and went all the way to pound town."

"Gross. Don't call it pound town."

Amy sticks her tongue out at me. "I'll spare you the details."

"Please do. Thank you."

"But it was a *good* night."

Once my camera is set up, I tell her to lean on a nearby tree. "Try not to be too aware of the camera. Rest your hand against the trunk lightly." She follows the instructions, but something still feels off as I look at the pictures, trying to figure out what is missing. "The lighting might be better over there. Let's try this tree instead."

She leans against a tree that's not being overshadowed by a building while looking off into the distance. The clouds above break up a bit, allowing the sun to peek through. The rays bring out the copper tones in her hair. She looks wistful, and it's exactly what I was hoping to capture.

"Perfect. Let's try some of you sitting. Here, hold this leaf."

I snap some pics of her posing with different props and some candid shots of her feeding the ducks and looking at the sky. She asks about Nana, and I tell her about how my grandmother has started teaching a baking class at the community center.

"Leave it to her to get a life after I leave town," I joke, but guilt sparks. Because I was too fragmented to take care of myself, she had to give up her life. Nana was once the highest scorer for her bowling league; she would knit blankets for those in need, and she volunteered for the city every weekend. When I moved into her condo, all of that stopped. Now she is able to get back to her hobbies.

"Jess! Amy!"

Abel runs down the path toward us. His long hair is braided, swinging behind him like a pendulum. He's wearing only black joggers and white tennis shoes. No shirt. His tattoos and toned chest are on full display.

"Damn," Amy says.

Damn is right. Shit.

"Hey, Abel." I put my camera in my bag as an excuse to look away from him and his exposed abs. My cheeks are heated, and my throat has suddenly become dry.

"What are you guys up to?"

"We're taking pictures for Jesse's class." Amy steps closer to Abel, smiling up at him. "Wanna join?"

Lord, help me.

I pray that Abel says no. If the person who constantly makes my heart somersault is around, then I won't be able to get anything done.

"Nah. Thanks, though." Abel gives his attention to me. I look away from him again so I don't get lost in the man's dimples. "I just wanted to ask Jesse out."

"Me?" My brain stutters to a stop. "Why?"

This is the first time someone has formally asked me out. My ninth-grade boyfriend kissed me during a game of spin the bottle at a birthday party, and then we were kissing every weekend, with a promise that I wouldn't tell a soul about what we were doing. With Benji, I learned about him liking me from a friend of a friend who told Alan, who then relayed the message to me. A week later, we were holding hands in the cafeteria and making out in the back of my dad's Mazda.

How should I respond? And what happens when he finds out I'm ace? It's well-known that Abel has slept with more people than I can count on my fingers and toes.

What if he expects me to be just another number in his repertoire? Fooling around with Abel would be fun, but I know myself. I would grow attached.

SHADES OF US

Not only that, but I still don't understand *why* Abel would even want to go out with me. There's nothing special about me.

"Jesse?" Abel says.

I shake my head, clearing my thoughts. "I'm sorry. What?"

"So, what do *you* say? Would you like to go on a date with me?"

"Yes!" The word doesn't leave my mouth.

I glare at Amy.

Abel shoots Amy an uneasy half smile before turning back to me. "What do you say?"

Can the world swallow me so I can avoid answering? I should tell him that I'm not looking to date right now, but the words that come out of my mouth are, "Sure. Sounds fun."

I would love to say that the only reason I agree is because it would be too awkward to refuse him after Amy already said yes, but there's something about Abel that draws me in, and I'm powerless to stop whatever it is.

Chapter 18

Toby's late, which makes me fidgety as Amy, Shelby, and I wait in line for snacks for the free movie night the school puts on every other Saturday. His tardiness adds to the nervousness that has been brewing inside since seeing Abel at the pond earlier. I still can't believe I said yes to being asked out by the campus rock god.

I'm so nervous to tell Toby about being asked out, but I don't know why. He'll be ecstatic to learn that there has been more progress with Abel and that he's one step closer to winning fifty dollars. But there's an underlying voice in my head that's screaming, *Don't tell him!* I have no idea why that voice is there. Honestly, I'm afraid of what it means. So it's best not to think about it too much.

"Jay!"

Everyone in line turns to stare at Toby. He's still wearing the jersey and shorts he wore to play basketball in the park near campus. His megawatt, ten-mile-wide smile is in place. Something in my stomach flips.

Stop. We can't go there.

Toby stands near us but off to the side. He's late, and a massive line has already formed, so he doesn't try to cut in. "Get me popcorn and a pickle. I'll go find seats."

My stomach flips again as Toby darts off.

We get our snacks and go look for Toby in the ballroom, where the school has set up a projector, a screen, and a hundred uncomfortable plastic chairs. When we find Toby, he's stretched out across four chairs, typing on his phone. He sits up as he spots us and snags the pickle and popcorn from me.

"Thanks, Jay."

Toby smells like sweat and his citrusy cologne. I forcibly direct my thoughts to pouring M&Ms into my popcorn.

"How was your day?" Toby asks, taking a bite of pickle and immediately following it with a handful of popcorn.

"Oh, Jess had a *very* good day." Amy laughs and winks.

I wish I was sitting next to her so I could elbow her.

Toby looks at me, but I don't meet his gaze. "Oh? What happened?"

"Abel asked me out." I tug on the sleeves of my hoodie.

"I'm not surprised."

"Abe was so excited when he came back earlier," Shelby chimes in unhelpfully.

Toby takes another bite of his pickle-popcorn combo. "What did you say?"

"He said yes!" Amy squeals.

"*You* said yes."

Amy flips me off.

"You're going?" Toby asks. I half shrug, half nod in response. "That's surprising."

"Why?"

"'Cause the last time we talked, you were dead set on not dating anyone." There's an edge to Toby's voice.

Why does he sound upset?

I can't explain how weak I am for Abel and his tattoos. Honestly, it sounds silly when I think about it. "It's like you said: I like him, and he likes me. So why not?"

"I'm just surprised is all."

Why does he sound so bothered by it?

"You're not getting those fifty bucks now," he tries to joke, but he looks away from me.

My chest constricts.

Amy and Shelby excuse themselves to the bathroom.

I stare at Toby's profile as he stares at the blank screen ahead. All around us, people are laughing and talking about the movie, but I barely hear any of it. All I see is Toby and the tightness around his mouth that shows he's clearly displeased.

"If that's what you want, Jesse, then I'm happy for you," he finally says.

There's definitely something wrong. Toby hasn't called me by my full name since our first day at the university.

"Toby, what's wrong?"

"Nothing." He takes another bite of his pickle. He still hasn't looked at me.

It's hard to get air into my lungs. The static in my brain is getting louder.

"Do you not want me to go out with Abel? You've been trying to push us together since that party."

"I'm fine. I want you to go. It's going to be great."

Why is Toby so upset? What changed? The lights turn off and the projector turns on, and the whole room falls silent as the opening credits start before I can ask him anything else.

After the movie, Toby and I say bye to Amy and Shelby and head back to our dorm. I want to talk more about the weird feeling between us, but Toby keeps talking about the movie.

I didn't pay attention to the movie at all. All I can focus on is how weird Toby is being.

Why?

Why?

Why?

The static in my brain is loud but manageable.

I play with the sleeves of my hoodie as we walk. It's calming me a bit.

"Can you believe they killed off the main character? What was that ending?"

Toby rants until we're back inside our room and changed into our pajamas.

"Toby, are you mad at me or something?"

Toby's on his bed, reaching for one of the five books he's reading. "Why would I be mad at you?"

"About Abel."

He freezes. "Just surprised. That's all."

"You're not mad."

"No," Toby says, but I feel like he's lying. "I promise." He yawns and puts his book back on his desk. "I'm tired. Night."

Before I can say anything else, Toby rolls over, facing away from me. I stare at him for a long time, unable to shake the feeling that something happened between us when Amy brought up me being asked out by Abel.

Why? What happened?

I'm probably overthinking. Telling myself this is the only way to quiet my staticky brain a bit and remember what Doctor Hartland told me: "Sometimes the reaction we *think* people are having is not what they are truly feeling. Sometimes when people say they're fine, they really do mean that they are fine."

Toby's fine.

It's fine.

I'm overthinking.

"Good night, Tobe."

After turning off the light and lying back down, I stare up at the ceiling. The conversation between me and Toby plays over and over in my head. What could I have possibly said that would cause Toby to react the way he did?

Chapter 19

I told Doctor Hartland about Abel asking me out during our session earlier today, and she reminded me how great it was that I've opened myself up to the prospect of dating. She reminded me of breathing techniques if I get too anxious throughout the night on our date tonight. We talked about taking things slow and allowing myself to be present in the moment with Abel, not letting my negative thoughts command me. Honestly, after talking to Doctor Hartland, I feel a little hopeful.

Toby lies on his bed reading manga. There's still tension between us, but neither of us has brought up the night of the movie since it happened.

"Are you sure I can't bring my headphones?" I ask, looking at myself in the full-length mirror attached to the bathroom door. I'm wearing my favorite black jeans, a maroon long-sleeved shirt, a denim jacket that's covered in a variety of patches and pins, and a pair of gray high-tops. The white shirt seems like a better choice, though.

"You can't take your headphones, Jay."

"You'll call me with an 'emergency' if I send you the code word, right?"

"Parsnip?" Toby doesn't look up from his book, but his lips curl at his own joke.

"No! Pineapple!"

Toby puts the book down and stands in front of me. "Jay, you're going to be fine. You don't need your headphones or code words. Just be your awesome self."

My mouth goes dry as I look into Toby's honey eyes. "I'm not awesome."

"Fine. Just be yourself, even if it's not awesome."

His response makes me laugh, calming me slightly.

Toby's phone rings. His face lights up when he looks at the screen. "Maddie! Hey!" He goes back to his bed with his phone pressed between his shoulder and his ear. "I miss you!"

My alarm goes off, signaling that it's time to leave. I'm meeting Abel at the library and want to make sure I'm there on time. Toby mouths, "Good luck" while Madison chatters in his ear.

I'm surprised to find Abel leaning against the light gray wall by the door when I step out of the elevator in the lobby. He's playing with his lip ring, looking nervous.

"Hey," he says when he sees me.

"H-hey. I thought we were meeting at the library."

"I finished my paper early and had some time, so I figured I should pick you up like a proper gentleman."

My stomach flips, and I bite the inside of my lip to keep from grinning. We fall into step side by side as we exit the building.

Abel is taller than me, which isn't much of a feat considering I'm only five-seven. He's the same height as Toby. I beat that thought back. No thinking about Toby. Not tonight.

The wind rustles Abel's ponytail. A black strand dances around his face.

"You're staring," Abel points out.

"Sorry."

"I didn't say I didn't like it."

I fight to keep my eyes on the quad and not stare at him, completely enthralled with the way the shadows dance across his face. Black lampposts line the pathways and bathe the area in soft yellow light. Leaves are starting to change colors on the trees, and the grass is browning in some spots on the lawns. Even though it's only five on a Saturday, the campus is deserted. It feels like Abel and I have stepped into a world of our own.

"Where are we going?"

"You'll see."

Abel leads me to a beat-up Tacoma with a tailgate covered in stickers in the library parking lot. He opens the passenger door so I can slide into the cab then goes around and gets in on the driver's side. As soon as he starts the engine, heavy guitar riffs blare through the speakers. He adjusts the dial so the guitar drops to the background.

"Sorry. I forgot I had the volume turned up that high."

The song switches to a slow, chill hip-hop song that I don't recognize.

"Weird," I say without meaning to.

"What's weird?"

"I never pictured you listening to stuff like this. Before I visited your house, I thought you only listened to rock."

Abel pulls out of the parking lot. "I like all music, regardless of genre."

"Me too! I'll listen to anything as long as it makes me feel something."

As Abel drives, we discuss our favorite singers, which helps me relax. We head into town, to a park where a festival is taking place. Booths and food trucks are set up, and a cover band is playing "Vienna" in the gazebo.

Abel climbs out of the truck and puts on a painted leather jacket over his Rob Zombie shirt. He rounds the vehicle to open the door for me. As we walk, my head swivels, trying to take in everything as we stroll between the white tents. The sun is setting, so vendors are turning on lights, and children laugh and scream as they run by shooting each other with toy guns. The smell of fried food makes my stomach rumble.

"This is the annual Apple Pie of My Eye Festival. Everyone from Freemont and the neighboring towns comes to celebrate fall's favorite fruit."

"Isn't fall's favorite fruit pumpkin?"

"Pumpkin is a squash."

"Whatever."

His warm chuckle does funny things to my insides that make me question why I ever thought going out with Abel Ryan was a bad idea.

"People bring their best apple pie for the mayor to judge. The winner gets a feature in the paper and bragging rights. Oh, and a ribbon. We missed the judging, but the night is my favorite part anyway."

"How often do you come to the town's festivals?"

"I love them, so I try to make it to every one. I've been coming since I moved here three years ago. We're set to play at the Fall Festival in October."

"I'll be there."

Abel looks away, ears turning red, and I feel a little proud of myself for making the drummer of Poisonous Winter shy.

We get in line for tickets, and Abel challenges me to ring toss. He wins three out of five rounds. We move through the games, and Abel wins most of them. On the last game, there's a stuffed blue

T-Rex that calls my name. Abel and I shoot balls at clown heads for three rounds, and Abel knocks down ten of them, which allows him to win a large prize. He asks the staff to get the T-Rex down.

Abel thrusts the blue animal at me. "For you."

"Really?" I ask, bouncing on my toes. My whole face lights up as I hug the T-Rex.

Abel leans down, whispering, "You're so cute."

"What's next?" My face flushes.

"Think you can beat me at ring toss again?"

"You're so on!"

Abel takes my hand as we find the booth. His fingers are warm and callused from playing the drums. My brain buzzes with so many feelings I'm not even sure what they all are; it's hard to focus on anything other than Abel's tattooed knuckles and the feeling of our intertwined fingers.

Chapter 20

"This better not become a thing," I complain, pulling my favorite gray-and-white hoodie over my head. "We've only been here for a month and a half and you've dragged me to two other parties already."

"Yeah," Toby replies, tying up his dreads, "but you survived."

I glare at him, but the look doesn't seem to faze him.

Doctor Hartland and my previous therapists have given me tools to help cope in social situations, such as counting to five while deep breathing and mentally preparing myself before entering the house. They have helped negate some of the social anxiety I feel when being in crowded places. Even so, I would still rather stay in the dorm and play video games or edit my photos for my photography club project. Mingling with people is exhausting.

"Ready?"

"No."

I kind of wish there was something I could force Toby to accompany me to so he could make up for dragging me to these parties. He needs to pay me back for sitting in the corner of a stranger's house, getting migraines from blaring music.

As we head out the door, Toby swings an arm over my shoulder. He smells different than usual, spicier, like there's pepper or something in the new cologne Madison sent him. I prefer the other cologne he usually wears.

"We won't be there long if that makes you feel better, and I promise to stay by your side the whole time."

"I appreciate it. Benji was a big party person, and like a dutiful boyfriend I would tag along, but he would always abandon me. I wouldn't see him again until it was time to go home."

"Please tell me I don't do that. You would tell me if I made you uncomfortable like that, right?"

"You don't."

Toby gets drunk, but he always stays where I can see him and periodically checks in to make sure we don't need to leave.

"Actually," I say, "you're pretty stuck to me like glue."

"I told you that you wouldn't be able to get rid of me that easy."

We arrive at the sorority house and enter a throng of people dancing to 90s music. The party is the same as the other parties we've been to. It's the same people, the same music, the same drama. I grab a soda and a stack of cookies from a table before heading to the couch, where Amy's sitting with some guy. I keep my distance from them, giving them their privacy as they flirt with their noses practically touching. She acknowledges me with a nod before suggesting that she and her date find somewhere more private.

"I'll be back," she whispers to me.

Toby, Shelby, and Abel find me. Abel's face lights up when he sees me, and it's fucking adorable. He sits on the arm of the couch at my side. The rest of the couch is fairly crowded, so when Toby sits on the other side of me, he's almost in my lap. I don't particularly *mind* that he's this close, with half of his ass on my thigh, but we're not going to explore what that means. Shelby leans against the wall, nursing a can of beer.

"You made it!" Abel says, leaning into me. "Do you want me to get you anything?"

"No." I'm feeling brave, so I put a hand on Abel's bicep. "Stay here."

He leans closer. I get lost a little bit in the smell of his cologne and his flowery shampoo and forget for a second that other people are around.

"How long until I can start bugging you guys to go home?" I ask.

"Two hours," Abel says. "And one dance with me."

Next to me, Toby's body tenses.

"Fine. *One* dance, but not to this. What the hell is this?"

"Techno? Country?"

"It's awful."

We talk for a bit, and Abel steals one of my cookies. After a while, the song changes to one that I actually know.

"If you want that dance, this is your only chance," I tell him.

Abel stands, holding out a hand. He smirks. "Sir, may I have the honor?"

There's a heat in my stomach that kind of makes me feel like I'm going to throw up but also makes me giddy. I follow Abel to where other couples are dancing in front of the large flat-screen TV mounted on the wall.

After putting my arms around Abel's neck, I slide my fingers up into his hair. It's just as soft and silky as it looks. His hands are on my waist, moving in motion with me swaying my hips.

"I didn't know you could move like this."

"I've had lessons," I joke.

Looking into Abel's deep brown eyes, the party seems to fade. My mind fills with this buzzing, but it's different from when I'm anxious. Instead of panic, I feel elated, excited. Abel pulls me closer, and my beath hitches. My body arches on its own, pushing into the man before me. Abel's eyes dart to my lips, which part under the attention.

"Can I kiss you?"

The buzzing in my brain grows louder. I hesitate for a moment, but then I nod.

Time slows as Abel bends toward me. Everything narrows until there's only Abel Ryan. All I hear is Abel's breath and my breath. All I feel is Abel's body against mine and my heart pounding in my chest.

His lips are soft and taste a bit like chocolate and beer. He kisses gentle and slow, like he's exploring my mouth, and I savor the way his lips feel against mine.

My heart hammers. We kiss at a languid, leisurely pace as if we have all the time in the world and nothing is going to end this moment.

Abel pulls back, places one more kiss on my lips, and then steps back completely. His hands are still on my waist, but there's space between us. I mourn the loss of his mouth on me.

More. I want more.

A slow smile creeps onto Abel's face, followed by his ears turning red. "Wow."

"Wow indeed." My heart is still beating double time.

The song ends and is followed by another techno-country-something that makes my ears bleed.

"Come with me outside?" Abel asks.

"Sure." I slide my hand into his, turning to tell Shelby and Toby where we're going. Shelby flashes a thumbs-up, but Toby looks away when my eyes meet his. He stands and walks away.

My heart plummets. *What's wrong with him?*

I don't have time to find out. Abel leads me in the opposite direction, past a spiral staircase and out onto the front porch. We sit on the steps, and Abel takes out a vape.

"Are you having fun?"

I nod, intertwining Abel's free hand with mine. I'd never admit this out loud, but the way our hands look together is starting to become an obsession of mine.

"We'll do something quiet and low-key for our next date."

"I've been wanting to rewatch *Lord of the Rings*. Maybe we could do a movie night?"

"Anything you like."

"And pizza."

"Is it even a date if there's not pizza involved?"

"Don't mock my love for pizza." I hit his arm with my free hand.

He laughs. "I wouldn't dare. It's one of the essential food groups."

We sit in silence for a moment as Abel vapes. The crisp breeze blows, ruffling his hair. "Shit. it's getting cold."

Without a word, I remove my beanie and place it over his head, covering his ears. "You southwestern folk really need to learn how to dress warmer. Where's your jacket?"

Abel's wearing a long-sleeved shirt and black pants with so many holes in them they shouldn't even really be called pants.

"Jackets? What are those?"

I roll my eyes.

"I never see you without one," he says to me. "Even when

school started, I remember you wearing a denim jacket on the first day."

"You remember what I wore?"

"Denim jacket, joggers, and a black shirt."

Amazing. I have no idea what Abel was wearing that day. All I remember is being enthralled with the way the classroom lights seemed to turn his black hair midnight blue.

Being next to Abel makes me feel so plain. Everywhere I go on campus, people gossip about Abel Ryan, the hot drummer. He is beyond popular; some people in the donut shop were talking about Abel and how their daughters had followed Poisonous Winter since the beginning. How am I supposed to compare to Freemont's drummer god?

"Can I ask you a question?"

Abel puts his vape back in his pocket and takes my hand again. "Shoot."

"Why do you like me?"

"Hmmm . . . It was your eyes that got me at first. They're kind. Plus you're cute. You're genuine and sarcastic. You're funny and seem to really care about the people who are in your circle."

His answer is unexpected and makes me shy. I look away from Abel out to the quiet street filled with cars.

He nudges me with his shoulder. "And you? What do you like about me?"

"Tattoos."

Abel snorts. "That's all?"

"That's what got me at first."

"And now?"

And now it's more than that. He's funny. He's smart. It's adorable watching his ears turn red when he's embarrassed and the way he plays with his lip ring when he's nervous. Despite his scary, punk-rock appearance, he's a gentle soul.

"Still the tattoos."

"In other words, you're not going to tell me?"

"Maybe one day." I stand, holding out a hand to Abel. "Ready to go back in?"

"Fine. I'll let you off the hook for now, Jesse Lancaster, but next time you have to tell me one thing you like about me."

"Deal."

Two hours later, Toby is too smashed to even stand. Shelby and Abel help me take him outside. The three of us barely make it to the front lawn without Toby falling over.

"I'm not going to be able to walk him to the dorm like this."

Abel helps lower Toby to the ground as he sings "Jingle Bells" loudly. "Do you want me to come with you?"

"No. It's okay. You have to meet Zack , right?"

"I do, but I can just text him that I'm going to be late."

"I'm going to go make sure Amy gets home okay," Shelby says and leaves.

After pulling out my phone, I order a rideshare. "They'll be here in five minutes. Go. We'll be fine."

Abel hesitates. "Are you sure?"

"Yes."

He leans forward, kissing my cheek. "Text me when you get to your room."

I salute him and push him lightly in the direction of his truck. As Abel walks away, I sink on to the grass next to Toby. He looks up at me all glassy-eyed.

"Y-you kissed Abel Ryan."

"I did."

"Why?"

"'Cause I like him." I so did not want to be having this conversation with Toby while he is drunk. "You thought it was a good idea if we went out."

"I didn't think . . . I didn't think . . ." He pauses, and confusion washes over his face. "I forget."

My heart squeezes at the sadness in Toby's voice. What the hell is it that Toby didn't think? Is starting something with Abel so wrong? Where is this guilt coming from?

The rideshare comes, and I push Toby into the back seat before sliding in. As the woman drives, Toby scoots closer until he's in the middle. Our hands touch, causing me to jolt at the sudden contact. Toby rests his head on my shoulder, and my throat goes dry. My heart squeezes.

The feelings that have been building over the past weeks come bubbling to the surface. The thoughts that I have been forcing myself to not think about take over. I have developed a stupid-ass crush on my roommate.

Chapter 21

"I should have stuck to my rule," I explain to Doctor Hartland at our session on Wednesday. I had to reschedule since I'm visiting Nana this weekend. "Things are getting complicated."

"We can't control our feelings. All we can do is make decisions based on them."

With a huff, I sink further into the chair. "And what the hell am I supposed to do about the fact that I currently have a crush on *two* guys at the same time?"

"You have several options. One, you can tell Toby how you feel—"

"No, thanks. He's got a girlfriend. It's not like my *feelings* for him can really go anywhere."

"Then decide what you want to do about Abel." Doctor Hartland sips her coffee. "You can either keep going down this path with him or you can end things with him."

That last suggestion is against the question. I *like* Abel. Even though I said I wanted to go back to my rule, there's no going back now. I want to give dating Abel a real chance.

"This sucks."

"Feelings are never easy. Remember what I keep telling you: focus on the things you can control. You can't control the fact that you have feelings for two people at the same time, but you can control how you respond to those feelings. Just make the right decision for yourself, whatever that may be."

SHADES OF US

I huff again.

The session ends with me just as confused as when I walked into the office. Doctor Hartland's to blame for this situation. She suggested I be open to new experiences, and look where it's got me.

>> <<

"Jay!" Toby calls from his car, which is parked three spots away, when they pick me up after my session. Shelby and Amy are in the back seat waving at me frantically. I head toward them, sliding into the passenger seat after I open the door.

"Hey."

"We brought your camera bag," Toby says, pointing to the back seat where my bag and tripod are between Amy and Shelby.

"And snacks!" Shelby shakes a bag of chips in my face.

"Gimme." I wrestle the bag from her hand and put a fistful in my mouth. "Yum. I haven't eaten since breakfast."

"Why not?" Concern laces Toby's voice.

"Been too busy. I had to meet with one of my professors after class because I couldn't get an article we needed to read to open on my laptop, and then I had to come straight here."

"There's a granola bar in my backpack." Toby reaches down, digging through the bag at my feet. He finds the bar and hands it to me. "Much healthier than chips."

"Thanks, man."

Toby reaches over, patting my knee in response. My pulse ticks up several beats.

We drive out to the woods on the outskirts of Freemont to take pictures. Once we reach the destination (a small camping area with a trail map and bathrooms), I set up my camera while Shelby adjusts her outfit.

She's dressed in a wide-brimmed hat and a black dress.

I didn't plan on spending my evening taking pictures of my friends, but they were bored and wanted something better to do than sitting in our dorm room watching reruns of old 2000s shows.

As I photograph Shelby, Amy and Toby sit on the hood of his car and talk about how Amy has sort of started seeing one of the basketball players on his team. Despite trying to tune them out, Toby's voice and laugh keep distracting me.

After I photograph Amy, it's Toby's turn. Toby's wearing one of my red-and-black flannel shirts, black ripped jeans, and tan boots. His dreads are tied back, showing his open and honest face with no obstructions. He looks too fucking good.

I wipe my sweaty palms on my sweats. "Ready?"

"What do I do?"

"Act natural. Pretend I'm not here."

Toby looks beyond nervous. I wish I had some words of encouragement to calm him, but since I'm just as nervous, my mind has drawn a blank.

Toby poses as I instruct, learning quickly what looks best. There's a moment where he looks directly at the camera as I line it up to take a picture, and his gaze sears into the lens. Into me. I stop shooting and lower the camera. Our eyes meet, and I'm enamored with the way the sun cuts across his brown skin and the way the flannel hugs his shoulders.

Toby chuckles, breaking whatever spell he's cast. "Are we done?"

"Not yet."

I raise the camera and snap ten more pictures. My favorite shot ends up being one of Toby when Amy calls him a camera hog and he looks behind the camera at her with his eyes full of amusement and sticks out his tongue.

Soon after that, his phone rings. He pulls it from his pocket and smiles softly.

Madison.

He answers with a cheerful, "Hey, Maddie! I miss you!"

I hate this jealousy I have of Madison. It's not like I deserve to feel this envious about their relationship. Madison and Toby have been dating since they were twelve.

Focus on Abel. You like him, he likes you. Easy-peasy.

As Toby talks, Amy and Shelby help me gather my camera equipment.

"Can we *please* go get coffee after this?" Amy complains. "It's been four hours since my last dose. I'm having withdrawal."

Toby laughs at something Madison says, catching my attention. He's pacing on the driver's side of the car as he talks on the phone. He laughs again. My gut clenches.

When will this feeling go away?

Chapter 22

"You must be Toby!" Nana exclaims as he and I exit his beat-up white car.

We have a four-day weekend that the school is calling fall break. Toby didn't want to stay in the dorm by himself all weekend, so he tagged along with me to visit Nana.

Toby runs to Nana and wraps her in his arms like they're life-long friends. She laughs and holds him in one of her rib-crushing hugs.

"Betraying me already!"

"Oh, hush, Jesse," she scolds, swatting at my arm before pulling me into her chest.

Nana leads us inside her condo. She's already decorated for Halloween, even though October only started three days ago.

It's odd having Toby inside this space that is so much a part of me. I nervously drum my fingers against my thigh as he looks around at the tchotchkes, family pictures, and Nana's troll doll collection. He spies a baby picture of me on a table and beelines to it.

"This you?"

Sheepishly, I nod.

"You were cute."

Nana makes a fuss about how hungry we must be and disappears into the kitchen.

After Toby looks at all the pictures in the living room, he turns to me. "Show me your room."

I lead Toby down the hall while twirling my septum ring.

Toby explores my room with wide eyes while I stand in the doorway. I'm too afraid to be in such a small space with him while he looks at and judges all the personal belongings I've kept in boxes and totes. After looking around, Toby heads to the wall that has a picture of my parents.

"They look happy."

"They were."

His eyes flick to me, and I drown in the light brown of Toby's irises. "Your mom does that same raised eyebrow thing you do."

I don't really know what to say to that. "Do you want to see where I grew up?"

"If you're comfortable with showing me."

We eat the snack Nana prepared and then tell her we're heading out. As we walk out the door, I text Abel to tell him that we've arrived in Plainsburg. Toby follows me through the park behind the condos to head into town but stops in the middle and looks up at the branches of the trees intertwining against the sky. He looks serene with his hands in his back pockets and his dreads loose and falling against his long-sleeved navy-blue shirt.

"Do you think there's life out there?"

"Like aliens?"

"Yeah."

Lowering myself onto the grass, I pull my knees up to my chest. Despite knowing Toby is interested in aliens—he collects anything he can find with aliens on it—I have never really talked to him about whether I believe in them. I thought Toby's thing for aliens was silly, like the way some people collect items that have llamas or cats on them. I didn't think I would be in the middle of a park in Plainsburg discussing the possibility of little green men with big black eyes flying above our heads.

Toby settles next to me on the grass. He's shivering from the evening breeze.

"You should have brought your jacket." I remove the puffer jacket from over my hoodie and hand it to Toby.

"I can't take that, Jay."

"Don't be difficult. I'm hot anyway."

Toby doesn't argue further and puts on the jacket. "So, do you believe in aliens?"

"Probably? Humans are just tiny specks on a tiny ball in this big-ass black nothingness." I sigh, playing with a string on my hoodie. "It's kind of stupid and narcissistic to think human beings are the only life-forms in the whole universe. I don't think aliens are green, though." I laugh, kicking Toby's alien shoe with the tip of my high-tops.

He's quiet for a few moments, elbows resting on his knees. "That's exactly what I think," Toby finally says and smiles, and once again I'm disarmed by him. "But think of how cool it would be if they were green!"

"You're so weird." I climb to my feet. "Come on."

We walk half a mile to my childhood house. The sun is setting, bathing the blue home in golden light. The lawn is unkempt and overgrown. A layer of dust has settled on the windows.

My heart sinks at seeing it.

"Are you okay?"

I nod, but I'm far from okay. Memories of Dad mowing the lawn flash in my mind. Mom would sit out on the porch and talk to our neighbor, Sharon, for hours while I played in the yard. The apple tree I fell out of when I was seven still stands tall and proud.

"I never told you this, but I fucked up my parents' funeral. I got really, really drunk the morning of and kind of lost it." *How am I only eighteen and have had so much shit happen to me in such a short span of time?* "I don't remember much of that day, to be honest, but what I do remember is shameful. I screamed at the funeral director, couldn't get through my speech, and was too drunk to carry my dad's casket, so my cousin had to step in. Nana said I got in a fight with my cousin, and I punched him."

"Jesse."

"I was off my meds and drunk all the time during those days. Honestly, it's a miracle I didn't do worse damage."

We sit on a bench on the sidewalk near the house. Toby wraps his hand around my cold, numb fingers. I focus on the feeling, unable to really look at him.

What comes next is the worst, but now that I've opened the floodgates, everything comes pouring out. I want Toby to know every part of me, even all the messed-up, broken pieces I'm trying to put back together.

"A week later, I tried to kill myself." I pull up the sleeves of my hoodie, revealing the long vertical scars that trace up my arms. This is the first time I have ever willingly shown my scars to anyone.

Toby takes one of my wrists, flipping my arm back and forth as if checking for more scars, evidence of other attempts. Fortunately, Toby can't see my legs. Those scars can stay a secret for now.

The space between Toby's eyebrows is scrunched. I hate that I'm the one making his face look like that.

"That's the only time I attempted suicide," I assure him. "Nana found me, and I checked myself into SunnySide. I was there from May until the end of July."

Toby pulls me to him, crushing me in a hug. I breathe him in; he's wearing a new cologne that I like, bergamot mixed with something woodsy. The smell is relaxing.

"I'm sorry you went through that," Toby whispers. His breath tickles the side of my neck, but I hold on to him like a lifeline. "I'm so glad you're here and that we met."

When I pull out of the hug and sit properly on the bench, I look up at the house before me. "I'm supposed to decide what to do with it."

Toby rests his arm behind me and crosses his left ankle over his right knee. "Do you know what you want to do with it?"

I shake my head.

We sit in silence until the sun sets and the streetlights come on. The porch light at Sharon's house goes on, and I'm pretty sure I can see her looking at us from her window. She's probably on the phone with Nana gossiping about us.

"Jesse?"

"Hmm."

"Promise me that if you ever feel like that again, you'll tell me." He pauses, his eyes darting away from me. "I can't imagine not having you in my life."

I want to call him out for being cheesy, but the truth is, I can't imagine not having Toby in my life either. We've known each other for less than two months, but something about Toby pulls me in like a magnet. It feels as if we have known each other our whole lives. Everything is easier with him around; I feel more relaxed, happier. Whenever I'm near him, the static in my brain goes from a ten to a three. I cherish every moment I share with Toby. My roommate has quickly become one of the most important people in my life.

"I love you, man."

Toby smiles, punches my shoulder, and says, "Ditto."

Chapter 23

"Hey, Scout, you got a visitor!" Wendell yells from the front of the shop.

I wipe my hands on my apron and remove my headphones before exiting the kitchen, where I've spent the last two hours frying and glazing donuts. Wendell's is short-staffed, so I'm filling in for Fran on my day off. Abel and I are supposed to be seeing a movie, but I found it hard to say no when Wendell called and asked if I could cover Fran's shift.

Entering the front of the shop, I expect to see Toby, who visits almost every day that I'm working, often staying until my shift is over so we can walk back to campus together. Instead, Abel stands off to the side of a small line that has formed in front of the cash register. He's dressed in gray sweats, a black hoodie, and sneakers. His hair is tied up as if he's been running. His smile makes his cheekbones sharper. My breath hitches.

"What are you doing here?"

"Wanted to say hi."

I lead Abel to one of the booths, and he slides in beside me, so close that our legs brush. He smells like a combination of cloves and sweat; it's intoxicating. Without thinking too much about it, I reach for his hand, intertwining our fingers. We've only been on three dates . . .well, one couldn't really call them dates (besides going to the Apple Pie of My Eye Festival). They were more like hangouts; either we'd chill at the Poisonous Winter apartment or get lunch or coffee at the school. Going to the movies this evening was supposed to be our second official date.

I should have told Wendell I was too busy to come in to work. Spending the day with Abel sounds a lot more appealing.

"I was jogging nearby, and I wanted to see you," he says. He plays with the ring on my pointer finger with the hand I'm not holding. "If you get off early enough, maybe we can catch another time for the movie."

"Definitely. We close at eight, and I can be out of here by nine."

Abel whips out his phone and pulls up showtimes. "Oh! There's a showing at nine-thirty."

His eagerness is fucking adorable. Does he show this part of himself to anyone else? Normally he appears collected, confident, cool.

"Perfect."

Abel smiles in this way that makes my skin erupt in goose bumps in a very good way that I can't really describe. Sometimes it's hard to believe that someone as beautiful and as wanted as Abel Ryan is interested in me. There must a fluke in the matrix, because how can someone like *that* be interested in someone like *me*?

"I'll be back to pick you up at nine."

"Okay."

Abel leans over, planting a kiss on my cheek. Heat blooms where his lips touch.

I duck my head, too shy to look him in the eye. "Go away."

Abel chuckles and exits the shop. I watch him through the window until I can no longer see long black hair swinging in the breeze.

After a few moments, I go back to the kitchen to continue frying and glazing donuts. Wendell gives me a look as I pass. I refuse to make eye contact with the man, but his gaze bores into my back.

Working in the kitchen is a lot better than working the register. In the kitchen, I can listen to music for my entire shift, and no one really comes back here to bother me. I can do my job and go home — no need for small talk, no need for a customer service smile. Working in the back all the time would be ideal, but Wendell has all the employees on a rotating schedule.

Nana thinks working for Wendell is helping my social anxiety, but working is annoying. I would rather not have to listen to strangers chatter about their lives. Call me a dick, but I don't really care that Becky finally got braces at thirty, and I'm sure her date didn't care either. Other people's lives aren't particularly interesting to me.

Toby and Abel are different in that regard. They love to be around people. Abel likes to party and mingles with everyone he comes in contact with, and Toby likes to people watch. He says they help him develop characters for his stories. I think he's just nosy. How the hell I ended up crushing on two extroverts is beyond me.

My crush on Toby *cannot* be thought about. It *has* to be unimportant. Nothing can come of it. Lock it in a box and hide it in my subconscious.

I'm with Abel.

Perfect Abel with his perfect cheekbones.

I like him, and he likes me. We can have something uncomplicated.

Focus on Abel. That's perfectly acceptable.

I thought about it a lot after talking to Doctor Hartland. I'm honestly surprised at myself that I decided to remain in a situationship with Abel. It would be so much less complicated to just cut ties and pretend we never kissed at that party and I am not completely enthralled with the softness of his hair and the sharpness of his jawline. But that's the thing, I am enthralled. And as much as I would have loved to stick to my no-dating rule, we all know that rule was a waste of breath. I am a man who is often controlled by his hormones, and my hormones *really* like other men who show interest in me, especially when said men are covered in tattoos.

A ping interrupts the song I'm listening to while glazing blueberry-lemon donuts. The ping is different from the sound I use for text messages, which I usually ignore while working. This ping is from Facebook, and no one ever messages me on there.

I wipe my hands and pull out my phone, curious to see who the hell is contacting me. It's a name I don't recognize: Kelly Piers. Normally, I leave my message requests unread until I have time to go and delete them or ignore them completely; most of the time they're either spam or assholes from high school who didn't say two words to me for all four years of that torturous time but now want to know why I tried to take my own life. But something tells me to at least scan the message from Kelly before dismissing it.

Dear Jesse,

My name is Kelly Piers. I lived in the same building as your parents when they were attending their senior year at Westbrook. They helped me out in one of the hardest moments of my life. I will never be able to thank them enough.

I'm so sorry. I don't know how to say this in a way that won't hurt you: I'm your biological mother. I hate that you're finding out this way, and I went back and forth on whether I should contact you or not. Your parents were supposed to tell you when you graduated high school, but I just found out they didn't have a chance to tell you before they passed.

I'm so sorry for your loss, and for springing this information on you. I just feel like it is time to tell you. You deserve to know.

From the pictures I have seen of you over the years, it seems that Monica and Aaron loved you very much. I could never ask for anything more. That is all I have ever wanted for you.

I don't know what else to say to make this better. I want to tell you the whole story face to face. I'm living in New York City, and I would love to meet you.

If you ever want to meet up, please reach out, but there's no rush or obligation.

Hoping to hear from you,
Kelly

I'm fucking shaking so hard that it's nearly impossible to read anything after, *I'm your biological mother.*

I'm adopted.

I'm fucking *adopted.*

They never told me. My whole life, and no one ever said a word. Not even Nana. Why would they keep that from me?

Still shaking, I punch in Nana's number.

"Hell—"

"I'm *adopted*?"

"Jess—"

"Tell me the truth."

Nana sighs heavily. "Yes, you're adopted."

"Were you ever going to tell me?"

She dodges the question by asking, "How did you find out?"

"Kelly messaged me on Facebook."

"Ah."

"Were you ever going to tell me?"

"Your parents were going to tell you over the summer, but then they—they died." Her voice rises with every word, and I hate that I'm the one causing her to lose control. "And then you tried—tried to—you went to SunnySide. How could I tell you then? After you were released, you were so determined to start over and have a clean slate. I couldn't mess that up!"

"Okay." My voice is small. I called her to be angry, to accuse her of keeping this secret, but now I feel guilty for making her breathe so heavily I'm afraid she's going to hyperventilate. "I'm sorry, Nana."

"Where are you?"

"Work."

There's no fucking way I can go on that date with Abel now. I can't handle being around anyone, especially him. I don't want to have to explain to him why I'm fucking losing it. He can't see me like this. He doesn't need to know about all the fucked-up parts of me yet.

I should text him and cancel, but I don't. The thought of having to type the words is mentally exhausting.

I'm so fucking tired of going off the deep end. I'm so tired of all the bullshit. I finally thought I caught a break, and now here is another thing to fuck everything up. When will I be able to breathe? I just want to feel like the weight of the world is no longer crushing me. When do I get to be free of this shit?

"I have—I have to go back to glazing these donuts, Nana."

"Jess-bug."

I hang up on her. Something I have never done in my life.

I'm adopted.

I collapse to the floor, and my back hits the chrome counter. The cool metal sort of calms me. My breath comes out fast and uneven, and I'm still shaking. The darkness is trying to set in and take hold. I'm trying the calming techniques that Doctor Hartland taught me—the self-affirming mantras, counting to twenty—but they're not working. For some reason, my brain has forgotten what comes after twelve.

I'm adopted.

A few moments later, Wendell comes into the kitchen. He finds me still on the floor, counting to twelve over and over. It's not working. The darkness is seeping; the static is getting louder and louder.

I'm adopted.

"Your nan called," he says. "You're going home."

"No, I—"

"That's not a suggestion, Scout." He sighs. "I'm sorry you found out this way."

I squeeze my eyes shut. I don't want to be here anymore. I don't want to feel anymore.

Where's my razor?

The need to cut burns deep inside of me. My hand twitches for the release, to purge out the darkness through cuts on my thigh. If I feel physical pain, then the mental pain goes away, even if only for a short period of time.

I'm adopted. No one told me. No one cared enough to tell me. Why? Why didn't they tell me?

I don't look at Wendell, unwilling to see his pity. "Okay."

I fumble in my pockets for my keys, but my fingers aren't working.

The darkness pushes in. Everything is black.

My brain is too loud.

I long for a razor to offset the black with red. It's been almost six months since I last cut my leg, but the urge still rears its ugly head. It'll probably never go away.

"You can't go home alone in this state," Wendell says. His voice sounds muffled by the chaos in my brain. "I'll call Toby."

I want to protest. My roommate—my *crush*—can't see me like this. He can't know that I'm this broken.

But I don't. I can't move. I can't speak. I can't think.

Darkness. Static.

Wendell reaches for my phone on the counter and goes through my contacts.

Twenty minutes later, Toby arrives, and I'm still in the same spot, contemplating grabbing a knife from one of the drawers and going to town on my leg, but Wendell hasn't left me alone. He knows better than that; I'm sure Nana warned him.

Toby is here. Toby is seeing the broken pieces of me. He's seeing the darkness.

No. Please, go away.

"Jay."

The sound of his voice releases everything that has been building for the last thirty minutes. The darkness recedes a bit and I see him. He's dressed in his practice uniform, a single dread falling over his face. His honey eyes are full of concern. I just fucking sob as he looks at me. Something inside of me begins to loosen. The urge to cut begins to fade just because he's here.

I reach for him, and he gathers me in a hug. I'm shaking again, but my head doesn't feel simultaneously heavy and floaty like it did just moments ago. I hug him back so tight I'm sure a few of his ribs probably crack. I turn my face into his neck, inhaling his cologne mixed with sweat. The static is getting quieter. It's still there, but it's lower now, as if someone has turned down the volume.

"Jay," he says again.

I can't say anything. I'm afraid if I open my mouth, I'll vomit all over him.

Hold me. I hug him tighter. *Please, just stay here.*

Chapter 24

In the days since I found out I'm adopted, everyone wants to talk about it, but I can't. I can't even get through life right now without the darkness and static closing in. I'm either avoiding Nana's calls or hanging up on her the second she mentions it. Doctor Hartland doesn't even know about the message or the darkness. I cancelled our session this morning.

It's too much. Everything is too much.

"Are you sure you want to do this?" Toby gestures at the house in front of us, which has music blaring from within. "We can just go back to the dorm, order Chinese food, and watch something."

"Let's do it." I pull Toby behind me and lunge into the party.

The first hour of the party is the same as usual: I find a corner to hide in while Toby mingles but keeps an eye on me.

A pink-haired girl approaches Toby and hands him a cup of something. He downs it, turning his back to me.

With my watchdog distracted, I leave my corner, wandering through the throng of people. I don't want to think. I don't want to feel.

"Want some?" someone says. They offer me a cup of a dark purple liquid with edible glitter swirling in it. "It's good."

I don't give a fuck if it's good or not. I down the drink in one gulp.

The dude is right. It's great: it tastes like grape and burns my throat.

SHADES OF US

Someone passes me another one of those galaxy drinks as I meander through the party. I take the drink and go back to wandering around.

When Toby finds me, I'm sitting on the top step, drinking my third cup of the purple drink. He looks frantic and a little angry.

"There you are! I've been looking for you!"

"I was wondering when you would find me." My words slur. "Tastes like a grape popsicle. Try some." I thrust the cup at him.

He takes it, but he doesn't drink.

"Jesse."

I hate when he calls me Jesse.

"Don't say my name like that. Let me do this. Be fucked up for one night so I don't feel anymore."

It's either this or a razor to my thigh. This seems less destructive.

"Jess—"

"Toby, if you're going to mom me, then go away."

Toby sighs, conflicted. "Just be careful," he finally says after a long moment.

"Yes, sir." I down the rest of the contents.

The world is starting to tilt, but I welcome it.

I pull Toby down the stairs to the dance floor, jumping and flailing my arms. The static in my brain is loud and jumbled. It's disorienting. The darkness blinks on the edges of my vision.

Keep dancing. Keep drinking. Don't think. Don't feel.

Toby looks startled as I pull him to me, setting my hands on his waist, but he dances along.

I wish I could kiss him.

Abel's on the edge of the dance floor. I haven't talked to him since that day. I sent him a shitty message canceling our date and never replied again. I'm sure Toby's explained the situation by now. Abel can't see me like this.

I can't be in here anymore. The darkness is pressing in. It's too much. Tears begin to burn my eyes.

Reaching for Toby's hand, I lead him from the house and walk until we're down the block. Toby's quiet. The only sound is my huffing and puffing.

The tears begin to fall.

I have to stop. I lean against a lamppost, facing away from Toby. My heart beats too fast. The air catches in my lungs. All I see is darkness. All I hear is static. It's getting louder and louder by the minute.

"Are you okay?" Toby asks. He tries to touch me, but I recoil.

"No."

The words I've been hearing since I read Kelly's message play in my mind over and over.

You're adopted.

You're adopted.

"I don't know who I am anymore. I was perfectly okay without knowing I was adopted. Why did Kelly have to ruin my happy ignorance?"

"The only way to find out the truth is to talk to Nana or Kelly."

"I don't want to."

"Can I hug you now?"

I nod.

Toby wraps me in his arms, and for the moment I feel safe. The static recedes a bit. The darkness loosens just enough so I can see his face. He's crying.

I'm sorry. I'm so sorry you have to take care of me.

"You can't avoid this forever, Jay."

"Stop being the voice of reason. It's annoying."

"Are you ready to go back to the dorm?"

"Yeah."

"Promise me you'll call Doctor Hartlandin the morning. She needs to know about this."

"I promise."

I can't tell if I'm lying or not.

Chapter 25

Almost a week after the party, I'm still very much avoiding the subject of Kelly and adoption. I think Nana has finally gotten the hint, so she's stopped bringing it up when we talk on the phone. The only people who seem to want to talk about it are Toby and Doctor Hartland, so I have been avoiding them both. I canceled my last session with Doctor Hartland and have been dodging her calls. With Toby, it's much harder to avoid him, but I've been returning to the dorm late or staying the night with Amy. She doesn't pester me to talk.

I'm also avoiding Abel, but for a different reason. I can't let him see me like this. The image of me that he's built up in his head can't be ruined by all my flaws. He keeps calling, but I don't answer.

On Wednesday, I wake up, and everything finally catches up with me. The darkness fully takes hold. The world is too much. My brain is too fucking loud. The pills aren't helping. My limbs feel heavy. I'm tired. God, I'm so fucking tired.

I go to class on autopilot, not really talking to anyone or listening to my professors. I have lunch with Toby and Amy but don't talk to them either. I don't eat. Right after class, I return to the dorm, where I put on my headphones and crank up the music, but even that doesn't drown out the static.

I'm so fucking tired.

I fall sleep.

SHADES OF US

When I wake again, I'm the same. Everything is the same.

It's later now; the sun has set.

Toby's in the room, hovering like a mother bird; he tries to get me to eat or play video games, but I can't. I don't care about either. Ignoring him, I roll over in my bed and go back to sleep.

On Friday, he tries to get me to re-engage with society by asking me to go with him to get coffee.

"Come on, Jay, getting out will help you feel better."

"I'm fucking fine!"

I'm so far from fine, even I'm scared. The razor calls to me day and night. My dreams are filled with letting my blood spill just so I can feel something other than this numbness in my soul. I haven't actually done it. Yet. My promise to Mom is the only thing stopping me; I can't let her down.

"Just leave me alone, Toby."

On Saturday, I manage to put on a new pair of joggers and heat up a cup of ramen in the community microwave for breakfast. I start up the PS5 and play games until I go cross-eyed. Toby has basketball practice, so he's going to be gone for most of the day.

In the afternoon, Amy and Shelby stop by, but I don't let them in.

I open the door wide enough that I can see their worried faces. "We brought you that soup you like from Bodie's."

Amy hands me a bag with takeout containers.

"Thanks." My voice is hoarse from not using it for days.

"We're all here for you, Jess. Don't forget that."

This conversation is exhausting.

"Abel's been asking about you." She pauses. "He's worried about you."

"I'll call him later."

133

But I don't call him that night.

Nor on Sunday either. I'm supposed to meet my photography club group at the library to work on our project, but I can't bring myself to go. I text Craig to tell him I'm dropping out of the club. He calls me, but I don't answer.

It isn't until I wake up on Monday that I feel better. Not a hundred percent, but better. The darkness blinks at the edges of my vision, and my brain is still too loud, but it's manageable. A/AA is meeting for dinner, and though I tell them I'll meet them for the next one, I decline the invite. I'm not at a point where I want to deal with people yet.

I have missed my morning classes and decide to skip my afternoon classes as well. The Dark Episodes always take a lot of energy out of me. Today will be for recharging.

Toby sits up in his bed, reading with his headphones on. When he sees that I'm awake, he smiles at me tentatively.

"Hey," I croak.

"You fucking scared me, Jay."

He's looking at me all intense and concerned. Guilt runs through me for causing him to worry so much. I hate myself. I hate that my brain doesn't work right and that God fucked me over when he was handing out serotonin. I hate that I'm the cause of this Dark Episode by refusing to talk about Kelly and the whole adoption thing. But even with that knowledge, I still don't want to talk about it.

"I'm sorry."

"No need to apologize. I just want to understand what happened." He slides off his bed and joins me on mine. I pull my green comforter up to my chin. I'm not naked underneath or anything, but having him my bed while I'm having all these feelings for him is making me so nervous, even the backs of my knees are sweating.

"What *was* that, Jay?" His eyes burrow into me. He's too close to be looking at me like that. I look away. "I mean, you're normally an apathetic asshole—"

"Thanks." I hit his shoulder and smile—my first genuine smile in days.

"—but it was like someone had taken your batteries out. I know it's been hard for you lately, but I've never seen anything like that."

It would be nice to have coffee; this is a lot to be talking about right after waking up.

"I call them Dark Episodes. Everything just becomes too much, and my body shuts down."

"Don't the pills help with that?" He reaches over and places a hand on my knee. I want so badly to lace our fingers together, to feel the warmth of his palm against mine, to take some of his strength to replenish what I lost over the past few days.

"They do, but they're not a fix-all." I sigh, running my hands through my hair as I try to gather my thoughts to figure out how to explain this to him. "Think of it like having a cut that won't stop bleeding. You can bandage it, but the blood will seep through. The cut will never fully heal. Sometimes the blood may take a very long time to seep through the bandage, but it will always make it through eventually. If something terrifying or life-altering happens—like, I don't know, finding out I'm adopted—the blood will seep out quicker."

Toby's quiet as he thinks about what I've said. "And what about the anxiety?"

I let out a humorless laugh. "That's a whole different ball game, dude. I'm a big fucked-up ball of apathy and angst."

"Are you ready to talk about the adoption thing?"

"No." We fall into silence for a few moments. "I didn't mean to scare you."

"It's not your fault." He squeezes my knee. "Coffee?"

"Yes, please."

I get up to take my first shower since being pulled into the darkness. I avoid looking at myself in the mirror as I set up my toiletries and get undressed. I don't want to see the zombie that stares back at me.

Before placing my phone on the sink, I shoot Abel a quick text.

I'm sorry 4 disappearing 4 days.

It's been rough.

Twirling my septum ring, I wait for a reply. His response is immediate:

Don't worry.

You can tell me when you're ready.

He's still here. He still cares. Ghosting him for weeks had me worried that he would hate me. I still don't want him to see the broken parts of me. I'm not looking forward to it, but I will have to explain what happened.

There's also a message from Greg, saying that Toby explained what happened and asking if I want to reconsider dropping out of the club. I don't text him back.

Abel sends me another message.

I miss you.

The noise in my brain goes from a twenty to a ten, the daily level that I'm able to deal with.

Finally, normalcy.

Chapter 26

On Tuesday, I sit in front of Doctor Hartland'sdesk. She had a cancellation and was able to squeeze me in at 10:00. I'm missing class to see her, but this is probably more important than the quadratic formula.

"Tell me about what happened."

I play with my wallet chain as I tell her all about drinking at the party, and the darkness and static that consumed me for days.

"How do you feel now?" she asks.

"Better. Normal." Well, what passes for normal for me these days.

"And you've been taking your pills?"

"I didn't during my Dark Episode, but I did yesterday and today."

She makes a note in her notebook. "Now that you're feeling better, how do you feel about finding out you're adopted?"

"Really cutting right to it today, aren't you, Doc?" I sigh and run my fingers through my unkempt hair. "I feel like I was starting to find my footing in the world again, and it was ripped out from under me with one message. I can't even explain how betrayed I feel that my parents never told me, and they're not even here to talk to about it."

"You have your grandma."

I don't reply to that.

SHADES OF US

"You want answers, Jesse, and going to your grandma is the best place to go for those answers. You're not ready to confront Kelly, so here is another source for helping you come to terms with this life-altering news you've received."

She's right, but I *really* wish I could just pretend this wasn't happening.

Doctor Hartlandlooks at her watch. "Our time's up. Talk to your grandma, Jesse."

A headache starts behind my eyes as I walk to the bus stop. Toby texts me to meet him at the science building when I get back to campus.

As I ride the bus, I think about what Doctor Hartland said. I know I need to talk to Nana, but the thought terrifies me. When I talk about it, then it becomes real. Living in ignorance sounds a lot better than confronting the fact that my whole life is a lie.

Fuck!

I pinch the bridge of my nose. I don't want to deal with this. I'm so angry at my parents for never telling me that I was adopted, and at Kelly for ruining everything. I wish she never contacted me. Why couldn't she have just left well enough alone?

When I arrive at the science building, Toby's leaning against the hood of his car while Amy and Shelby are sitting on the curb eating corn dogs. The Poisonous Winter van is parked in the spot next to Toby's. The band is sitting in the van with the side door wide open. Mahara and Sebastian playfully argue while Zack and Abel goof around.

My headache starts to dissipate when I see them.

I wave at Toby, and his eyes follow me as I beeline for Abel. Abel pushes his hair out of his face as I approach, and Zack slinks away to go bother Amy and Shelby.

"Hey," Abel says.

"Hey."

He wraps his arms around me, and I melt into him.

"You had us all worried," he whispers in my ear.

"I'm sorry."

He kisses my cheek and then pulls back to look into my eyes. "Are you okay?"

"As I can be." I'm not okay, but he doesn't need to know that. "I'm sorry I missed our date that night."

"We can reschedule."

He doesn't push me to tell him why I disappeared, and I appreciate it. I'm going to tell him everything today. As much as I only want to show Abel the good sides of me, this whole adoption thing is forcing me to come clean about how broken I am.

Will he still be interested when he realizes I'm not a functioning human being?

I hug Abel again, finding comfort in burying my face in his chest and inhaling his scent.

"Can we go now?" Amy asks.

I pull out of Abel's arms but keep my hand in his. "Where are we going?'

Toby's eyes meet mine, but he looks away. His facial expression is tight. "You'll see."

"Do you want to ride in the van or with Toby?" Abel asks. "I'm good either way."

"Toby." I need to be near him to feel grounded and safe. Out of all the people here, he makes me feel the most at ease.

"Are you okay with that?" Abel asks Toby.

"Sure. The more the merrier."

Amy, Toby, Abel, and I pile into Toby's car, while the rest follow in the van. I sit in the back seat with Abel, which is weird for me. Usually, I'm up front with Toby. Being in the same small space with both of my crushes has me beyond nervous. My fingers drum against my thigh. For some reason, my brain has decided to focus on my chipped nail polish. I have the urge to pick it all off and paint my nails when we get back to the dorm, but I don't. Partially because I don't want to leave polish peelies all over Toby's car, but mostly because it bothers me if my nails are unpainted for longer than thirty minutes.

Abel takes my hand, probably to make the drumming stop. I turn my focus from my nails to his tattooed knuckles and his fingers wrapped around mine.

Amy turns on the radio, flipping from station to station.

"Wait! Go back!" I yell, making Abel jump. Amy does as I ask. "Sweet Child O' Mine," my mom's favorite song, crackles through Toby's dying speakers. A soft smile spreads across my face as I hum along. Memories of my mom belting the lyrics at the top of her lungs while she made cookies or when we went on road trips fill my mind. I haven't been able to listen to the song since my parents died, but I need this after the week I've had with my Dark Episode. I need the reminder of them and their love for me after everything that has happened.

When the song ends, Amy changes the station, and we all sing along with the pop song she lands on.

We pull into the parking lot of an arcade. Toby glances over his shoulder and grins at me like he's proud of himself or something.

"An arcade? What are we, six?"

"Seven," he replies, sticking his tongue out at me. "I bet I can kick your ass at air hockey."

"Doubtful."

"Abel, Amy, place your bets on who you think is going to win," Toby tells them.

"Toby."

"Jesse."

"How dare you bet against me, Amy!" Feigning shock and betrayal, I place my hand over my heart.

She shrugs. "I'm just here for the pizza."

We exit the car and enter the rundown brick building. The interior is dimly lit with a pizza parlor on one side and games on the other. The whole place smells like pepperoni and feet.

"What kind of pizza do you all want?" Toby asks, walking backward toward the counter. "I'm buying."

"Can you get plain cheese?" Abel asks. "I'm vegetarian. I can pay—"

"Keep your money, Ryan." Toby seems friendly toward Abel, but there's something off about his voice. I can't put my finger on what it is. "I'm the one who invited you all out on this excursion."

"Driving ten minutes to play *Pac-Man* is hardly an excursion," I quip.

Toby mockingly flips me off and goes to order pizza with Shelby.

As the others go to check out the games, Abel and I walk hand in hand to claim a table. "I didn't know you were vegetarian," I say, and then I realize that when we've hung out, he's always ordered something without meat. "How did I not know that?"

"There's still a lot we get to learn about each other."

I don't know what to say to that, so I blush and look away. My eyes land on Amy, who is playing *Dance Dance Revolution* while Mahara and Sebastian take pictures in a photo booth. Zack leans into the booth, ruining their shots.

"I'm excited to learn."

"Learn what?" I turn back to Abel, confused.

"Everything about you."

No, you aren't. You'll run away if you know.

But it's as good a time as any to tell him why I disappeared. "I'm sure Shelby's told you that I have depression and anxiety."

He nods.

"I'm taking meds for them, but sometimes everything gets to be too much, like when I found out I was adopted, and they kind of take over." I need something to focus on, so I play with his fingers. "I don't mean to, but I sort of shut down and can't function until I come out of it."

I don't tell him about the scars on my thighs or my attempted suicide. One day, I'll show him all the sides of me, but exposing myself like that to him right now is too terrifying.

"That must be scary for you."

No one has ever worded it like that, but he's right. It's as if I lose control of my body and my mind and become nothing, just a shell. I want to break free of the episode, but I can't.

"I'm used to it." Lies. I'll never get used to it.

Abel reaches up, cupping my cheek. "Thank you for trusting me enough to share this with me. I know it can't be easy."

My heart swells with affection for this man before me. I lean forward and kiss him, a quick peck on the lips to show my gratitude for being with me.

Shelby screaming Abel's name grabs both of our attention. She's at the edge of the arcade, jumping up and down pointing behind her. "They have that shooting game you like! Remember? The one we played at the arcade in Philly?"

Abel holds up a finger to her before turning back to me. His eyes are warm, causing butterflies to flutter in my stomach. "Do you want me to stay here?"

"No. Go play with Shelby."

"Are you sure?"

I nod and gently push him out of his chair. "Go!"

He stands, practically running over to where Shelby's bouncing up and down in her combat boots.

Shortly after, Toby comes to the table from the restroom. He slides into the booth next to me.

"I saw you talking about something important with Abel."

"Hmm. I told him about why I disappeared."

"How was it?"

"Honestly, not as scary as I thought it would be."

Toby's silent for a few moments. I want to know what he's thinking, but I don't pry.

"Ready to get your ass kicked, Lancaster?" he says after a few moments.

"Not going to happen."

He laughs.

Before we stand, Toby places a hand on my arm. The fabric of my jacket keeps his fingertips from touching my skin, but I can still feel his warmth as if there is no barrier between us.

"I'm glad you opened up to Abel." He seems off again. What is going on with him? "He's a good guy."

Abel and Shelby are yelling at their game and shooting their fake guns. A sort of lightness fills me as I look at him.

"He is, isn't he?"

Chapter 27

Unfortunately, I'm unable to see Poisonous Winter play at the Fall Festival. I have to make up two tests I missed during my Dark Episode. After the first test, I send Abel a good luck text, then I have twenty minutes to kill before the next one and decide to stop by one of the coffee stalls near the art building.

A group of girls whisper as I pass their table, their eyes darting to me.

"That's him. He's the one dating Abel Ryan."

Obviously, going out with Abel means I would be gossiped about, but I don't like it. The whole school doesn't need to know who I am. As soon as the barista hands me my coffee, I hightail it out of there as fast as I can, but Val is right behind me. I haven't talked to anyone from my photography club since dropping out. Sheepishly, I greet Val with a small wave.

"Jesse!" She greets me with an enthusiasm I'm not expecting. She's not upset with me for abandoning our group? If it were me, I would be pissed. "Come sit with me."

I follow Val to an empty table under a tall maple tree. Val tucks a strand of blue hair behind her ear as I sit down across from her.

"We miss you in the club."

Rubbing the back of my neck in embarrassment, I reply, "I'm sorry for just dropping everything on you and Kat."

She waves her hand dismissively. "No sweat. We heard what

happened; no one blames you." She looks at her phone. "Oh, shit, I have to go. I'm meeting my history partner. Are you coming back to the club?"

"No. I don't think so, not now anyway." Even though I stayed in A/AA, going back to the photography club seems like too much at the moment; I can't focus on extra projects while this Kelly thing looms over me.

She stands and begins walking away, throwing over her shoulder, "Your spot is always open if you change your mind."

I want to ask how she found out about everything, but she's gone before I can form the question.

After my second test, I head to Nana's earlier than I planned to. Riding the bus from Freemont to Plainsburg is incredibly boring, so I crank up my music and fall asleep the second the bus leaves Freemont.

Nana's sitting in a plastic chair near the railing when I arrive. Her eyes are closed, and she has a book on her chest.

"Are you just gonna sit there when your grandson came all this way just to see you?" I ask, climbing the stairs toward her.

She jumps, startled. "Jess-bug!"

"Hi, Nan."

She wraps me in her arms, immediately making me feel safe. After several seconds, she pulls back, looking hesitant. We haven't properly talked since I found out about being adopted. She wants to talk about it now, but I don't want to. I have already talked about things with Toby and Doctor Hartland until I was blue in the face. Honestly, the whole thing is making me so exhausted.

Nana doesn't push, she just takes me by the elbow and pats my arm. "Let's get you inside."

Nana chats about Old Tom, her next-door neighbor for the

past six years, as I follow her inside. Apparently, they had a romantic dinner last weekend. Thankfully, she spares me the details. When we enter the condo, I head straight for the couch to lie down, but my phone buzzes as soon as my ass hits the cushion. I groan at the simple inconvenience of pulling my phone out of my pocket. It's a text from Toby.

Everything's going to be okay.

Stay strong, Jay.

Toby wanted to come with me, but he had basketball practice to prepare for the first game of the season. The fact that he's in my corner comforts me more than anything else in the world right now.

"Text from your fella?" Nana asks as she brings me a sandwich.

I blush and hastily put my phone back in my pocket. "Nah, just Toby."

She purses her lips. "I thought you were into Abel."

"I am."

Her lips purse even more. She knows what this smile means; she can tell that Toby is more than just my roommate.

"So—"

"I don't want to talk about it."

Nana nods with her lips still pursed in a judgmental way. "Whatever you decide, Jess-bug, I'll support you. Abel seems like a nice fella." She pauses, and I suddenly find my sandwich very interesting. "And I really like Toby."

"Helpful, Nan. Can we watch TV so I can pretend my life isn't totally fucked up right now?"

"Language, Jesse Lancaster."

"Sorry, Nan."

Nana and I settle in for a night of popcorn and comedies. Throughout the night, I text my friends and Abel. He sends me a picture of him at the Fall Festival.

Wish you were there.

I send back:

I'll make it up 2 U. Promise.

Nana and I end up watching three movies and don't go to bed until two in the morning.

I open Facebook as I crawl into my sheets and go to my messages. I haven't replied to Kelly's message, but she can tell that I've read it. What does she think? It's been weeks, and I still haven't said anything.

I wish Mom and Dad were here to tell me what to do.

The next morning, I'm still unsure about what I should do. Should I visit Kelly, or do I pretend my life is just the same as it always was?

Nana goes to work at the library, leaving me to pace my room alone with my thoughts.

Hours pass as I pace back and forth throughout the condo. I'm pretty sure a hole has been burned into the rug from my tracks.

I have nothing. I have to talk about this shit with Nana when she returns tonight before I can make any decisions. Part of me is curious to get to know Kelly, but the other part wants her to stay out of my life.

Eventually, I get sick of my own thoughts and head out to the balcony. The balcony is so small it barely has room for a single chair, but somehow Nana's made it work. I turn on my playlist and open Toby's copy of *Brave New World*.

Toby is insisting that I read it before the end of the semester or we can no longer be friends. He's just kidding, but even the thought of losing him is just so fucking depressing. What would I do without him?

My phone buzzes with a message from Shelby.

WE LUV U!

I don't reply to her right away. She's texted me the most out of everyone. I should probably say something before she has a heart attack. I like her message and tell her I love them too.

Chapter 28

Nana is busy cooking when I go back inside. The sun has set, and I've lost my light to read. She's going all out on the food, making my favorite meal: roast chicken, corn, and mashed potatoes.

"Slice the apples for pie," she instructs.

Having something to do helps distract me from the weight on my chest that makes me feel like I can't breathe.

Shit. When was the last time I felt like I *could* breathe?

Did I take myself out of SunnySide too early? Everything was so much easier in there. Probably because I spent so much time in a drug-induced fog while adjusting to my new meds, and everything was so structured I didn't really have to make decisions for myself. I should try having a routine instead of freeballing my life, but that seems unlikely. Planning is not something I'm good at.

Nana and I sit down for dinner, food sprawled out before us like we're feeding an army.

"Dig in, Jess-bug."

I'm not hungry but pull the potatoes toward me and pile a bit on my plate. For several long minutes, the only sound is metal clinking against ceramic. When there's nothing left to put on my plate, I finally ask Nana the question I've been dreading for weeks.

"Nana, what happened with my parents and Kelly?"

She sets down her fork and sits up straighter, propping her elbows on the table as if bracing herself.

"Kelly lived across the hall in your parents' apartment building. She was fifteen when she got pregnant with you. At the time, your mom had just graduated college and was working at Wendell's while your dad finished his degree and worked full-time at the bookstore." She stops to sip her wine. She's stalling, but I don't call her out on it. "Kelly's parents gave her an ultimatum: Have the father take responsibility or get rid of the baby. But they were clear on one thing, abortion was not an option.

"The guy that got Kelly pregnant was a deadbeat. He had tricked her into sleeping with him and then refused to believe you were his even though Kelly had been a virgin. She decided to give you up for adoption and wanted you to have a good family. According to her, your parents were the best people she knew. She refused to give you up to anyone else. Your mom was over the moon and agreed right away. She knew it would be hard, raising a kid right out of college, but she felt like it was fate.

"I was against it at first—they were young and struggling with money and finding stable jobs—but your mom already loved you, and you weren't even born yet. She just knew you were supposed to be theirs."

The static in my brain grows loud again. Thinking of my friends' encouraging messages is the only thing keeping it at a level where I can think.

"H-how come they never told me?"

"They wanted to. They wanted Kelly to be involved in your life, but her parents were very against it. The three of them made a plan to tell you when your graduated high school, but then your parents—they—" Her eyes begin to glisten.

I reach across the table, taking her hand. "It's okay, Nan."

"Soon after you were born, Kelly's parents moved her across

the country, and your parents lost contact with her until you were eight." She sniffs and blinks back tears. "She lived far away, but they sent her pictures and told her everything about you." Nana sniffs again. "I was hesitant to tell you about her after everything that happened."

My parents loved me. They gave me everything I ever wanted. The anger I've been feeling isn't about me being adopted—not really. It comes from being kept in the dark. I wish I knew. I was angry at Kelly for coming out of the blue and upending everything I knew about myself, and at Nan for hiding this from me.

"Are you going to meet her?"

"I don't know."

This isn't something that can be ignored, but damn do I wish I could erase her message and pretend nothing has changed.

"Whatever you decide." Nana pats my cheek affectionately. "I'm behind you no matter what."

The static gets louder and louder.

I need to call Toby or Abel to hear their voices. They're the only ones who can quiet everything inside my brain.

Excusing myself from the table, I head to my room. Then I pull out my phone and dial.

"Jay." Toby picks up after the second ring as if he were waiting for my call.

"Toby."

Everything rushes out of me. I tell him everything Nana told me and sob into the phone. Toby's voice soothes me, telling me that we're going to figure it out together.

Chapter 29

The next few days pass pretty quickly. I go school, work at Wendell's, and bullshit with Toby and the Poisonous Winter crew. Abel and I finally have our date but spend most of the movie making out and feeding each other popcorn. My feelings for him grow with every moment we spend together. He's smart and funny, and so fucking nice. He's probably the nicest person I have ever dated.

Now it's Thursday night, and I'm being forced to go out. According to my friends, Halloween is not an excuse to hide in the dorm. Abel, Toby, and Shelby are forcing me to dress up and join in on the annual Poisonous Winter traditions.

A squeal comes from the bathroom.

Oh, and Madison is joining us too. She flew down, deciding to miss her classes so she can spend Halloween weekend with Toby. She's super nice, but I hate the tightening in my chest that started the second she landed yesterday evening. It's been getting tighter and tighter the longer she's here.

There are moments, like when they are kissing or cuddling on Toby's bed, when I want to crawl out of my skin.

Stop fucking pining!

I try to focus on my costume instead. My brown hair is covered by a shoulder-length blond wig, and I found an awesome pink-and-gray jacket online. On my shoulder is a flame-shaped plushie that Amy has drawn a face on.

The plushie is smiling at me. "I feel really pathetic, Calcifer."

The door to the bathroom opens. Madison and Toby emerge amid a bellow of steam that smells like apples. She smiles at me sheepishly. She's dressed in one of Toby's shirts and a pair of his shorts.

"You look great!" she exclaims.

"Thanks."

Toby is still displaying his "I just got laid" smile. My chest tightens even more.

"I can't wait to see what Shelby and Amy look like," Madison says.

Madison and Toby start to get dressed. Their costumes are a devil and a fallen angel. Toby wanted to join our trio as one of the characters from *Howl's Moving Castle*, but Madison vetoed that. She wanted a couple's costume, so he came up with gender-bent Mario and Princess Peach, but she vetoed that as well. Personally, I was all for the Mario-Peach idea.

Madison brought everything they'll need for their costumes from California. The coolest thing about Toby's are the wings Madison found at a thrift shop in LA. They're black with beautiful sleek feathers, and they're fully functional when Toby presses the button on his chest.

We left our door open a crack so Amy and Shelby are able to enter without us having to answer it. They arrive as Madison is putting makeup on Toby. Amy looks fabulous in a slinky black dress, costume pearls, and a very, *very* wide-brimmed hat. Shelby's wearing a frumpy blue dress with a gray braided wig and a straw hat.

"Sophie, you look stunning."

Shelby twirls. "Why thank you, Howl."

"What about me?" Amy asks jokingly.

I bow gallantly. "Beautiful as always, my dear witch."

She giggles.

We spend the next hour taking selfies and reciting lines from the movie while Madison and Toby finish getting ready.

"Are you done messing around?" Toby asks when Madison finishes his makeup.

She's done some sorcery with the gold face powder she brought with her. It really highlights the structure of Toby's face. With the black lipstick she put on him, the temporary tattoos, the ripped pants, and the safety-pinned shirt—*shit*. It's a whole different side of Toby.

Let's just say, Toby dressed as a fallen angel really does something for me.

I have to turn away from him before I start drooling. The need to sit down is strong.

"Ready!" Madison says.

She also looks amazing. She has on a tight red dress, black heels, and horns atop her immaculately styled hair. She used pink to highlight her face and she's wearing a red lipstick that looks killer on her.

"The both of you look so hot!" Shelby stares closer at their makeup. "I love what you did with Toby's face. It looks better than usual."

He flicks her on the arm.

They really do look hot, like the popular couple that everyone is jealous of in a teen movie.

"You okay?" Toby asks me. "Your face looks weird."

"Your face looks weird!" I retort, since there's no way I am going to tell him what is truly going on.

You need to get over him. He's not available.

I know. I know.

He raises an eyebrow at me. "Are you ready to go?"

I nod and shuffle out the door behind Amy and Shelby. We head out to the parking lot and find the band's van, where our friends are waiting for us.

Chapter 30

Poisonous Winter's traditions are pretty simple. First, they go trick-or-treating, and then they head to the woods to spend the night looking at stars and eating all the candy they scored. It's simple and effective. My two favorite things.

Honestly, I'm happy they're not dragging me to one of the three parties happening tonight. I'll do anything to be anywhere where there are not a lot of people gyrating all over each other.

Abel and I sit in the very back as Mahara drives the van. She doesn't celebrate Halloween, so she's been dubbed the designated driver of the evening.

Zack and Sebastian sit up front with Mahara. They're dressed up as Steve and Blue from *Blue's Clues*—well, if Steve wore black skinny jeans and combat boots instead of khakis and sneakers.

"I will never wear khaki!" Sebastian yelled when they were planning the costume. "I will not be caught dead in dad pants!"

It's surprising how many people give us candy. There is only one lady who refuses, swatting us away like flies.

"Wait until your father hears about this!" she yells as we run away. "It was cute when you were in high school, Shelby and Sebastian Winter, but you're adults now! Grow up!"

"Never!" Shelby yells back.

We hit a few more houses before Mahara drives us out to the woods.

"Is this where you kill us?" I ask.

Abel leans over and stage-whispers, "And then we eat your corpses."

He's dressed as Death and has covered the backs of his hands and his neck with black liquid latex. Someone painted his face to look like a skull, and he's wearing blackout contacts. His hair is woven with small fake bones we found at the Halloween shop in town. He looks awesome.

"Cool," I retort. "Start with my butt, it's the only fatty part on my body." Realizing how sexual that sounds, I blush. Everyone laughs. "I didn't mean it like that!"

On the other side of me, Toby shifts.

Heat rises to my cheeks. Would I actually die if I threw myself out of the van as it travels at thirty miles an hour? "I hate you all."

Embarrassed, I reach up to twirl my septum ring, but I took out all of my piercings for my costume because that is the type of commitment being Howl deserves. Instead, I tug on the sleeve of my coat.

Abel places his hand on top of mine on my thigh.

Mahara drives us to the lake. We pass a sign that says NO ENTRY AFTER SUNDOWN. She gets us as close to the edge of the water as she can without the van giving us problems when we want to leave later.

We all exit the vehicle. Zack and Toby go off to find some firewood while I stand at the edge of the water and look up at the stars. The sky is so clear, it's almost like I can reach up, snag a star, and put it in my pocket. How fucking cool would it be to own a star?

The rocks crunch behind me. I turn to see Abel walking toward me. He's smiling at me with such warmth, it radiates off him.

SHADES OF US

"What are you thinking about?" he asks when he reaches me.

"Stealing a star from the sky."

He looks up at the night sky and then back down at me. "Why would you want to do that?"

"I would be the only one in the world who had one."

He just looks at me. I hate that I can't figure out what he's thinking. He probably thinks I'm weird. Part of me wishes I were having this conversation with Toby. We have conversations like this all the time, and I never have to question what he's thinking. Toby and I are the same type of odd—he gets my weirdness.

Abel steps closer, wrapping his arms around me. "You're so cute," he whispers. "Can I kiss you?"

I nod. He leans forward, and his lips brush mine. An unusual sound emerges from the back of my throat as I press closer and put my arms around his neck, deepening the kiss and exploring his mouth. He tastes like Red Bull and Twizzlers. I kind of like the combination. I surprise him when I deepen the kiss; he makes an odd grunting sound and pulls me even more into him. There's not an inch of space between his body and mine.

My dumb brain suddenly decides to become aware that others can see us. Despite enjoying the kiss, I pull back and look over to where the rest of the crew is.

Everyone is doing a piss-poor job of pretending they haven't just witnessed Abel and me sucking face. They've all suddenly found the trees on the other side of the van to be interesting. But Toby is staring at us openly. It's dark, but some sort of shadow contorts his face.

My lungs constrict.

Abel lets out an embarrassed little laugh. His ears are red. "Do you—do you want to stay the night tonight?"

Although I have hung out at the PW apartment a handful of times, I've never stayed over. Anxiety bubbles up at the idea of it.

"I'm ace," I blurt out.

"Okay, we don't—"

"I'm asexual, which means I'm not going to have sex with you." I don't know why I'm defining what being ace means; it all just tumbles out of my mouth. My head buzzes. My breath comes out raspy and quick. The dial in my brain is slowly cranking up in volume. There's an itchiness under my skin that I need to scratch, but there's no way for me to relieve it. My vision begins to blur, and everything falls out of focus.

"Hey, hey." Abel takes my hand. I don't register the feel of his hands in mine. He must be able to tell that I'm the edge of panicking because his voice is low and calming. "Hey, I get it, okay? We don't have to have sex. I just want to be near you."

Why? Why does he want to be near me? I'm broken. My brain doesn't work right. We're *never* going to have sex. Why does he want to be with someone like that? Hell, why would anyone?

My breath comes out more rapidly. My body feels too hot and too cold. My heart pounds, trying to jump out of my chest.

"Jess?" Abel's voice sounds distant, even though he's right here. He's still holding on to me.

I try to focus on the feeling of his hands in mine.

Abel is here. He is here. Breathe.

But my thoughts are still racing. Benji didn't want me. I was too broken for him. *I can't take care of you anymore, Jesse.* He's right. No one should have to take care of me. I don't want to burden Abel like I did Benji.

Distantly, outside of my freak-out, I hear arguing.

I focus on that. On the back of Abel's head, his long black hair.

I still can't make out who he's arguing with or what they're saying; all I can hear is the noise in my brain.

Breathe. In. Out.

I close my eyes. My thoughts spin.

I can't take care of you anymore, Jesse.

Warm hands cup my face, and I open my eyes. In front of me are brown eyes winged in gold and black shadow.

"Hey," Toby says. "You're okay. You're okay."

"I'm broken."

"You're not broken." Toby's fingers flex at my temples. I try to shake my head, but he keeps me immobile, grounded. I focus on him, on his eyes, on the pressure of his fingers on my head. "You are a beautiful person. Say it."

"I can't."

"You can."

"I'm a beautiful person." The words are a lie. I'm broken.

"Keep saying it." He pulls me into a hug and squeezes me tight. I wish I could stay wrapped up in him forever, but over his shoulder there's Abel. He looks confused and a little terrified.

I squeeze my eyes shut, feeling guilty for freaking Abel out. My whole body sags, tired from my anxiety attack.

"Breathe," Toby whispers in my ear.

I breathe in.

I'm not broken.

Breathe out.

I'm not broken.

I repeat it over and over, adding in Toby's *I'm a beautiful person.* Eventually, I start to sort of believe it.

Mom's words come to me as I calm down: *Some people want sex, and some don't. You don't, and that is as valid as people who do. Someday, there is going to be a boy who sees you for everything you are.*

"I'm not broken," I whisper out loud.

"No, you're not." Toby pulls out of the hug; his eyes are shining with tears.

My brain is quieter now. The itchiness under my skin is less noticeable.

"You okay?"

"I'm exhausted."

Toby smiles softly. It's dim compared to his normal smile. I wish I could do or say something to bring out his usual megawatt smile. I could really use it right now.

Seeing that I'm back to my normal self, Abel steps forward. "Jess, I—"

"I'm sorry you had to see that."

He looks stricken. "No, Jess, I'm sorry."

Toby steps away and goes back to Madison. A chill settles around me without his arms around me, but Abel closes in, providing warmth. He takes my hands, and I look at our intertwined fingers, focusing on how every single fingernail is black.

"Are you okay?" Abel asks.

"I'm fine. I want to stay with you tonight."

"You don't have to."

He still looks worried. I kiss his cheek. "I want to."

He looks like he's going to argue but ends up saying, "Okay."

I hug him so tight I'm afraid he's going to break, but he doesn't complain. He kisses the top of the blond Howl wig. He's whispering something in Spanish, but I can't make out what he's saying. His voice rumbles where my ear is pressed into his chest. It's soothing.

Our friends are all seated around a bonfire. They keep

glancing at me worriedly. Toby's concerned face watches Abel and me closely. Madison says something to him, and he turns away, gracing her with a ghost of his signature Toby smile.

After several long moments, Abel and I join the others and roast marshmallows. No one brings up my panic attack.

We return to the PW apartment after dropping Toby, Madison, and Amy at the dorms at two in the morning. Everyone is too tired to say anything more than good night before heading to their rooms.

"I'll let you shower first," Abel says, handing me a towel and some clothes to change into.

My stomach churns with nerves as I take the items from him and head to the bathroom.

Since I know Shelby and Zack also have to get in, I shower quickly. The hot water loosens the residual effects of my panic attack. I take a moment to smell the two different men's body washes in the shower and find Abel's. I squeeze a dollop out onto my hand and begin washing.

When I enter the bedroom again, Abel's peeled off all the latex and has washed up in Mahara and Sebastian's shower. He's lying on his bed dressed in gray shorts and a tank top.

"Are you comfortable sleeping in the same bed with me?" he asks. "If not, I can sleep in Zack's bed."

"Where would he sleep?" I don't like the idea of Zack and Abel sharing a bed.

"On the couch. He's already offered."

"No. I'll sleep with you."

I climb in beside him, beyond nervous to be under his covers, but I need his warmth right now.

"I want to tell you something." His voice is low, comforting.

"Hmm?"

"Since you told me something super personal today, I wanted to share something with you. I have been in several relationships and situationships, but nothing has ever lasted more than a few months. Every single person has broken up with me."

"You've never broken up with someone?" I find it hard to believe. Not only is he attractive but he has a great personality.

"Nope. I've never even ghosted anyone."

"Tell me about your last relationship."

"Janine. She didn't want to make long distance work. Which is fair, I guess, considering she was going to study in Europe."

"Europe? Wow. I always wanted to go there." I yawn, barely able to keep my eyes open. I want to talk to Abel more about this. I knew of his sexcapades, but his actual relationships are new information to me.

"Go to sleep," he says, kissing me on the forehead. "We'll talk more in the morning."

He pulls the blanket up to my chin, and I snuggle closer to him, wrapping an arm around his body.

I'm asleep within seconds.

Chapter 31

The first couple weeks of November come and go. I have another Dark Episode around the time of my mom's birthday, but it only lasts two days. Toby spends those two days worrying and talking on the phone with Nana. I don't even know when they exchanged numbers. Craig and Greg call me and ask again if I'm going to return to photography club, but I decline. Even though the club would be a good distraction from the whole adoption thing, I left my group in the lurch when I abandoned the first project. I'm still too embarrassed to face them.

After I get over myself, the crew and I have a friend date to a pizza place and a movie. Since Abel and I flirt the entire time, I miss what the movie is about.

That weekend, we're all sitting in the stands in one of Westbrook's gyms, cheering for Toby. It's his first game of the basketball season, against the Black Ivy University Reapers.

Here's the thing: I don't know shit about basketball. In fact, my headphones cover my ears, blasting music because this loud, stinky, too-bright gym is giving me a headache. But Toby is my friend even though some of us don't like loud, stinky, too-bright gyms. On the plus side, Toby looks *way* too good in his Westbrook Hawks uniform.

I'm squished between Abel and Shelby on the uncomfortable bleachers. Shelby's holding up her phone for Madison to see the court. They're all cheering wildly and sporting Westbrook colors: navy blue and yellow.

"Never took you for a sportie," I tell Shelby when she's calm enough to sit down.

"Sportie? I don't think that's PC, Jesse Lancaster."

"I couldn't think of the word."

She laughs. "Your number fourteen is peeling off, by the way."

Sure enough, when I reach up, blue paint flecks fall off my cheek. Toby painted his jersey number on my cheek before leaving this morning. "So everyone knows who you're rooting for," he said.

"They'll know," I retorted. "We're roommates, dumbass, otherwise I would never be caught dead in a gym."

Around me, people go into a frenzy as one of Toby's teammates scores a basket.

Eventually, I begin to see the appeal of live sports and join in on the cheering whenever our school has the ball or scores. I still have no idea what's going on, but I cheer hard and loud when Toby shoots a three-pointer that wins the game.

The team hoists him into the air in victory. There's a big, dopey, proud smile on his face. Just when I think I'm going to get over this crush on Toby, he does something that my brain finds adorable, and I get all warm and fluttery on the inside.

I wish my heart would . . . I don't know . . . stop finding my roommate so attractive.

Abel's hand is on the bench next to me, and I intertwine our fingers, reminding myself that Toby is unavailable, and Abel is here. I'm going to make things work with him.

Chapter 32

The next weekend, I leave after my shift at Wendell's and head down to Plainsburg on my own, borrowing Toby's car for the weekend. I find it too quiet without my friends around, so I kick on the radio and start blasting my playlist. The first song that comes on is a hip-hop song that Toby snuck on there when I wasn't looking. I haven't removed it, even though I keep telling him I have. It's one of the songs that played at the first party we went to together.

It's midnight when I pull into Nana's condo, due to an accident on the highway that slowed down traffic. Even though it's late, she's standing outside her condo in just her pajamas and robe.

"Nana!" I chastise, exiting the car. "It's dangerous to be out here by yourself this late!"

"Oh, hush up, Jesse," she answers while wrapping me in a hug. "I'll kick anyone's ass who tries to attack me."

"I have no doubts, Nan."

We go inside but don't stay up late talking like usual. I'm tired from my shift and driving, and I want to shower because I still smell like fried dough and sugar. Nana's tired from dealing with her work frenemy, Peggy, who tries to tell Nana what to do even though Peggy is younger and has been at the library for less time. Despite Nana's annoyance with her, they spend every Saturday morning walking together.

When I enter my room, there's a folded black shirt on my bed with an alien printed on the front. It's smiling at me like it's greeting me.

"Oh, that sweet boy must be missing that. I found it shoved under your bed," Nana says, putting her chin on my shoulder.

"Please don't call him 'sweet boy.'"

She laughs. "Why not?"

"You'll inflate his ego!"

"He's not even here!"

I stare at the alien, who is still smiling up at me. I'm having some weird-ass feelings about Toby's shirt being in my space, even though his clothes are *all* over our dorm.

"He'll know," I tell her.

Nana tuts at me. "You like him, don't you?"

I hate that she knows me so well. "I'm too tired to have this conversation."

"Okay, Jess-bug." She kisses my temple and leaves.

Picking up the shirt, I turn it over so the judgy alien can't look at me anymore. Then I text Toby and settle on the bed.

U left ur alien shirt @ Nana's

Two seconds later, he replies.

Toby: *Harold! Bring him back!*

Me: *Of course U named it*

Toby: *Shouldn't you be sleeping?*

Me: *Can't sleep w/o ur snoring*

Toby: I. Do. Not. Snore!

He then sends me a gif of someone snoring.

I send him a bunch of middle finger emojis, smiling the entire time.

Just as I'm about to put the phone down, there's a beep. A message comes in on Facebook from Kelly.

Hey Jesse,

With the holidays coming up, I felt like I should reach out again. I would love a chance to tell you my side of the story. I'm not trying to pressure you, but I was wondering if you have given more thought to possibly meeting up.

We're going out of town for Christmas, but I will be around before or after. I totally understand if this is too much for you, and if you don't reply back, I'll take that as a no and will stop contacting you.

Again, I'm not trying to put pressure on you. I just want a chance to talk, to get to know you.

Wishing you the best, Kelly.

I really don't want to deal with this right now, but it's time. It's been over a month since she sent me the first message.

I call Toby.

He answers immediately.

"What's up?"

"Kelly messaged me again."

"And? What did she say?"

"She wants to know if I'm going to visit her." I reach up to play with my septum ring.

"And are you?"

"Yeah." Saying this one word to Toby makes it feel really real. I'm going to meet my birth mother. "I want to see what she looks like and hear her side of the story."

"Are you sure?"

"I think so. It will bug me if I don't meet her at least once."

"Whatever you decide, Jay. I'm here for you."

I wish he were physically here. I could use his calming presence right now. "Thanks, man. I gotta go talk to Nan."

"See you on Sunday. Don't forget Harold!"

"I'm not going to forget your shirt, weirdo. Bye."

As soon as I hang up with Toby, I make my way down the hall to Nana's room. Her room is full of knick-knacks she's been collecting since she met my grandpa in the 1970s. Stepping into her room is kind of like taking a step into the timeline of her life. There are pictures on her dresser from when she was a little girl, and photos of my dad when he was growing up. A photograph of my grandpa hangs over her bed—she says it's so he can watch over her while she sleeps.

She's watching her ancient portable TV when I enter. She looks away from her show, face full of concern.

"I heard," she says.

"Are you eavesdropping?" I crawl into the bed with her, pulling her box of crackers into my lap and digging out a handful.

"You talk so loud, Jess-bug. The neighbors heard." She turns the TV down so the voices of the actors are nothing more than low buzzing in the background. "Are you sure you want to meet Kelly?"

"You don't think I should?"

She looks off into space for a moment, thinking. I stuff another handful of crackers in my mouth. "I just think it's going to be a lot.

You just got out of an institution. You're doing really well in school. You've made new friends, and you're getting back on track." She pauses, wringing her hands. "I just don't want to see you go back to that place, Jesse. It was scary as hell seeing you like that."

The mere thought of going back there scares the hell out of me too. The drinking, not eating, being off my meds. In those days, I couldn't look in a mirror because I was disgusted by the person who looked back at me. I was a shell of a human and couldn't even recognize myself.

But I feel stronger now. I feel mentally prepared to meet Kelly, to face this head-on as Doctor Hartland said. People are in my corner who will have my back if things get too tough. Besides, I can't put Nana through that again. She's had to deal with shell-Jesse once; she shouldn't have to do it again.

"It's not going to be like that, Nan."

She sniffs, tears glistening in her eyes. "I'm worried that if things get to be too much, I'll actually lose you this time."

I take her hand. It's thin, frail, and cold. Her hands are always cold even in the middle of summer. "You're not going to lose me. I promise. I'm okay."

She sniffs again. "Okay."

I end up falling asleep not long after while watching TV and holding Nana's hand.

>> <<

On Sunday morning, before I head back to campus, I go to Bonnie's Bakery to grab coffee and Nana's favorite cinnamon rolls. The line is long, and I curse, falling in behind a man in a three-piece suit on the sidewalk in front of the bakery.

"Jesse?" someone says as they walk by.

Benji.

He looks good. His red hair is perfectly coiffed. His chest and arms are more toned, and he's dressed in a well-fitting jacket and jeans. He's holding hands with someone with curly black hair and a mustache.

The second I see him, everything in my brain begins to fritz and freeze. The urge to run away builds and builds until it consumes me.

"H-hey, Benji."

The last words he ever said to me replay in my head: *We just don't work, Jesse. I get it now that you are never going to want sex, but it's not just that. I can't handle your bizarre episodes anymore. It's too much. I can't take care of you anymore.*

"How are you?" At least he has the decency to sound sheepish.

"Fine." I reach for my headphones and place them over my ears. "Nice to see you, Benji, but I was just leaving."

"Weren't you—"

"Nope."

The urge to run finally wins, and I scurry off as fast as my feet can carry me. My head is buzzing. "Novocaine" by Fall Out Boy cuts through some of the noise, but even the guitars and drums can't drown out Benji's voice in my head saying "I can't take care of you anymore" over and over again.

Shut up!

Shut up!

My chains slap against my thigh as I cut through the streets. The blackness at the edges of my vision is getting thicker and thicker. Sweat beads on my forehead.

I can't take care of you anymore.

I know. I know. I know!

Doctor Hartland helped me realize how Benji's rejection of my sexuality has shaped a large part of the hatred in myself. She said something that has stuck with me since that session: "Don't let what people think about you define who you are. Benji was not able to understand you, but you have so many people who love you. Don't use Benji's words against those people. The way he reacted is not the way others will react. You just have to let people in to show you that." She told me to repeat a mantra whenever I was being too hard on myself.

I am worthy of love.

I am worthy of love.

I think of Toby and Abel, my friends, and Nana. These people know me. They love me. They accept me.

This is helping. The blackness begins to seep away, and my vision clears.

I am worthy of love.

I don't know if I believe it, but it's helping. The noise in my brain is quieter now.

Nana's building is just ahead, and I let out a relieved breath. Walking the rest of the way, I count my steps to ground myself even more. A light breeze kicks up, and I close my eyes for a moment.

Inhale.

Exhale.

I climb the stairs and open the door to the condo.

"Jess-bug? I thought you were getting coffee."

My legs give out, and I collapse on the couch. "Benji."

Nana stands from her chair and hugs me.

The panic recedes as I focus on the pressure of Nana's arms around my shoulders and the feeling of the couch's fabric beneath my fingertips. I count the ticks of the clock hanging above the TV set.

Inhale.

Exhale.

"I'm good, Nan. I'm okay."

She pulls back, eyeing me. "That must have been a shock for you."

Of course it was. I haven't seen Benji since before Mom and Dad died. He didn't even bother coming to the funeral. He sent me a card saying he was sorry for my loss. That was it. After a two-year relationship, all I got was a lousy card at the lowest point of my life.

Nana and I spend the rest of Sunday in her apartment, eating day-old pasta and watching old movies like *Casablanca* and *Breakfast at Tiffany's*.

Neither of us brings up Kelly or Benji. I'm pretty sure I got my tendency to avoid big, complicated problems from her. Best to sweep it under the rug and pretend it doesn't exist.

I contemplate calling Toby or Abel and telling them about Benji, but I decide not to. Both of them are busy. Toby is at a basketball camp, and Abel is practicing with Poisonous Winter all weekend. They don't need to be worried about me too.

As the sun begins to set, Nana walks me out to Toby's car so I can drive back to Freemont.

"Call me when you get back," she says. "Let me know when you decide to visit Kelly."

It's the first time she's brought up Kelly's name since Friday night. I give a vague nod.

"Love you, Jess-bug."

"Love you too, Nana."

The second I pull out of the parking lot and turn the corner at the end of the street, I'm thinking about Kelly. When should I contact her? What should I say to her when I see her? Is this a bad idea?

Even when I reach the highway, I still have no idea what to do, but weirdly I feel uncharacteristically optimistic about meeting the woman who gave birth to me.

Chapter 33

On the Monday night before Thanksgiving, the crew gathers at the PW apartment—well, everyone except Mahara and Sebastian, who flew to Chicago to visit Mahara's parents.

"Welcome to Friendsgiving!" Shelby exclaims as she opens the door. She's wearing a flapper dress, and her makeup is done in a 1920s style. She requested that we dress in ridiculous costumes for the event, so we're all wearing something we found at the thrift stores around town. Amy is wearing one of those dinosaur balloon suits, Toby is dressed in a cat costume he found for 75 percent off after Halloween, and I'm dressed like a giant pink bunny, very much giving off *A Christmas Story* vibes.

The apartment is decorated in a mix of Halloween, harvest, and Christmas decorations. Abel (Wolverine) and Zack (I have no idea who he's supposed to be) are playfully arguing over the stove. I beeline for Abel, sneaking a peek at the food on the table: there's everything from elote to steamed dumplings to chili.

Abel pulls me into him as I approach, kissing the top of my head. I bury my face in his chest; since he's been busy with school and band practice, I haven't been able to see him much, and I miss his scent. He draws small circles on my back, continuing his argument with Zack.

"Michael Keaton is *the* Batman!" Zack argues.

Abel lets out a frustrated sound that makes me chuckle. "Are you serious? We've been friends for so long, how did I not know you were so blind? Val Kilmer!"

"You're both idiots," I interject.

Zack opens his mouth to argue, but Shelby comes into the kitchen with a look on her face that gets them to shut up and continue cooking.

"Come help me set the table, Jess." She pulls me out of Abel's arms and leads me to a small round table they have set up in their living room—which only fits because the armchair is out on the balcony and the couch is pushed to the side of the room as far as it can go.

Shelby hands me a stack of "Happy Birthday" plates and begins setting out plastic cups with SpongeBob on them.

"No turkey and fancy china?"

"Nah. None of us actually celebrate Thanksgiving. We use Friendsgiving as an excuse to dress up—"

"As I suspected."

"—*and* get shit-faced. On the actual day, we sleep in and watch movies." She pauses, and her face suddenly turns serious. "We have a gig in New York on December fourteenth. It could be your chance to meet Kelly."

My hand, holding one of the SpongeBob cups, begins to shake. "I'll let you know."

Shelby gives my shoulder an encouraging squeeze but says nothing else.

Once everything is ready, we all gather around the table, with me squished between Toby and Abel. We're packed so tight around the table that there's no way we're going to get through this meal without accidentally elbowing our neighbors multiple times. Every time I move, some part of me touches Abel or Toby, which is going to be the cause of me combusting.

What have I gotten myself into?

I should have sat next to Amy.

"The chili's vegetarian," Abel tells me. "Tell me what you think."

Toby's knee bumps mine. He smiles at me sheepishly. "Sorry, Jay."

Has anyone ever died from being too consumed by their hormones? I feel too warm and blame the bunny suit. Would it be too dramatic to light it on fire when I return to the dorm?

I eat in silence, mumbling my confirmation that the chili is, in fact, really good. As I'm spooning some sort of cabbage salad into my mouth, Abel accidentally knocks my elbow, and the salad falls back to my plate.

"Oops, sorry, babe."

A blush heats my cheeks.

There's a collective "Ooooh" from Shelby, Amy, and Zack. Next to me, Toby stiffens. I can't look at him. I stare at my cabbage salad.

Abel leans over. "Sorry, slip of the tongue."

"No worries." I clear my throat. "I don't mind you calling me that."

Abel's returning smile is beautiful.

We all go back to eating for a few moments, and then Amy stands. She wrings her hands nervously. "So, um . . . I want to thank you all for being my friends. I know we haven't been friends for that long, but you all have become like a family in the past few months." She pauses. Her eyes well with tears. "I can't tell my own family yet, but if I don't get this out, I think I'm going to explode." Tears slide down her cheeks. Shelby rubs her arm. "I'm—I'm agender, and I would really appreciate it if you all could start using they/them for my pronouns."

There's no hesitation from us. We all stand and give Amy the biggest, warmest group hug they have ever received. We're all a crying mess.

Amy's right: We're a big, weird, messy family.

Chapter 34

On the Sunday after Thanksgiving, I'm lying in my bed, eating shitty ramen noodles and watching *Demon Slayer* when there's a knock on the door. For a moment, the thought crosses my mind that maybe Toby forgot his key, but he isn't supposed to be back until Monday. It couldn't be Amy or Shelby because they both went to New Jersey for a concert and won't be back until Tuesday.

I flop out of my bed, slurping noodles on the way, and open the door to see Abel. He looks exhausted. His hair is in a messy bun, and he's wearing an artfully bleached black shirt and sweatpants.

"When did you get back?" I step aside to let him into the dorm.

"Twenty minutes ago." He kisses my forehead and makes himself at home on my bed. He's only been in my room twice before this; usually we hang out at the PW apartment. I like all the space and having Shelby around to tease. "I had to leave early because I couldn't handle Mom and Dad fighting anymore."

I sit on the bed with him, tucking my arm under his head. He's told me a little about his home life but hasn't shared major details. All I really know is that his parents fight a lot, and his little brother has to act as a mediator between them.

"How was your weekend at your grandma's?" He changes the subject.

"Good. I talked more about Kelly with her. We had a really long conversation about how I feel about the whole thing."

SHADES OF US

"And?" Abel begins drawing little circles on my arm. It's very distracting. "How do you feel?"

"I feel betrayed, Abe. I feel like everyone has been lying to me, and there's no one I can scream at about it."

"Scream at me."

"What good would that do?"

He shrugs. "Would it make you feel better?"

"No. It wouldn't."

"Can I tell you what I think?" He looks at me with uncertain dark-brown eyes, like he's afraid to overstep.

I nod.

"Yes, it's shitty that your parents and grandma didn't tell you that you're adopted, and yes, it's shitty that you had to find out from a stranger, but you decided to meet her. Hear her out. The worst that can happen is you don't like her and you guys don't develop a further relationship."

He's right, but it doesn't alleviate the betrayal or confusion I feel. I'm afraid to confront this big part of my life since I still have no idea who I am. What if I am more like this stranger than my parents? What if Kelly is an addict or a criminal? What if I become her? What if she's just using all of this as an excuse to use me in some way?

"But none of that could be true," Doctor Hartland said when I brought my concerns up in one of our sessions. "Kelly could just be a person who wants to see what a wonderful man you are becoming. She may not have a hidden agenda. You'll never know unless you meet her."

Those words were the catalyst for me making the final decision to meet Kelly. All the unknown about who she is has caused my mind to overthink and come up with worst-case scenarios.

Abel reaches up and brushes hair out of my eyes, catching my attention. I intertwine our fingers. Looking at the tattoos on his knuckles has become a safety blanket. If I feel overwhelmed, I count the stars that take up each of his fingers over and over. Fifteen in total, combining both hands.

"We're all here for you, Jess."

"Thanks."

We watch the rest of the episode of *Demon Slayer* in silence. Abel's eyes begin to close, but when I reach for the remote, he's alert again.

"Sorry, I just wanted to turn off the TV."

"Can I ask you something I was thinking about this weekend?"

"Sure."

"I know we've been seeing each other casually for a while now." He pauses, looking unsure of himself. "Would you wanna make it official?"

"Yes," I answer without thinking.

If I think, then I will talk myself out of it. Toby's face will enter my mind, and we can't have that. Lock that shit in a box and throw away the key.

"Really?" His smile is as bright as sunshine. "Oh, shit! Yes!"

He leans toward me, peppering kisses along my jaw, lips, and cheeks. His excitement makes me laugh. I push him off of me and lean over him, taking in everything about him. His dark-brown— nearly black—eyes, his high cheekbones, his full lips. His kindness and his unwavering dedication to me even when I disappeared for days on end.

I lean in and kiss him, pouring every ounce of adoration into the kiss. I'm not good at expressing how I feel when it comes to romance, so I try to convey how much he means to me with my lips. The kiss is sweet, chaste, slow, and sensual. His fingers go into my hair, curling at the back of my head. His tongue dances with mine. Everything feels light.

Even my brain is quiet.

I pull back and push his hair away from his face. He chuckles. "Wow."

I kiss him again.

You're really special, Abel Ryan.

And now we're together.

How the fuck did I pull this off?

Chapter 35

The two weeks after Thanksgiving are filled with studying for finals and work. I don't see Abel at all because we're so busy, but he texts me every day with flirty messages and sweet comments.

Toby's been MIA since I told him about becoming actual boyfriends with Abel. When I do see him, he's either heading out the door or already asleep. Usually, he waits for me after class so we can get lunch together, but lately he keeps texting me with excuses as to why he can't meet up.

Sorry. Team meeting.

Have to finish this paper.

I already ate with the team.

I might be overthinking, but I'm pretty sure he's avoiding me for some fucking reason. Part of me wants to ask him about it, but when I actually do see him, he seems normal, so it might just be my brain trying to find problems where there are none.

Despite that, I still go to his games to support him. At the last game before the winter break, the basketball team loses to Westbrook's biggest rivals, which puts Toby in a bad mood. He keeps blaming himself for the loss since he missed the final basket that would have put them ahead. Amy and I take him out for burgers, and that seems to calm him a bit. I've learned that food is Toby's weakness; it's the best way to cheer him up or get back in his good graces. He's all smiles by the time we leave the restaurant and even suggests we go see a movie. Amy tells us they can't; they have to meet with a tutor so they can ace their algebra final.

As we walk to the theater, Toby slings his arm over my shoulder. All around us, the city sparkles with holiday decorations. The lampposts of downtown Freemont have been twisted with garland, and lights are strung around the window of every store.

"This is romantic," Toby jokes, squeezing my shoulder.

I was just thinking the same thing. Abel would like this. We could go to the candy shop and try Christmas treats.

But hearing Toby saying those words to me causes my heart to flutter.

I brush the feeling off by rolling my eyes at him and pushing him off of me. "You're such an idiot."

When he's acting like this, it's easier to pretend I'm not worried something is wrong between us. *I'm overthinking. Everything's fine.*

Chapter 36

On Friday morning, after my last final, we are all standing around the van as Abel and Sebastian throw bags inside.

"Two minutes," Abel reminds me as I talk to Toby and Amy.

"Bring me back something," Amy says, squeezing me in a hug. "I want an 'I love NYC' shirt."

"Those are so touristy."

"Yeah, well, I've never been there, and that's what you get someone who has never been."

I pull out of the hug and kiss their cheek. "Fine. I'll bring you a tourist shirt."

"Thank you!"

They dart off to say goodbye to everyone else. It's just me and Toby. He keeps playing with his hair, and his eyes dart from my face to the space behind me.

"Are you okay?"

"Yeah, man." He runs a hand over his loose dreads, flipping them from one side to the other. "Good luck."

"Jess!" Shelby calls. "We're leaving with or without you!"

I hold up a finger to tell her to wait. "Are you sure you're okay?"

Toby nods, but it looks forced. "I'm good. Go."

"Jesse Lancaster, don't make me count to five like you're a child!" Shelby's laughter drifts toward us from the open door of the van. I know they're all anxious to get on the road, but I can't leave Toby when something is bothering him. He's never uneasy, and I hate seeing him like this. His nervousness is crawling under my skin and making me jittery.

He pulls me into a hug. My arms automatically come up around him as natural as breathing. "Call me for anything, Jay. You got this."

We've hugged many times over the last few months. We've hugged in excitement and in sadness. He's hugged me when I've needed grounding and to calm me down. But this hug feels different. He throws his whole weight into it, enveloping me with his arms. His face is tucked into my neck like he's afraid to let me go. And it *lingers*—this is the longest hug we've had to date.

When he pulls back, he's blushing and very awkward. It's a look I have never seen before.

A small part of my brain begins to feel a sliver of hope, but I shut it down. Don't unlock that box; it needs to remain closed.

It doesn't matter what that part of my brain may be feeling. Toby is taken. I am taken. We can be nothing more than friends.

When I turn toward the van, everyone is looking at us. Abel looks obviously, and rightfully, pissed.

Ugly, bile-inducing guilt drops like lead in my stomach as I walk toward the van.

"What was that?" Abel whispers harshly as I climb into the seat next to him.

"I don't know what's going on with him." I chew on my bottom lip. Why is Toby acting so weird?

The rest of the band pretends like they can't hear our conversation as we pull out of the parking lot. Fuck, this is so awkward.

"Do I have anything to be worried about?"

I swallow. "Of course not. Toby and I are just friends."

Abel nods. "Okay." He takes my hand. "I believe you."

Chapter 37

Though New York is only a few hours from Freemont, we stop in Philly for the night to visit Zack's parents.

I sleep for most of the hour-long drive, leaning my head against Abel's shoulder, and wake up just as we pull up to a small white house with yellow shutters and a small garden. It looks cozy and quintessential, not at all the type of house I pictured Zack growing up in. For some reason—probably because he told me both of his parents are world-renowned artists—I pictured him living in a modern, artsy penthouse on the top floor of a high-rise.

As soon as Zack turns off the engine, the screen door of the house bangs open and a plump woman with salt-and-pepper hair runs out onto the lawn, followed by a tall, skinny man and what looks like a hundred dogs.

"Zackery!"

"Hi, Mom," Zack says as we all enter the yard through a small brown gate.

Zack's mom crushes him to her chest before he's even through the gate. When she releases him, she squeals over the rest of the crew.

His dad is much more subdued, clapping Zack on the shoulder. "How was the drive, son?"

"Fine. How is your art show coming along?"

"Fine."

"Abel! You're still wearing those awful holey shirts? And those spikes on your jacket—they nearly took my eye out when I hugged you!" Zack's mom chastises him, but she's still hugging him. She's too short to even reach the spikes on the shoulder of Abel's jacket.

Once she releases him, she turns to me, her face beaming. It seems Zack takes more after his dad; they're both calmer, while his mom seems to be a ball of energy. "You must be Jesse!" She pulls me into a hug before I can answer. "We're so happy you're here." His mom reminds me of Nana. She places a hand over her heart. "Oh, look at those dimples! And those pretty blue eyes! You must have all the boys fawning over you!"

My face heats. "Thank you?"

Abel pulls me to his side. "He's got me hooked."

I hit his chest. "Shush."

"Oh, aren't you the cutest pair!" she squeals.

"Let the boy breathe, Martha." Zack's dad steps forward. "I'm Peter. Welcome."

I shake his proffered hand. There's paint under his fingernails, and his palm is callused from wood carving.

"We put you boys in the basement, and the girls in the guest room."

"Mom, Seb and Mahara are practically married. They should be in the guest room."

"Don't say we're married," Mahara says. "Not for another five years. It's all planned."

"Of course you planned it out," Shelby teases. "As long as I'm still maid of honor."

"You're not even invited," Sebastian retorts.

"Children, enough." Zack's mom shakes her head. "This is how the sleeping arrangements will be for tonight."

"That's great, Mrs. Cameron," Sebastian replies.

"Always so polite, Sebastian. I was hoping after three years of friendship, more of that would rub off on Zack."

"Thanks for making me look like a bad son, Seb."

Sebastian shrugs with a smirk. "Can't help it. Parents love me."

"Come inside," Peter interrupts before they can start messing around again. "Martha's made lamb stew and baked tofu for Abel."

We all enter the small house, which is definitely not designed to hold six dogs, two adults, and six college kids. The walls are plastered with original artwork by Zack's parents, as well as pictures of him from babyhood until now. Behind all that is awful floral wallpaper that I'm sure was hung before any of us were born.

Dinner is delicious and loud. It's clear Zack's parents view the PW crew as their own children. They dote on the band and scold them when they reveal their latest mistakes and blunders.

After dinner and a round of Monopoly, Mr. and Mrs. Cameron head up to bed. As soon as we hear the door shut, Sebastian and Mahara sneak out to the backyard. Zack and Shelby fire up his Wii U and start playing *Just Dance*. Abel comes over to where I'm sitting on the floor by the couch, flipping through a book I pulled from the bookshelf.

"Come outside with me?"

"Okay." I put the book on the couch cushion and take the hand he's reached out to help me stand.

He leads me to the front door. The air is beyond chilly; it feels like it's going to snow. Abel seems unbothered by the cold but does still zip his jacket. I'm shivering in my hoodie and ripped jeans.

He climbs the ladder attached to the rear door of the van and sits on the roof. The metal is freezing as I lower myself down next to him. He pulls me more to his side, rubbing my arm to warm me up. We watch the stars in silence for a few moments.

"About earlier—"

"No sweat. You told me not to worry, so I'm not going to worry." He leans against me. "I know you're close with Toby."

"Why?"

The word comes out of my mouth without me meaning to. If I had this problem with Benji, it would have resulted in a huge fight. Why does Abel seem so calm about the whole thing?

He seems to understand what I'm asking. He places his fingers under my chin, turning my head toward him. He looks at me—*into* me—with heavy-lidded eyes. His breath fans my face. My stomach tightens, but I can't tell if the feeling is pleasant or unpleasant.

"Because I love you."

I stop breathing for a few seconds. My brain halts. My heart beats in overdrive.

"What do you mean you love me?"

"Exactly what I just said." His thumb traces my cheek. "I love you."

"Why?"

His gaze is intense. I can't look away.

"Does love really need an explanation?"

I just look at him, not really knowing how to respond. He has to be joking. But he's not. There's sincerity in the depth of his deep brown eyes.

I can't say the words back to him. As much as I like Abel, I'm just not there yet.

"Abe."

The only thing I can think of to do in that moment is kiss him, hard. He falls back against the roof with me lying on top of him. His hands go under my shirt, tracing my back before traveling lower to grip my ass. I arch into him, and our hips grind together. He moans around my mouth.

"Jesse. Is this okay?"

"More than." I want to do this for him. Even if I don't want sex, I want to see his pleasure; watching my partner let go brings me happiness.

I trail kisses from his mouth to his neck. He uses his hands on my ass to control the rhythm of our hips as he nips at my jaw.

I still don't fully understand why he says he loves me. But my heart and brain are synced for once: they are overjoyed to be loved by someone like Abel Ryan. Maybe one day, I can reciprocate those feelings.

As we get lost in each other, it begins to snow.

Chapter 38

We eat breakfast with Zack's parents early the next morning and then hit the road again. Something has shifted between Abel and me since fooling around on the roof of the van. I feel more sure of my relationship with him, and it seems like he's more sure of me as well. The events of last night released the things that were holding me back from committing to my feelings for Abel.

He sleeps as we drive, lying against my chest while I braid his hair. Shelby keeps looking at us pointedly, giggling whenever I make eye contact with her.

"It's nice seeing you two like this," is all she says.

"Don't point it out," I say. "You're gonna ruin the moment."

We arrive at IUG, a trendy bar in Brooklyn, after checking in early to our hotel. The band has a sound check at twelve-thirty, so we spend the next hour and a half sitting around and watching the other band rehearse. The bar has an industrial feel to it with neon lights painting the interior brick, concrete, and metal with a rainbow of colors. Tables are set up in the center of the floor with black leather couches lining the walls. Shelby and I are sitting on one of the couches while the rest of the band sits at a table nearby. The staff of the bar is working hard to get things set up for the show that night. Besides PW, there's another band playing, called Tri-PROMISE. PW has played with them before and are acquaintances with the members.

"When are you supposed to meet Kelly?" Shelby asks me.

"She said she was free all day. I just have to call her and let her know a time to meet."

"When are you going to call her?"

"I should probably call her soon, right?"

"Right."

"Poisonous Winter!" someone calls from the stage. "You're up!"

Shelby stands and pats my knee. "Call Kelly."

Abel comes to kiss me before following everyone else on stage. "Good luck today, Jess. Call me if you need anything. I'll see you later."

I nod. "Break a leg."

After they get settled on stage, they start playing one of their most popular songs, "What's Left Unsaid," which was written by Shelby after she broke up with her first girlfriend. I watch them for the first song, mostly focusing on Abel and the way he moves his sticks. Seriously, I could watch him drum for hours.

After they finish "What's Left Unsaid," I head out of the bar. Outside, the sun is too bright after being in the dimly lit building. I blink rapidly, trying to get my bearings, and pull out my cell phone.

But I don't call Kelly.

"You're stalling," Toby says when he answers.

"I'm sorry. I can't hear you. What am I doing?"

"Stalling," he replies in the same smart-ass inflection I used.

I smile. "What are you doing?"

"Amy and I decided to go have coffee in town, and then they want to go thrifting."

"Come pick me up! I love thrifting!"

"I know you do, but you got shit to do. I'll see if I can find anything for you." There's a pause, a heavy thing that I'm not sure what to do with or why it's there. "Be brave, Jay. Call Kelly."

SHADES OF US

"I will. I just have to work myself up to it."

"You got this."

We talk for another twenty minutes as I walk around Brooklyn. One of the bookshops I pass is selling exclusive signed copies of Brett Cable's new book. Brett Cable is one of Toby's favorite authors, so I don't even hesitate to stop in and get him a copy.

The whole time I'm exploring Brooklyn, Toby keeps telling me to get off the phone and call Kelly, but he doesn't seem to be in a rush to let me go either.

"Where are you now?"

"I'm at a park," I reply, settling on a bench. "I'm going to call Kelly now."

"I'm proud of you, Jay. You'll tell me everything when you get back tomorrow, right?"

"No. I was going to let you live in suspense for the rest of your life."

I can almost feel him rolling his eyes through the phone. "Pain in the ass. I'll see you tomorrow."

We hang up, and I dial the number in my phone that is saved as "???." Putting Kelly's actual name and number in my phone made everything feel too real, too confusing, so I had Toby change it. The three question marks are fitting, considering I have no clue what the hell is going to come from all of this.

The tightness in my chest clamps down with every ring.

"Hello?"

"Ke-Kelly? This is Jesse."

"Jesse. Hi." I try to tell her mood by the tone of her voice, but the truth is she may be my birth mother, but I don't know shit about her, so I can't read her voice. "It's good to hear from you. Would you like to meet for coffee now?"

"I—I'd like that." My anxiety is ramping up the longer I talk to her. I squeeze Toby's book in my other hand; the hard spine keeps me tethered. "Where should we meet?"

Kelly gives me the name of a café that's not far from the park. With every step I take in that direction, my pulse ticks up, and my hands begin to shake. Sweat beads on my back and forehead. The static gets louder and louder. I try to remember the words of encouragement Nana, Abel, and Toby have been giving me all week, but my mind goes blank.

From across the street, I see her sitting at one of the tables on the café patio. She's hard to miss. Her hair is the same shade of brown as mine, and her eyes are big and round like mine. There's no mistaking that this woman is my biological mother. It looks as if she's been there for a while. There's an empty plate in front of her and a book on the table.

The sight of her makes my vision tunnel, and the world tilts.

Run.

It's the only thing that breaks through the static in my mind.

Run! RUN!

I run. I don't know where I'm going, but I can't stop. Barreling into people and objects, I keep running. Everything feels flipped upside down, and the ground feels unstable. Sweat pours from me, staining my clothes.

I stumble over a crack in the sidewalk, fall, and then get up quickly. I ignore the stinging in my hands and knees, the blood dripping down my leg, and just keep going.

Chapter 39

When I finally get my bearings, the sun is beginning to set. I breathe in and out, counting to calm down further. Nothing around me looks familiar, but I still have a few hours left until I have to be at the bar to watch Poisonous Winter perform.

I pull out my phone to pull up my location in reference to the bar. I'm a few blocks away from the hotel we're staying at for the evening, so I stick around the area, checking out random shops and bakeries to pacify my craving for sugar. The last shop I end up visiting sells vintage clothes, and I find a Michael Jordan jersey that Toby will love.

Toby's called me three times since we talked this afternoon, but I haven't answered. I text him that I will call him later and not to worry.

After grabbing some tacos from a Korean-Mexican fusion food truck, I head to the hotel and drop my purchases on the bed I'm sharing with Abel before heading back to the bar.

The place is packed when I arrive. It seems most of the people are here to see Tri-PROMISE, but several are wearing Poisonous Winter shirts as well.

I find a table near the back just as the lights go low and a guitar riff rips through the air. The bar fills with screams, and lights illuminate the stage as Sebastian takes his mic and begins the opening line of "Burn," one of their more upbeat and popular songs. I'm exhausted from my panic attack and marathon running earlier, but I force myself to not feel it, to not think about the whole Kelly thing, so I jump around and scream the lyrics along with Sebastian and half of the venue.

Poisonous Winter play their most upbeat songs, raising the energy inside of IUG, but after the fourth song, Sebastian takes the mic to address the crowd.

"How ya doing, Brooklyn? You guys having fun?" His questions are met with a crescendo of screams. He beams. His blond hair sticks to his forehead with sweat, and he looks very much like the famous rock star he'll soon be. "We're going to slow things down now. This new song was written by my sister. I hope you guys enjoy."

Sebastian and Shelby switch places. She takes center stage, and Sebastian picks up her bass, slinging the pink strap over his shoulder.

The venue buzzes with confused excitement. Shelby sings background vocals for her brother, but she's never been front and center like this. She looks beyond nervous.

"This song is called 'Red Harmony.'" She takes a breath and begins to sing. Her voice is eerie and beautiful, low and breathy at the beginning. She draws tears from my eyes as she tells a story about love, loss, and jealousy.

"There is nothing left here . . ."

That line guts me. I can feel the pain and longing from Shelby's words deep in my heart. Something about the loneliness of her lyrics resonates with me.

The tempo builds as Shelby reaches the chorus, holding a beautiful high note that leaves my jaw on the floor. The note ends, and the crowd erupts into cheers, even as Shelby continues to sing.

Once the song ends, the entire bar starts applauding. My heart swells with pride for her. She sang so beautifully.

Shelby breathes heavily as she finishes, clutching the mic for dear life. She's crying, but there's a look of relief on her face, as if singing the song was almost cathartic.

"Th-thank you," she says into the microphone, wiping her tears. "We are Poisonous Winter."

They exit the stage. There's a lull after their set while the crew prepares the stage for Tri-PROMISE.

My phone rings. I pull it out to see Toby's name on the screen and leave my spot to take the call outside. I lean against the brick wall and answer the phone. The night is freezing, as if it's going to snow. My breath comes out in puffs.

"I chickened out," I say instead of telling him hello. "I don't know what happened, but I couldn't do it."

"Are you okay?"

Truthfully? No. "Yeah, I'm okay."

"Are you at the bar?"

"Yeah. I just watched PW's set. They were amazing."

There's a pause. "Jay?"

"Hmm?"

"Are you sure you're okay?"

Tears begin to well. "I don't know." A breeze blows, and I zip my flannel jacket higher. "For the past week or so, I have been so confident about meeting Kelly. Everything would be fine—I was going to get answers—but the second I saw her, I freaked out and ran."

"Where did you go?" Panic sets in his voice.

"Nowhere. I just ran."

"Shit. You should have called me."

"I wish you were here." The words tumble out of my mouth

unbridled. I clear my throat. "I have to go. The next band is going on."

Before he can say anything else, I hang up.

"There you are." Abel leans out of the door to the bar. He's still sweating from playing, which makes his black shirt cling to his chest. "You okay? How did it go with Kelly?"

"I don't want to talk about it."

He doesn't say anything, just sticks his hand out for me to take. "Come on. The next band is about to go on. We'll talk when you're up for it."

I close the space between us and follow him inside. He turns to me in the small entryway, which is covered in posters for local musicians, and wraps his arms around me, and I kiss his cheek.

"You guys were awesome."

"Thanks. I broke one of my sticks."

"I saw. It was cute how you threw it behind you."

He cups my cheek, his thumb caressing the skin. A million questions burn behind his eyes, but he doesn't ask a single one. Instead, he says, "Come on."

Tri-PROMISE has already taken the stage when we rejoin the PW crew. We spend the next hour getting lost in their music.

Chapter 40

The ride from New York to Freemont is loud: Zack and Sebastian fight over the radio, and Shelby spills her cheese puffs after our second stop at a gas station. Abel and I sit in the back, cuddled together, talking and listening to music. I told him everything that happened when we returned to the hotel after their performance. He comforted me and gave me advice, saying that I should reach out to her again when I feel more comfortable.

I decide to message Kelly. Not knowing exactly what to say, I end up sending:

Sry about yesterday

She replies quickly.

I understand how hard this is. Let me know if you want to try to meet up again; I'm here for you.

I don't text her back.

We arrive at campus a little before sunset. The PW crew drops me off in front of my dorm, and I kiss Abel before they go back to their apartment.

When I get to my room, it's shrouded in gray, dusky light and smells like burnt popcorn. Toby's not around, but his things are everywhere. It's strange; he's usually really good about picking up after himself. Sometimes he even cleans up after me.

I pull out my phone and call Toby.

"You're back!" His voice sounds weird; it's thick with emotion, like he's been crying.

"What's wrong?"

"Nothing," he lies. He sighs. "I found out something about Madison."

"Where are you?"

"The pond."

"In the middle of December?" The pond has sort of become our place. We sit on one of the benches before and after class, and on weekends we bring coffee and talk about everything and nothing. "Stay there. I'm going to meet you."

"Bossy, but okay."

I hang up and drop my bag on the floor before sprinting back out the door and into the cold.

When I get to the pond, Toby is sitting on a bench with a bucket hat pulled over his ears. His back is toward me, and the last bits of sunlight create a golden halo all around him.

I close the distance and sink onto the bench beside him. His eyes are swollen, and his face is splotchy. A tear trails down his cheek.

"What happened?"

"I found out Madison has been cheating on me." He sniffs. "Last night, Chaz called me while he was drunk, and he spilled everything. They've been hooking up behind my back this entire time."

"Oh, shit." Scooting closer to him, I place a hand on his knee in an attempt to comfort him. "T, I'm so sorry."

He sniffs again. "I called Madison, and after denying it for nearly twenty minutes, she confessed. It started back in September. Can you imagine, Jay? This whole time, she has been playing me for a fool. We've been together for years. How could she do that to me? Fuck." He dashes his tears away. "I told her last night that I needed to think about everything, but I called her back this morning and ended things. I can't be with someone who would break my trust like that."

"You broke up with her?"

He nods and wipes his tears again. "No matter how much I love someone, I can't be with a person who lies to me like that. I'm forgiving, but I don't play when it comes to that shit."

"I'm so sorry, T."

I pull him into a hug and hold him as he cries. His whole body shakes as he sobs. My heart breaks for him. I hate seeing him so upset.

We hug for a long time until the sun has fully set and the lamps turn on, bathing the pond in yellow light. Toby pulls back and wipes the last of his tears. He looks at me with a watery smile.

"I'm sorry."

"Hey, you've taken care of me plenty of times, it's only polite that I return the favor." I wipe a lingering tear from his cheek without thinking. "You okay?"

"I need to take my mind off everything. Take me somewhere?"

Normally, I would suggest we go back to the dorm, but I know just the thing to get his mind off Madison.

"Marla from my A/AA club is throwing a Christmas party. Want to go?"

"You're suggesting we go to a party? Who are you? Did you get body snatched when you were in New York?"

"Shut up." He cackles like he's the funniest person to ever live, so I push him backward. "Do you want to go or not?"

"Oh, we're going."

We stand and head to Marla's house, which is only a short walk from campus. She and her roommates have decorated the outside of their three-bedroom home with so many lights that aliens could probably see it from space. The inside is decorated from floor to ceiling with a tree, lights, plastic snowmen, garland, and a hand-painted sign that reads: HAPPY HOLIDAYS WESTBROOK!

The air smells heavily of cinnamon, alcohol, perfume, and body odor.

"Jesse!" Marla calls. She already looks drunk. Paxton holds her up because one of her heels broke, but she doesn't seem to be standing still long enough for him to take it off for her.

"Hey! Great party!" I yell over a modern pop version of "Santa Baby."

"Aw, thank you! The others are around here somewhere, make sure you say hi!" She takes a drink from whatever is in her cup. "Food and drinks are in the kit—" The song switches from "Santa Baby" to a rock version of "You're a Mean One, Mr. Grinch," and Marla's eyes go wide. "Oh! I love this song! Pax, come dance with me!" She jumps around, dragging Paxton behind her.

"She's not normally like that," I tell Toby with a laugh. "When she's sober, she's really quiet. At the last dinner, she got buzzed and wouldn't stop talking about different species of plants."

"It's always the quiet ones who know how to party."

We enter the kitchen laughing, and Toby has his arm over my shoulder. Zack is leaning against the counter, picking at a tray of cheese and crackers.

SHADES OF US

"Hey," he says. He eyes Toby and me. His stare makes me squirm. "I didn't think you were coming."

"Some shit went down with Madison, so I forced Jesse to take me out," Toby explains. He leaves me to get a drink from the counter behind us.

Zack eyes me up and down. I don't like it; something about the look feels hostile.

"Are you pissed about something?" I ask.

He shrugs, leaning forward and whispering, "Don't hurt Abel."

Offended, I step back from him. My face contorts. "Why the fuck do you think I'm going to hurt him?"

Zack shrugs. "Call it a hunch."

I get in his face, hissing, "I'm not planning on hurting Abel. I genuinely *like* him."

Toby joins us again. He steps in front of me, blocking me from Zack. "Leave him alone."

People are starting to stare. I pull on Toby's sleeve before things get more heated.

Zack raises his eyebrows at us. "Hmm. Enjoy the party." He leaves the kitchen.

Toby turns toward me. "What the fuck was that about?"

Confused, I shake my head. "I don't know."

"Fuck it."

The scenario plays again in my mind even as Toby pulls me out to the living room, and we spend the next hour or so dancing to different Christmas songs. Some Top 40 songs are mixed in, but I only know a handful of lyrics to like five songs. We don't see Zack for the rest of the night.

After dancing, we find a place to sit by a fire pit and roast marshmallows. I yawn as my fifth marshmallow catches fire.

"Okay, party monster, time to leave," Toby says after "Frosty the Snowman" starts playing for the third time since we arrived.

I stand, leaning against him as my legs don't seem to know what upright and walking are. "Can we stop somewhere? I'm starving."

Toby leads me to the door. "How can you be hungry? You just ate like eighty-four marshmallows."

"Are you laughing at me right now?"

"I would never, Jay." He then has the audacity to actually laugh. "Usually you don't eat this much."

He's right. Though I have gained back all the weight I lost after my parents died and my attempted suicide, my appetite still isn't what it used to be. In high school, I was able to scarf down two cheeseburgers, and now I can barely finish one.

As he orders a rideshare, I rest my head against his shoulder, too tired to keep my eyes open. "Maybe I *was* body snatched."

"Nah. I would know if you weren't my bestie, Jesse."

"Don't say stuff like that when I'm too tired to come up with a sarcastic comeback."

"What do you want to eat?"

"Nachos, a Coke, and a cookie."

"Very specific."

A green Versa pulls up to the curb, and he drags me to it. I slump against the seat, leaning against Toby as he closes the door.

"Good night?" the driver asks.

Ugh. He's one of those drivers that talks.

I groan and bury my head more in Toby's arm.

"It was great," Toby answers. "How about yours?"

"Can't complain."

"Can we add a stop? There's a fast food place down the road, right?"

I doze off as Toby and the driver talk, their voices lulling me to sleep.

Toby wakes me again when we're back at the dorm. He carries the bags of food and drags me beside him as I sleepily sip my drink. When we're inside the room, he sets out my nachos and fires up *Death Note*. As soon as we're done eating, I crawl into bed without changing into pajamas. I'm out within seconds.

Chapter 41

The next morning, Toby and I wake up late. We don't have time to lounge around and grab a cup of coffee like we wanted before Shelby needs to take him and Abel to the airport. It's officially the start of winter break. I won't be seeing Toby or the PW crew for three weeks. The knowledge of that twists my stomach. These weirdos are my family; I can't imagine not seeing them for that long.

We change in a hurry. I have a pounding migraine, which builds as I grab my duffle and race out of the dorm.

"Are you going to be okay?" Toby asks while I massage my temples.

"I'll be fine."

We exit the dorm and head to the parking lot, where we find Shelby, Abel, and Amy. Shelby's leaning against her car, joking around with Amy. Abel starts walking toward me as soon as he sees me.

As I come to a stop in front of Abel, Toby keeps walking until he's next to Shelby.

"Call me when you land, okay?" I tell him.

"Of course."

My head throbs. I groan, reaching up to pinch the bridge the bridge of my nose and squeezing my eyes shut. Abel massages the back of my neck.

SHADES OF US

"What's wrong?"

"Migraine." Despite the headache, his touch feels so fucking good. When I look at him again, his brow is furrowed with concern. "I'm okay."

He kisses my temple. "Are you sure you're okay?"

I nod and walk toward Shelby and the others.

"Were you guys discussing how much you're going to miss each other over the break?" Shelby jokes.

"Ha ha, Shelby Winters, you're so funny."

"Right?"

"Actually, I was asking him if he wanted to take a shirtless pic of me with him to Plainsburg," Abel jokes.

Everyone except Toby laughs. He looks off into the distance.

"I hate you both."

It's too early for them and their jokes, so I head to Amy's car. Toby follows me. I lean against the car while Amy continues to joke around with Shelby and Abel.

"Here." Toby passes me a bottle of painkillers. I didn't even see him take them out of the room. "I figured you would need them."

"You're a lifesaver." Since I don't have any water, I shake two out and swallow them dry.

Toby leans against the car next to me. He's so close that our elbows brush. "I'm going to miss you, Jay."

"Me too. Promise you'll text me when you land."

"Duh. Tell your nana I said hi."

"Will do." I don't know why I'm starting to get choked up saying goodbye to him. We're going to see each other again soon; it's not like either of us is going off to war.

We hug briefly. I try to swallow the lump in my throat.

The others head over to where we're standing. Breaking the

hug with Toby, I head over to Abel, pecking his lips. Another lump forms in my throat.

Calm down. It's only two weeks. You can survive two weeks without seeing them.

When I pull back from Abel, Shelby steps forward. "I'm going to miss you guys. Text me or I will hunt your asses down."

"Shelbs, you don't even let us go an hour without texting you," Abel reminds her. "You are infamous for your double texts."

Shelby smiles as if proud of herself. "I have to make sure you don't forget I exist."

"Trust me, Shelbs," Amy says, pulling her into a hug. "No one can forget you."

"This is why you're my favorite." Shelby pats the roof of Amy's car. "Have a safe trip." She wiggles her eyebrows at me. "Don't worry about that shirtless pic of Abel, Jess. I have one in my phone from summer last year. I'll send it to you."

"Goodbye, Shelby."

They howl with laughter as Amy and I climb into their car. A BTS song starts playing as soon as they start the engine.

"Plainsburg here we come!" they squeak.

"Can we stop for coffee?"

"Have you just met me? Of course, we're stopping for coffee."

We talk as we drive. Amy tells me about the new boy they have been talking to; I tell them about what happened with Kelly and how I still plan on meeting her but don't know when.

Halfway through our drive, it begins to snow.

Three hours later, we pull into the lot of Nana's condo. She's waiting in front of the building, even though it's snowing. She jumps with excitement when she sees our car. Even though the windows are rolled up, I can hear Nana yelling, "Jess-bug!"

SHADES OF US

"Have I mentioned how much I love your grandma?" Amy says as they park.

I jump out of the car and run to Nana. "Are you crazy! You're going to hurt yourself!"

"Shut up and give me a hug." She pulls me into her arms. I can't help but chuckle as she fusses over me. "What do they feed you at school?" she complains, patting my flat stomach. "You're skin and bones."

I've gained the freshman fifteen and then some. I'm almost back up to the weight I was in high school before everything went to shit.

Amy honks at us before pulling out of the spot to drive to their parents' house. Nana waves.

"I have chicken noodle soup and homemade bread waiting." She loops her arm through mine and starts pulling me along. "Tell me everything."

I tell her about seeing PW perform and about Kelly, but the thing she asks the most questions about is Abel asking to be official. What happened? How did he ask? What did I say? Do I love him too? What about Toby?

She huffs at me when I deflect most of the questions by asking about Old Tom but tells me about her new man anyway.

My phone dings in my pocket with a message from Toby.

My first flight was delayed, but we finally boarded.

I have a middle seat.

Pray for me.

I send back a praying hands emoji.

Nana reads the message over my shoulder and gives me a knowing look.

"Not a word, Nan."

She pretends to zip her mouth and throw away the key.

Chapter 42

The first week of break passes quickly. I spend time helping Nana bake for her knitting club's potluck and for her book club's Christmas party, and I watch movies and talk on the phone with Toby, Abel, and the others.

On Friday, Nana's friend Sheryl and her grandson, Dylan, come over to decorate cookies. Dylan is a couple years younger than me. We used to be friends back when we were children, but then his parents moved to Baltimore, and we lost touch. They moved back to Plainsburg when Sheryl had her heart attack. Luckily, I don't have to worry about the awkwardness between Dylan and me for too long. Shortly after they arrive, Amy texts me that they are downstairs with their dad's Excursion. We have plans to go sledding with their cousins.

"Hey!" Amy exclaims when I climb into their dad's car. "It's been ages since I've seen you!"

We planned to hang out more since both of us are back in Plainsburg, but we've both been too busy. I haven't seen them since they dropped me off on Monday.

"When we get to my house, can you use she/her?" they say, their voice small and uncomfortable. "I haven't come out to my family yet."

"Of course, Ames. Whatever you need me to do, I'll do it."

"Thanks, Jess."

Amy pulls into the driveway of their parents' house. People are running around, loading cars with sleds, blankets, and various other items. A dozen kids run around the yard, throwing snowballs at each other. Amy's brother chases a handful of other kids.

"Wow. I didn't know you had so many cousins."

"My one uncle and aunt had seven. My Aunt Sherie and Aunt Daisy adopted two and had one through surrogacy and one from a donor. My other aunt and uncle had four and have one on the way. I told you I come from a big family."

"Amy! Amy! Play snowballs with us!

"Amy, who is this?"

"Amy, help me build a snowman!"

"Is he your boyfriend?"

Amy laughs. "Calm down! I would love to play snowballs and build a snowman, but I have to help my mom. This is my friend Jesse."

"Your boyfriend!" one of the kids exclaims.

"Definitely not." Amy looks at me for help. I just shrug. I have no plans to help them get out of this. It's too amusing. "Jesse has a boyfriend. He's in New Mexico right now."

"Oh!" The child's eyes go wide. "Is that why you're going sledding with us?"

"Yep!" I bend down to their height. "What's your name?"

"Molly."

"It's very nice to meet you, Molly"

She beams. "I like your nails!"

My nails are black as usual, but my left pinky is red and the right one is green to make them more festive.

"And I like yours."

Molly's are bright blue with glitter.

SHADES OF US

"Can I put glitter on yours?"

"You know," I reply, "I was thinking they could use some glitter."

"You don't have to indulge the kids. They'll get away with murder if you let them."

"Are you kidding? I love glitter, Ames."

They hit me. "You do not."

Molly takes my hand and leads me inside the house. Amy follows, introducing me to their aunts and uncles along the way. Amy's mom pulls me into a hug and wishes me happy holidays.

"Honey, I can't find the camera!" Amy's dad calls as he comes into the room. "Oh, hello, Jesse."

"Hi, Mr. Benson. My camera is in the car. I was going to take some shots for my photography class portfolio. Would you like me to send some to you?"

"Would you? Thanks, Jesse."

"Jesse!" Molly calls from the living room.

"Sorry. My manicurist is calling." I leave them and head to where Molly and Amy are sitting. Molly is painting Amy's nails a bright orange color. "Sorry, Molly, I was talking to Amy's parents."

"It's okay. I'll do yours next."

After a few moments, Amy switches seats with me, and Molly begins putting glitter over my nails. She chatters away happily as she works. There's more paint on the skin around the nail than on the nail itself, but I tell her she's doing an amazing job.

"All done!" she exclaims.

"Thank you. It looks so good!" I share a look with Amy, and we fight to hold back our laughter. They show me their nails; one of their fingers is orange all the way up to the knuckle.

After cleaning up, Molly runs outside, forgetting about us. Amy and I take the opportunity to go upstairs and clean up Molly's work. The bathroom is sleek and modern with a large tub and marble vanity. Amy finds nail polish remover and cotton balls in a storage basket on the shelf behind the toilet.

"Thanks for being so great with her."

"Of course. She's sweet."

We're quiet as we clean our fingers, but Amy's nervous about something.

"I keep thinking I should come out to them over the break," they say after a while, "but every time I open my mouth to do it, I can't."

"There's no rush. Do it when you're ready. I can't tell you everything is going to be golden when you do. Coming out is hard, and you never know how people are going to react, but the rest of the crew and I have your back."

Tears shimmer in their eyes. "Thanks, Jess."

"I love you, Ames. You know that. I'll be there for you no matter what."

"Jesse! Amy! We're leaving!" their mother calls from downstairs.

Amy wipes their face. "Come on. Let's go before they leave without us."

Chapter 43

Amy's cousins run us ragged. Hours later, all the adults huddle under a tree at the top of the hill where families from all over the city come to sled. It's fairly crowded, and Amy's cousins have made friends with nearly every other kid playing in the snow.

Amy's mom packed hot chocolate and cookies for everyone. We stand around chatting as the kids play, but Amy is tense. Their back is ramrod straight; they're still worrying over what we talked about in the bathroom before leaving. I wrap an arm around them, hopefully easing some of their nerves.

Amy's parents are going through the pictures I took, raving over them. I promised to send them as soon as they've been cleaned up and edited.

"You're so talented, Jesse," Amy's mom praises.

"Thank you."

"Mom. Dad. I have something to say."

I squeeze Amy's shoulder, letting them know that I'm by their side no matter what happens.

"What is it, Amy?" Their dad sounds concerned by the urgency in their voice. "What's wrong?"

"Nothing's wrong. I just . . . I wanted to tell you . . . um . . ."

Amy's mom takes their hand, waiting patiently for Amy to gather their thoughts.

"I'm . . . agender."

Their words are met with silence. Their aunts and uncles blink in confusion, except for Aunt Daisy and Aunt Sherie.

"Oh, sweetie! What are your pronouns?" Aunt Daisy asks.

"They/them, please."

"Of course." Aunt Sherie pulls Amy into a hug. "We're so proud of you, Ames. Is Amy still okay?"

They nod. Tears fall from their eyes. Even though they're hugging their aunts, their eyes never leave their parents.

"Mom? Dad?"

Their mom blinks. "I—I don't know what that means."

"It means I don't feel like I'm a girl. I feel like I'm genderless, just a person. I don't really know how to explain it in a way that would make sense to you, but this is how I feel on the inside. I'm me."

Amy's mom looks like she's processing, trying to understand where Amy is coming from but not quite wrapping her head around the unfamiliar term.

"You're a girl," their dad interjects. "You're my *daughter*."

Amy visibly freezes in their aunts' arms.

"Theo," Aunt Daisy admonishes.

"No. This doesn't make sense. Agender? They/them? What the fuck does that mean?'

"Mr. Benson—" I start to say, but Amy shakes their head at me.

They step out of their aunts' embrace and pull me by the hand. Their parents call after them, but Amy keeps walking until their family is nothing more than tiny specks in the distance. They find a rock and sit on it, and tears fall from their eyes.

"That was fucking awful."

"Give them time." I kneel before them in the snow, putting my hands over theirs. "I'm so proud of you, Amy."

"Thank you for being here. I couldn't have done it without you by my side." They pull me into a hug. "I love you, Jess."

"Sappy." I chuckle. "I love you too, but you're getting your tears all over my favorite jacket."

They laugh. Instead of pulling away, they hug me tighter. I let them hug me for as long as they need.

Chapter 44

On Christmas morning, the sound of my phone ringing wakes me. Still tired from staying up until 2:00 a.m. watching *It's a Wonderful Life* with Nan, without lifting my head from the pillow I fumble around for the device. I don't even open my eyes to see who's calling.

"Hello?"

"Hey, Jay. Merry Christmas."

The smile that spreads across my face at the sound of my roommate's voice is unconscious and instant. "Isn't it, like, seven there? Why are you up so early?"

"My siblings. I've been up since five. They're beyond excited to see what Santa brought them."

"And what about you? Are you excited to see what Santa brought you?"

"Despite my baby face, I stopped believing in Santa when I was ten." He chuckles. "My dad and stepmom threw me a hundred bucks last night. I'm good." The line goes quiet. "Jay. Madison is home for Christmas too. We had a talk the day before yesterday."

My smile fades. *Are they getting back together?* I shouldn't be worrying about this. It shouldn't matter. I'm with Abel.

But the thought of Toby getting back together with Madison guts me.

Please. Please. Please.

"Madison and her father came over for dinner a couple of nights ago, and Madison wanted another chance—"

My heart jumps to my throat. *No. Please. No.*

"I told her no." He clears his throat. "I explained I like someone else now."

My lungs constrict. Who the hell does he like? Why hasn't he ever told me about them?

"Jay?"

I clear my throat. "I have to go."

"Wait, Jay—I got you something for Christmas."

My stomach flutters. "You didn't have to get me anything."

"Well, I wasn't planning on it, but then you bought me all that stuff in New York. I didn't want to be a shitty friend. Plus, I had to one-up what you got me."

"It's not a competition."

"Everything is a competition, Jay." He pauses. "About Madison—"

"I really have to go, T. Nana is calling. We're supposed to meet Old Tom for breakfast."

"Oh." He sounds dejected. I feel guilty for dismissing him wanting to talk about Madison, but I can't talk about her. The thought of them makes everything inside of me churn like a stormy sea. "Okay. I miss you, Jay."

He's making it hard to get over my crush on him. There's so much I want to tell him, like how I miss him so much that I've been dreaming about him every night since coming home, and that I saw something at the store the other day that made me think of him, and I almost bought it for him. I can't say any of that. I'm with Abel. My feelings for Toby *need* to remain meaningless.

"Bye, T. I'll talk to you later."

"Bye, Jay."

As soon as I hang up with Toby, Abel calls me. The guilt is too much; bile rises up inside of me.

"Hey."

"Jess, Merry Christmas."

Two people shout in the background on his end.

"Your parents are going at it again?"

"Yeah. Third time since yesterday."

This is another reason I can't break up with Abel. He told me that seeing his parents fight every day was making him lose faith in love; not only that, but he has been broken up with so many times that it is starting to take a toll on his self-esteem. I can't be the person who catapults him into believing that love doesn't exist.

The thing is, I like Abel so much that I know one day I *could* love him. I don't *want* to break up with him. What we have is easy; I'm afraid to let it go. The loneliness inside of me when I moved to Freemont was terrifying, and I don't want to go back to that.

"Are you okay?" I ask.

"Fine. I was thinking about leaving the day after tomorrow and going back to Freemont early."

"Do you want to come to Nan's? She wants to meet you."

"I would love that, but after talking to my brother, I'm going to stick it out after all. Derek's scared."

I feel bad for Abel's fifteen-year-old brother. He's alone in the house with parents who are constantly at each other's throats. It must be petrifying to be in such a hostile environment.

"You should take him out."

"That's a good idea. We were thinking of going to the crest."

"Has it snowed there at all?"

"Flurries here and there, but nothing like back in Freemont. I haven't had to really break out my jacket since I have been home."

"Abe, I'm hungry, but I don't want to go out there," Derek says in the background.

"Okay, Dee. Hold on. Jess, I gotta go. I'll call you later. Love you."

"Good luck."

We hang up, and I shoot Amy and Shelby "Happy Holiday" texts complete with gifs.

>> <<

When I emerge from my room an hour later, Nana's already showered, dressed, and making our traditional Christmas morning waffles. Frank Sinatra croons from the Spotify app on the computer, and the whole condo smells of cinnamon and waffle batter.

Old Tom sits on the sofa, reading one of Nana's knitting magazines. He's a nice man with graying hair and a huge bald patch on the back of his head. He has hearing aids and glasses. He looks nothing like my grandpa, who was rugged and still handsome despite his age before he died. Old Tom looks very much the seventy years he's been on Earth.

"Morning, Jesse."

"Morning."

Despite the coziness of the condo with the smell of breakfast cooking and the Christmas decorations, there's an ache in my chest, a reminder that this is the first Christmas without my parents. That reminder calls to the empty, numb feeling inside of me. The blackness doesn't settle over me like it does when I have a Dark Episode, but it's still there, blinking at the edges of my psyche.

Memories of Christmas with my parents play in my mind:

baking cookies, opening presents around the tree, drinking eggnog while we watched every holiday movie known to humanity. Every year, my dad would make a joke that this would be the year that he stopped buying my mom her favorite perfume, but then he always got it. He would pair it with an amazing gift, like the plane tickets to Greece he bought her the year before I started high school. He always put some mistletoe on her gift, and she would have to "pay" him with a kiss in order to receive her present. They were cheesy like that.

Fuck, I miss them.

"Jess-bug?" Nana says. I don't know when she came to stand by me, but her arms are around me, and she's smoothing the hair back from my face. Old Tom watches me from his position the couch. "You okay, bug?"

"I'm okay, Nan."

"Come on, let's eat."

Nana, Old Tom, and I head to the table, where she's set out waffles, fruit, and coffee. The coffee calls to me, and I have a momentary thought of drinking it straight from the carafe, but Old Tom pours some in the mug before me.

"Thanks."

"Of course."

I don't eat much. Nana doesn't comment but keeps an eye on me. I guess I'm not displaying anything that's cause for alarm, since she's not hovering that much.

After breakfast, we open presents. I got Nana this expensive cookbook she's been wanting. She got me a new beanie, a game, and gift cards to all my favorite fast food places. Even Old Tom got me something, a new phone case with Pikachu on it. The only thing I got him is a calendar for the coming year. What the hell else do you get your grandmother's new boyfriend?

SHADES OF US

We spend the rest of the day drinking eggnog and listening to Christmas carols. We're supposed to go to a Christmas dinner hosted by her knitting club, but the three of us end up falling asleep and missing the first two hours.

At seven, there's a knock at the door. Alan stands on the doorstep, holding a large tray of goodies.

"Hey, Jesse."

"Hey, man."

He kisses Nana's cheek. "Merry Christmas, Nan. My mom sent over everything she's baked in the last week."

"Thank you, Alan."

Alan turns to me, looking nervous. We haven't really talked since clearing the air; things still aren't how they used to be between us. I don't know what to do to get us back to being the dynamic duo we once were. The last message he sent me was about how busy he was with school. He doesn't even know that I'm adopted.

"Hey, man," he says, rubbing the back of his neck.

"Hey."

He steps closer, still nervous. Awkward silence stretches between us. I want to tell him about school, about Abel and the crew. I want to tell him about Kelly and to learn what he's been up to, but are we even still that type of friends? I don't know.

"We're having our annual New Year's Eve dinner if you want to come."

"Oh, you loved going to those, Jess-bug."

I didn't *love* going to them. Alan always asked me to go so he wouldn't be bored with his parents' and sister's friends. I haven't missed a dinner party at Alan's house since I was eleven years old.

"Sure."

"Great. You can meet Heather."

225

"Oh, right." Meeting Heather doesn't sound fun. From what Alan's told me about her, she doesn't seem like the type of person I would vibe with.

"Great. I'll see you New Year's Eve at seven."

"I'll be there."

Alan stays for a cup of coffee. We barely brush the surface of what's been going on with us. I don't tell him about the adoption and Kelly. That's not news I feel comfortable sharing with him.

Chapter 45

Alan's house is two stories with red brick and white pillars. Green ivy wraps around the front and sides of the house. He lives only three blocks from Amy, which is something I didn't really think about until seeing the cars lined up in the driveway and along the street, and I start planning an escape route to Amy's just in case.

The house is still decorated for Christmas, despite it being the thirty-first. His family has a tradition of not taking down their decorations until January sixth. My parents always took ours down on New Year's Day.

The white string lights bathe the cars in the driveway in a soft glow while people in their fanciest dress hurry up the icy walkway to the front door.

The button down I'm wearing is from Target, and I found the pink tie in a box of my grandpa's old things that Nana kept. My slacks are slightly wrinkled from being shoved in a tote in the back of my closet. Though I can't see it under the steering wheel, there's a scuff on my loafers, which haven't been worn since my cousin's wedding three years ago.

My phone dings with an incoming message.

U coming in?

When I look at the house again, Alan's on the front porch, welcoming his parents' guests and shivering in his tailor-made suit.

The cold air bites at my face as I climb out of Nana's car, lock the door, and exhale some of my nerves.

You can do this.

"Hey, man," Alan greets me when I approach the front porch. The smell of food wafts out from within the house. "Glad you could make it."

"Of course." I wipe my sweaty palms on my pants.

Alan smiles slightly, fingers tapping against his side. "Come in."

Inside, the warmth from the heater, the fireplace, and around fifty bodies immediately chases away the cold. One of the staff takes my coat and gives me a ticket before I follow Alan through the large five-bedroom house that is the setting for so many memories from fifth grade to high school.

The house itself is familiar yet foreign, kind of like the way I feel being back in Alan's presence. At one time, I knew every nook and cranny of this place, but it no longer feels like a second home. I don't feel unwelcome, but it no longer feels like mine and Alan's. It's just his. I'm simply trespassing through this space where his parents watch football and eat their Sunday dinners. I'm no longer a part of their family.

We don't say much to the older adults as we pass—most of them are doctors who work with Alan's father or lawyers who work with his mom. His sister, a graduate student of biology at Brown, is telling a story to anyone who will listen of how she traveled to Bangkok over the summer.

I forgot this feeling of insignificance I have when visiting Alan's house. His family is wildly successful, and Alan will one day become a famous director. The Jeffersons have an insane amount of ambition that I will never possess.

I still remember the way Mr. Jefferson's nose wrinkled when I told him that my dream is to be a photographer, and if that doesn't work out my backup plan is to become a teacher or something. My parents raised me to follow my dreams and to dust myself off and try something new if I should fail. They were very go-with-the-flow type people. The Jeffersons are determined to be the best possible in whatever field they put their minds to, no matter the cost. There is no plan B for them. You either make plan A work or you die trying.

But that level of ambition and perfectionism led Addison, Alan's sister, to have a mental breakdown in high school, and Mr. Jefferson has a secret love affair with cocaine. When we were twelve, Alan and I were sneaking around the house late at night during a sleepover, and we saw him doing lines through the crack of his office door. He still has no idea that we know. Alan made me promise not to tell anyone, and I have kept that secret to this day.

So, really, is all that determination and drive toward perfection worth it?

Alan leads me to the second living room, where people our age lounge around, talking and sipping watered-down fruit punch. I recognize them as the sons and daughters of the doctors and lawyers in the main living room. They're all engrossed in their phones and don't bother saying hello.

I stick to Alan's side as he crosses the room to a young woman with freckles, red hair, and a very pinched expression.

"Jesse, this is my girlfriend, Heather."

"Hi, Heather."

She raises an eyebrow at my offered hand but doesn't take it.

"Nice to meet you." Her tone makes it seem like she's addressing something stuck to the bottom of her shoe.

I drop my hand.

Heather is different from the girls Alan dated in high school. They were all bubbly—too bubbly, if you ask me—while Heather is ice queen cold.

Alan serves me a small crystal glass of punch, and we sit on the couch to converse with some of the other college students. They are all like Alan, ambitious to a fault. A few of them are rude and pretentious as fuck. One guy keeps showing off the Rolex he got for Christmas.

At the party last year, Alan and I made fun of these people for flashing their designer brands, luxury cars, and acceptance letters into prestigious schools, but this year he's fitting right in with them, showing off the Bulgari necklace he got for his birthday.

Lord, save me from these people.

As if answering my prayers, Mrs. Jefferson pokes her head in. "Al, could you go check on Rufus? The staff are too afraid."

"I can do it, Mrs. Jefferson."

"Oh, Jesse, honey, you don't have to."

"I want to. I haven't seen Rufus in forever."

She looks like she's going to argue more but quickly gives in. "He's in the guest room. So good to see you, honey."

"Are you sure?" Alan asks as the door shuts behind his mother.

"Yeah," I reply awkwardly. Hanging out with Rufus sounds a lot better than hearing about Thad's—not his actual name—watch again.

I stand and walk out of the room, not saying goodbye to anyone except Heather. She doesn't say anything back.

As I leave, one of the guys says, "That guy is such a loser."

I wait by the door to see how Alan responds, but he doesn't.

Upstairs, they have two guest rooms. One is being used as the coat room and has a staff member standing in front of it. The other has a sign on the door that says: DO NOT OPEN.

Opening the door with the sign, I nearly get bowled over by a brown-and-white Saint Bernard and have to gently push him to wrangle him back inside the room.

"Hey, buddy."

He licks my hand happily while I pet him. Then I pour some of his treats into my hand from the container on the dresser.

"Everything is fucked up, Ruf," I tell him as he inhales his treats from my palm. "I don't think Alan and I can go back to the way things were." He looks up at me with sympathetic blue eyes. "I messed up royally, huh, bud?"

It's my fault that everything is so messed up between us, and now neither of us knows how to get back to where we were before. Alan was my brother, but now we're two different people who don't recognize each other. We're walking on eggshells around each other. He doesn't want to say the wrong thing to me, and I don't want to say the wrong thing to him.

I stay with Rufus for so long that I end up missing dinner. At eight-thirty, the door opens, and Alan comes into the room. He's removed his suit jacket and loosened his tie.

"Thought you snuck out."

"Hmm. Keeping Rufus company. He looked lonely."

Rufus is currently sleeping on the floor at the foot of the bed while I play on my phone. I sit up as Alan sits next to me.

"We should talk."

I have been dreading this moment, but it's all I have been thinking about for the past hour. "Maybe we've come to the end of the Dynamic Duo."

Alan nods sadly. "I think so."

We're too different now. Honestly, the only reason we remained friends as long as we did is because we met when we were so young. We were trying to hold on to that. But we can't ignore the blaringly obvious situation: we are no longer each other's comfort.

"Is it okay if I message you from time to time?"

"Of course," Alan replies. "We may not be the Dynamic Duo anymore, but that doesn't mean that I don't want you in my life at all." He chokes back tears. "Childhood friends grow apart. It was bound to happen to us too."

"This sucks."

He chuckles sadly. "Remember when you used to tell me you were going to marry me?"

"Oh, don't bring that up!"

We stay in the room for a long time, hugging and crying. We promise to keep in touch as much as we can, but it's still painful, knowing that the days of our best friendship are officially over.

Chapter 46

The drive from Plainsburg to Philly in Amy's car gives me more than enough time to overthink how reuniting with Toby is going to go. What if he did actually end up deciding to get back with Madison?

You shouldn't be thinking about this.

But I can't stop thinking about how much it would hurt if Toby and Madison got back together.

And then the guilt starts. I'm betraying Abel by feeling this jealousy. Something needs to give: either I break up with Abel or I get rid of these feelings for Toby. I don't want to hurt Abel. He's been hurt so many times in the past; I don't want to be just another person who broke his heart.

This isn't fair to him, but I don't know what to do.

When I reach the airport, my palms are sweaty, and my knuckles hurt from gripping the steering wheel like it's somehow offended me. It takes me an hour to find a parking spot, and then I head inside to the baggage claim to pick up Toby.

Since it's late at night, there aren't that many people around. I'm able to kick one of my feet up on the seat next to me as I wait, but the other jumps up and down with nerves. A K-pop group Abel likes plays in my headphones, blocking out some of the noise in my head.

The hard beats and fast rapping in Korean quickly calms me down, and it's not long until my nervous foot tapping moves along to the beat of the song.

At some point while I'm waiting for Toby, I doze off. Someone shakes my shoulder, and I open my eyes to see the dazzling smile I have missed so much over the last few weeks.

"Fuck," I say, groaning as I sit up. "I was supposed to be jumping up and down, yelling your name as you walked through the gate."

"Instead, you're drooling over your favorite hoodie. I thought Amy was picking me up."

"They weren't feeling very good, so I volunteered. And I was not drooling."

His smile grows bigger. "Sure, you weren't."

I stand, still glaring at him, but not even a second later I pull the asshole in for a hug. He holds me tight, and the noise in my brain finally turns to silence.

"Did you miss me, Jay?"

"No." I hug him tighter. "You didn't even cross my mind the entire break."

"Lying's not a good look on you."

"Shut up."

He chuckles and releases me. "Let's get out of here."

I don't know what it is about Toby that makes me feel so calm. There has been this weight on my chest the entire Christmas break, but the second I looked into Toby's hazel eyes, that weight was gone. He's warmth and sunlight. Being near him calms the storm inside my brain.

The thought of how much he has come to mean to me over the last four months kind of scares me. I have never felt this way about anyone. I have never felt this *safe* with anyone other than my parents.

Despite how much I like Abel, I am undeniably in love with Toby.

Chapter 47

The Gamma Phi sorority throws a New Year's party five days late to ring in the new semester. The theme is '80s movie couples.

And that's how I find myself, on the Sunday night before school starts back up on Tuesday, dressed in a pink outfit like Andie in *Pretty in Pink*. Abel is dressed like Blane, wearing a thrifted oversized gray suit jacket and a blue button-up. He's added studs and patches to the blazer to make it look more alternative.

"I don't think I have ever seen you in so much color," Abel says as we walk across campus to the sorority house.

A breeze picks up, making me pull the pink, artfully ripped sweater I borrowed from Shelby tighter around my body. Abel told me to bring a jacket, but I didn't want to ruin the aesthetic.

"This feels weird. Where are my black jeans and beanie when I need them?"

"You don't look weird. You look cute." He leans over and kisses my cheek. "Like an adorable bottle of Pepto."

I elbow him away from me. "Go away."

He laughs, pulling me tighter into his side.

We arrive at the house. Parties don't give me as much anxiety as they used to, and part of that credit goes to Toby, since he's dragged me to almost every one that has happened since the end of August. My stomach still drops at seeing so many people crammed into one space, so I guess that feeling will never change. But at least

I don't have to pregame by counting to one hundred and using breathing techniques anymore.

"We're only staying until the countdown."

"Deal."

We trudge up the frozen grass and into the warmth of the house. Unsurprisingly, we are not the only Andie and Blane. A different Andie hands me a red Solo cup of alcohol. Abel quickly takes it, explaining to the girl that I don't drink. She apologizes and pours me a Coke.

We loop around the room and find Toby hanging out around a table with his basketball friends. He greets me and Abel with a nod but says nothing.

"Come on, Jesse," Patrick yells, waving me over. His eyes are already glassy. "Come drink with us.'

"Jay doesn't drink," Toby says. His voice is tight. I wonder if something happened before we got to the table.

Patrick's glazed eyes swing over me. "But why?"

"I make stupid decisions when I'm drunk. Decisions that get me in trouble."

Patrick shrugs. "Your loss, dude."

It really isn't, but whatever.

"Jesse! Abel! Toby!"

Amy bounces their way through the party. Their hair is straightened and then curled in waves, and they are wearing a blue vest, pink jeans, and a white shirt. They and Toby have dressed as Marty and Jennifer from *Back to the Future*.

"Hey, Amy," Abel says. "Drink?"

"Oh, yes, please!" They bounce on the balls of their feet while Toby fixes a drink.

We spend the next two hours talking and watching Amy dance

with Patrick. Toby insists on staying with his basketball friends, so Abel and I make our way to the couch. At one minute to midnight, the music cuts off, and the sorority sisters set up a countdown on the projector.

At fifteen seconds, everyone begins shouting the numbers in perfect unison. "Fifteen . . . fourteen . . ."

Toby stands next to Amy on my right. He's unsteady on his feet but is giggling and smiling like this is the best night of his life.

". . . three . . . two . . . ONE!"

The whole party erupts with cheers. Abel hugs me, drowning me in a kiss that tastes like chips, Coke, and alcohol.

He smiles as if he's a little dazed. "I'm glad I'm ringing in the new year with you."

"Idiot. Don't be such a sap." Turning to Amy, I find that Toby is no longer standing next to them. "Where's Toby?"

They shrug. "Bathroom, I guess. Happy New Year!" They kiss my cheek. "Pose for a selfie with me!"

Abel and I take a spot on either side of Amy, each of us kissing one cheek, which causes them to giggle as they take the picture.

Amy looks at the selfie. "This is too cute not to post!" they exclaim, furiously typing on their phone.

Both my and Abel's phones ding with incoming notifications, telling us that Amy tagged us in a post.

As the music starts back up, I take Amy and Abel's hands, heading to the dance floor. I catch a glimpse of the basketball team; they're surrounding Leo, who seems to be hoisting Toby off the floor. Patrick catches my eye.

Is he okay? I mouth.

He gives me a thumbs-up. *We're taking him to the dorm. Don't worry*, he mouths back.

SHADES OF US

Too late. I'm already worried.

Amy and Abel follow me as I head over to the team.

"Really, Jesse. We can take him back," Patrick says as I approach.

I slide a hand under Toby's arm, pulling him to his feet. Abel takes the other side. "How much has he had to drink?"

"A lot." Patrick pauses. "He ... um ... he's got a lot on his mind."

"Like what?"

"You should ask him that."

I nod in acknowledgment of Patrick's words and turn my attention to my drunk roommate. Toby leans heavily on me with unfocused and glazed eyes.

"Toby? T, you okay?"

Toby's head rolls until he's looking at me. "Jay!"

"We're going to go home, okay?"

"Okey dokey."

Abel and I begin dragging Toby out of the party.

My brain races with a million thoughts. Toby's been weird all night. He's been moody and has barely said a word to me. Patrick says he has a lot on his mind, but what could it be? We talk about everything, and I had no idea that something was bothering him. I hate that he's upset about something and hasn't told me about it.

As we walk, Toby starts singing a Billie Eilish song, horribly and off-key.

Once we get back to the dorm, Abel helps me get Toby into bed.

"Do you want me to stay?"

I shake my head as I pull off Toby's shoes. He's already falling asleep. "I'll text you later."

"Okay. Jess?"

"Hmm?" I fight to get Toby under his covers.

"I love you."

Guilt burns in my throat like bile. "Good night, Abe."

I can't look at him as he leaves, unable to see the pain that my dismissal causes him.

"Jay," Toby says as he falls asleep. He finds my hand and holds it as his eyes close and his breath evens. "Don't leave. Stay."

What the actual fuck is going on?

Chapter 48

It's impossible for me to focus in my new classes since I'm worried about Toby. Even though he told me nothing's wrong, something very clearly is. He's been withdrawn and not as bright as usual. He changes the subject whenever I ask what's on his mind. Not wanting to upset him, I don't press further. He'll tell me when he's ready, I guess.

Since most students are still in holiday mode, and the professors seem to know that the entire student body spent the entire weekend partying, all my classes spend the first couple of days going over the syllabus and introducing the course material.

Thank God for merciful teachers.

On Thursday, I ask Wimbley if I can rejoin the photography club, but she tells me that all the spots are taken and to try again next year.

Abel's turning twenty-one on Saturday, so I spend the week planning his birthday party, making sure everything is perfect. Since returning from the holidays, I have kind of been neglecting him, having been too consumed with my concern about Toby.

Shelby helps me order the cake and decorations. All I have to do is pass out the invitations. I ask Toby for help, but he refuses, saying he has basketball practice.

On Saturday, we have the party room of Bodie's decked out

in black and neon green, Abel's favorite colors. Zack is distracting him by taking him shopping while the rest of us set up.

The first guests arrive ten minutes early, so we tell Zack to go ahead and bring Abel to the restaurant.

"Toby's not coming?" Shelby whispers to me as we hide in the dark party room.

"He said he had basketball practice."

That's a fucking lie, since I saw Patrick with Amy earlier. I'm pissed as hell that Toby lied to me. He's been acting so weird since we got back from the holidays. He's spending more and more time out of the dorm; there've even been nights where he hasn't come back at all.

"He's here!" someone whispers.

"What are we doing here?" Abel says in the darkness. "You don't even like Bodie's."

"Surprise!"

The lights flick on, and Abel jumps, startled. His eyes meet mine, and I go to him, wrapping my arms around him.

"Happy birthday."

"You did all this?" he says in awe, looking around the room at the twelve million balloons, the streamers, and the banner that says, HAPPY 21ST BIRTHDAY!

"I had help."

"This is amazing. Thank you."

He kisses my cheek.

Amy puts a crown on his head and leads him to the chair at the head of the table. "Happy birthday, Abel." They hug him from behind. "Your birthday present is on order; it should be here by the end of next week."

"You didn't have to get me anything, Ames."

They hit his shoulder. "Of course I did."

All thirty of us sit at the tables around the room and begin ordering food. The waiters work diligently to make sure we're served efficiently. Our orders of shrimp and pasta are brought out in no time.

"This really is amazing," Abel whispers to me. "Thank you."

"Of course. You only turn twenty-one once."

After we eat, Zack starts bringing Abel presents. He has a huge pile since people we didn't invite somehow heard that we were having a party and have been stopping by since the afternoon to drop off presents for him. When Zack hands him a box wrapped in red paper, I lean toward Abel, whispering, "This one is from me."

Abel tears into the paper with excitement. When he sees what I got him, he beams. "Jess! This is awesome!"

He pulls out the album he's been wanting, but underneath that are the boots he pointed out to me the last time we went shopping. They're black, steel-toed with buckles. I even asked Wendell for an advance on my paycheck to get them in time for Abel's birthday.

"Thank you!"

He grabs my face, kissing me all over until I'm laughing.

Chapter 49

Another week passes where I don't see much of Toby. In that time, I reach out to Kelly to set up a time to meet again.

Outside of classes and going to A/AA, I spend a lot of time with Abel and Amy to take my mind off how mad I am at Toby. He's avoiding me; I even confirmed with Patrick that they haven't had as many basketball practices as Toby has said they've had. The real punch in the gut, though, is when I'm sitting in the cafeteria eating lunch, and the second my eyes meet Toby's he walks right back out the door.

I chase after him.

"Tobias Washington!" I yell as I run after him in the courtyard.

People stare after us, but I don't give a fuck.

I finally catch up to him when he turns the corner between the science building and the library and is met with a dead end. I accidentally crash into him, smashing him between the wall and my body.

"Ow. Shit."

We both slide down the wall. He pushes me off of him.

"What the hell, Jay!" He sits up, resting both of his arms on his bent knees. We're both breathing hard. "Why the fuck did you tackle me?"

"I didn't tackle you. That was an accident."

He's quiet for a moment while I press my hand to my head, making sure I'm not bleeding.

"Are you okay?" he asks.

No blood. "I'm fine."

"Good."

"What is going on with you?" I sit in front of him, ready to block him if he starts running again. "Why have you been avoiding me?"

"I haven't been avoiding you." He looks away from me.

"Liar."

He huffs. "Don't worry about it."

"T, come on." He's pissing me off again, but not only that, him not talking to me is making the static in my brain turn up. "Tell me what's going on with you."

"It's nothing, Jay. I need to work it out on my own." He closes his eyes as if he's in pain. "Please, stop asking me."

"T—"

"I'm serious. Please. I promise it's nothing bad."

He's so fucking stubborn; it's infuriating. I want to shake him to make him tell me what's going on, but it will get us nowhere. Once he's made his mind up about something, there's no making him budge.

"Do you promise to tell me what's going on with you eventually?"

He hesitates.

"Promise me."

"I promise." Toby leans back against the wall, putting his head against the brick.

I wish he would just tell me so we can work it out together. He's taken care of me so many times; why won't he let me take care of him?

"Where have you been staying?"

"At Leo's apartment."

"Are you ever going to come back to the dorm?"

He shrugs.

That response feels like a knife to my chest. "T."

"Eventually."

The urge to shake him grows.

"I reached out to Kelly," I say. "We're meeting up at the beginning of February. I know you're mad at me—"

"I'm not mad at you."

"Then why are you avoiding me?"

He doesn't answer.

"You're so frustrating." I have half a mind to just leave him here. Fuck being besties, I guess. "Anyway, can you come with me? I know you're avoiding me right now, but I can't do this without you."

I need you.

"I'll come." He reaches out, placing a hand on my knee. I revel in the touch, longing to reach out and intertwine our fingers, to gain strength from his warmth. "I promise. I'll be there."

Chapter 50

The road trip to New York is tense since there's still strain between me and Toby. He hasn't been sleeping at the dorm, and I was terrified he wouldn't show up this morning, but when I walked out to the parking lot, he was already waiting by Amy's car. He had a bag of his things with him; I guess he got them while I was in class. I take the back seat, pulling my headphones over my ears and staring out the window. Toby writes in a notebook the whole time, and Amy keeps glancing between us. They wanted to come to offer me support and to see the city.

I feel sorry for subjecting them to the rift between Toby and me.

A few hours later, we're on Kelly's street, and the nerves kick in. Toby turns in the passenger seat, placing a hand on my knee.

"You got this."

I place my hand over his, squeezing his fingers gently.

Amy finds parking, and we all get out of the car. Toby stays with me while Amy pays the meter.

"We'll met you at the café when you're done. Just text us."

I nod without saying anything; if I open my mouth, I'll vomit.

Without a thought, I wrap my arms around him. My nerves loosen but don't fully disappear. I wish he could stay with me, but this is something I need to do on my own. It's enough to know that if I freak out again, he'll be right around the corner.

I let him go and begin walking down the street until I find Kelly's house. She lives in a brownstone that's been decorated for Valentine's Day with heart-shaped lights and a giant heart made of tinfoil standing on the front steps to greet passersby.

After I knock, the door opens to reveal a petite woman with long brown hair and big brown eyes. "Jesse." Kelly's voice whooshes out of her in a breath, as if she has also been unsure about this meeting. Freckles dot her nose and cheeks, and her smile is warm and inviting.

"N-nice to meet you."

"Come in, but please be quiet; Titus is sleeping."

"Titus?"

"My son."

A prickle of jealousy simmers in my stomach. Aren't I her son too? She just gave me away like some unwanted *thing*, but now she has a whole other family. Another son. One that she kept.

"Oh."

She wrings her hands. "Come into the living room. We can talk about everything." She leads me through the bright blue and white rooms filled with pictures of their small family: her, Titus, and a bespectacled man that I can only assume is her husband. "Would you like anything? Water? A cookie?"

"I'm fine. Thank you."

I lower myself onto the light-gray couch in their living room. My leg starts bouncing of its own accord. Kelly sits in a rocking chair opposite me. She sits stiffly, halfway off the seat with her hands holding her knees. It's a bit of a comfort to know that she's as nervous as I am.

"I'm sure you have a lot of questions."

"Nana told me pretty much everything, but I want to hear it from you."

SHADES OF US

Kelly nods and grips her knees harder. "I was young, not even sixteen, when I got pregnant with you. My parents were religious and told me I had to get rid of the baby or get married. Your biological father was a POS, a senior in school who had coerced me into sex. He didn't even believe that I was pregnant with his child. Marriage and abortion were out of the question. If I tried to keep you out of wedlock, my parents made it very clear that I would be on my own. They would kick me out, and there was no way I could afford to raise a child.

"More than that, I wanted to be a doctor, and to do that I needed to focus on school. Keeping you wouldn't have given you or me the life we deserved. Adoption was the only solution.

"My family was neighbors with Monica and Aaron. I had overheard them talking about how they wanted children when they were married, but Monica couldn't get pregnant. She was so heartbroken that she wouldn't be able to give your father children, and here I was with a baby. I could give them this gift that they wanted so badly."

"They were barely in their twenties—why didn't you give me to, like, actual adults?"

Kelly sniffs as tears begin to pool. "I didn't want to give you away to just anyone. Your parents had helped my family through hard times, and I wanted to repay all that."

I don't know what to say to her. Is there anything I *should* say?

"Your parents were reluctant at first because your dad was finishing college and they were worried about finances, but I think the deciding factor was your grandfather. He told your parents to seize the opportunity, and he and your grandmother would help them in any way they could. If I remember correctly, your grandfather told them that you were meant for them, he felt it in his bones. That's exactly how I felt."

"Why did you reach out now? You've had eighteen years to contact me, so why now?"

"Your parents and I agreed that they would be the ones to tell you all about me when you turned eighteen, but then the accident happened. I didn't want to drop the bomb on you while you were still grieving, but . . . I just felt like it was time to meet you properly. Reaching out to you became this thing that just got bigger and bigger, and I couldn't think about anything else until I took those steps."

I just nod, unsure of what to say.

Kelly shifts in place, looking around her own house like she isn't entirely sure why she's here. "I hope you understand, Jesse."

"I do," I say truthfully. In fact, had I been in her position I would have done the same. Without Kelly's generosity toward my parents, I wouldn't have received all the love and memories they gave me, and those are worth more than anything in this world.

"I would like to keep in touch, if that's okay."

"Yeah. That would be nice."

My nerves ease, and we talk for another hour, then she sends me off with a dozen cookies. In that hour, Titus wakes up from his nap, and I get to meet the tiny two-year-old. He doesn't take to me, but I don't really know what to make of him either.

After being an only child for my whole life, I have a brother. Well, not really a brother, but something kind of like it. I guess.

Before leaving, Kelly makes me promise that I'll have brunch with her in the morning before going back to Freemont.

I walk to the end of the street and find Toby sitting outside the café we planned to meet up at.

"Where's Amy?"

"They got bored and went to that shop." He points to a boutique across the road. "How did it go?"

"It was great," I say and jump into the details.

Toby listens intently, interjecting here and there with questions and comments. Mostly, he just makes sure I'm okay.

>> <<

The next morning, the three of us head to Kelly's to meet her for brunch.

"Jesse!" she exclaims as she opens the door. The squirming toddler on her hip seems more interested in the sounds coming from inside than the three random college kids on their front step. Kelly shuffles us inside.

She leads us to the kitchen, where her husband is cooking a huge skillet of eggs. There is already an array of food spread out on the counters and table. "This is Arthur," Kelly says. "Artie, say hi."

Arthur turns with a smile; he has a glob of pancake batter on the front of his sweater vest. "Hi. Welcome to our home. Food's almost done."

"Thank you so much for having us," I say nervously. My social battery is already starting to run out. There've been too many big things happening at once, and I long for the comfort of my bed and video games. Toby squeezes my arm reassuringly. "You didn't have to do all this."

"Kell insisted."

She tuts at him. "You all help yourselves. We have coffee and juice on the table."

As Toby and Amy load up their plates, I can't help but watch Kelly and Arthur. They are so sickeningly in love and kind of remind me of my parents. What would my life have been like if Kelly had decided to keep me? Would she have met Arthur? Would she still have been this happy? Part of me is jealous that she is this happy without me in her life, but the other part of me knows that giving me up for adoption was the best decision for both of us.

Chapter 51

Valentine's Day is a holiday that I think is nothing more than an excuse for card companies to make money off saps who feel some need to have a special day to make up for all the stupid shit they've been neglecting to do for their loved ones.

Despite my dislike for the holiday, Abel is dragging me to a Valentine's Day dance being hosted in the Rosenberg Hall ballroom.

We're both dressed in maroon suits. My button-up is covered in silver spiderwebs, and Abel's wearing the boots I bought for him for his birthday.

The hall is decorated with way too much pink and red for my taste. There's a photo wall of balloons and hearts. A projector plays slides of couples around campus; Shelby has already warned me that there's a picture of Abel and me in the shuffle. For multiple reasons, I'm dreading seeing it.

We find Amy dancing with Patrick. They keep saying they're just friends, but I don't know; the way Patrick looks at Amy makes me think he wants to be more. I pull Abel to the dance floor as a slow song comes on and wrap my arms around his neck.

"Happy Valentine's Day."

He kisses my forehead. "Happy Valentine's Day."

We dance through two slow songs and then jump around to a remix of an old '90s song with Shelby, Amy, and Patrick. When that song ends, we all find a table, and Abel and Patrick go to get us drinks.

"Where's Toby?" I ask. He was supposed to come with Amy.

They shrug. "He ditched me the second we got here. He's been so weird lately. Patrick won't tell me what's up with him."

Besides texting here and there, I haven't seen Toby since coming back from New York. He slept in the dorm the night we returned, but the next day he went back to Leo's again.

The thought crosses my mind that I am losing him, and that scares the shit out of me.

I look around the ballroom for him. He's sitting at a table with Leo and some of the other basketball guys. He looks too damn good in a navy-blue suit with his dreads half up and half down.

Our eyes catch.

He looks away, which makes my blood boil.

He says something to Leo and then gets up from the table, heading toward the bathroom.

"I'll be back," I tell Shelby. "Tell Abel I went to the bathroom when he returns."

"Sure. Are you okay?" She looks to where I'm staring, but Toby is already out of sight.

"I'm fine. I need to pee."

I get up and shuffle my way through people, exiting the ballroom into the hall where the bathrooms are. The only other people in the hall are a group of girls who are sitting on the floor vaping.

When I enter the bathroom, Toby's at the sink washing his hands. He looks up at me through the mirror.

"Jay."

"Please," I beg. "Please tell me what I did to upset you. I can't take this silent treatment, T. Tell me what I did so I can fix it."

He turns, dragging a hand down in his face. "You haven't done anything, Jay."

"You're a fucking liar, Toby!" I yell. "What is wrong with you?"

"Jay. Just drop it."

He goes to step around me, but I block him.

"No! I can't drop it!" My hands vibrate at my sides. I take a step toward him. We're almost nose to nose, but he doesn't back down. "Please tell me what the fuck is wrong with you!"

He pinches the bridge of his nose and squeezes his eyes shut. "I'm fucking in love with you, okay?"

I take a step back. Oh. That was not at all what I was expecting. I don't know what to say to that. *Tell him that you love him too! Tell him!* I can't—I shouldn't.

He bends forward, putting his hands on his knees like he's run a marathon. His breath comes out in shallow gasps. "Are you happy now?"

"Toby—"

"I love you, Jay. That's why I've been avoiding you. It hurts every time I see you with Abel. I'm trying to get over you." He looks up, and his eyes catch on something behind me. "Oh, fuck."

I turn. Standing at the door is Abel, who looks stricken. His eyes dart from me to Toby and back again.

"Abel—" I reach out for him, but he turns and leaves.

Toby looks like he's seconds from splitting at the seams. Unsure of what to do, I step toward Toby.

"No. Go after him. I'm fine."

He's not fine.

"T."

"Go, Jesse."

I want to stay with him, to talk about this bomb he just dropped on me, but I do as he says and run after Abel.

Out in the hall, Zack is waiting. He blocks me with his body, his arms crossed over his chest. He looks down at me with a raised eyebrow. Guilt churns in my stomach, causing me to hang my head.

"I fucking told you not to break his heart, Jesse."

"I didn't say it back to Toby." I try to defend myself, but we both know it's futile.

"But you love him too. I can see it in your eyes." His lip curls. "Break up with Abel, Jesse. He deserves better."

He's right. I should have broken up with him weeks ago.

"Where did he go?"

Zack steps aside, pointing down the hall.

Abel sits on the floor, slumped against the wall. He's crying. My heart clenches. I can't believe I caused this. He looks up at me as I approach. He sobs harder when he sees me.

I slide down the wall next to him. We sit in silence for a little until Abel stops crying enough to talk.

"You know what Zack told me when I told him I was going to ask you to officially be my boyfriend?" He doesn't wait for an answer. He wipes his nose on his sleeve. "He said you seem like an awesome guy but to be careful. I thought he meant be careful because you were grieving and going through shit, but he was telling me to be careful because he could tell there was some sort of connection between you and Toby." He finally meets my eyes; now I look away, ashamed. "He just told me he's been sensing something between you guys since Shelby claimed you as our new friends. He saw that shit from the very first night we met you guys, but I was too stupid."

"Abe—"

He holds up two fingers, cutting me off with a look that says, *It's my turn to talk, and you better fucking listen.* "You're cute and sweet, and something made me fall for you, so I made a move. I knew you and Toby had some sort of connection, but I thought fuck it, maybe it's just some platonic soulmate shit. But ever since he and Madison broke up, that connection between you two has become this tangible thing, a string that ties the two of you together. Do you know how many nights I was unable to sleep because I kept thinking, 'Is Jesse going to break up with me for Toby tomorrow?'"

"Abel." My voice shakes; tears burn my eyes.

"Am I wrong?"

We both know he's not wrong.

"You're in love with him."

Tears fall from both of us. I stare at my chipped nail polish. "I am. I'm sorry. I shouldn't have led you on."

"Why did you?"

He looks so sad, and I hate myself for bringing this fallen, heartbroken look to his face. "Toby wasn't an option, and there was something I wanted to explore with you." I pause, using the sleeve of my suit jacket to wipe my nose. "I truly think our relationship could have been awesome, but when Toby and Madison broke up, it became harder to deny my feelings for him." I blow out a breath. "I'm so sorry you got caught up in all of that."

"Is that supposed to make me feel better?"

"No, but it's the truth."

He scoffs. "At least you're being honest now."

"Please don't hate me, Abel."

He scoffs again and looks off into the distance down the hall opposite me. "I'm used to it." His soft, sad words hit me powerfully.

My heart squeezes, and my guilt grows. "That was another reason I couldn't bring myself to break up with you. You've been hurt so many times before, and I didn't want to cause you any more pain."

"And yet, it *does* hurt. I fell in love with you, Jesse. If you knew you didn't love me, you shouldn't have agreed to be my boyfriend that night."

"Abel—" My voice catches. "I'm so sorry."

He clears his throat, wiping his face and smearing the black his eyeliner has left on his cheeks from crying.

"I'm so sorry. I'm so sorry." There's nothing more for me to say; it's really over. The past few months of dating, kissing, and getting to know each other have been reduced to this moment. I fucking hate myself for it.

He stands, looking down at me. "It's going to take some time to get over you and everything, but I don't hate you."

"You're a great guy, Abel. You deserve someone who truly loves you."

He shrugs bitterly. "Maybe love just isn't in the cards for me."

I was afraid he would say that. I'm wracked with sobs at his words. "Abel—"

Before I can say anything else, he walks off. His boots thud against the beige linoleum. Unable to stand, I continue to sit in the hallway, sobbing.

Chapter 52

I thought after our confrontation in the bathroom, Toby would return to the dorm or try to work things out between us, but another week passes without seeing him. Amy told me he found out about my breakup with Abel and asked Patrick how I was doing, but he still hasn't come to see me.

Patrick keeps me up-to-date on Toby as well. This probably isn't what he had in mind when he started dating Amy, but if he dislikes being the messenger between the two of us, he doesn't complain.

On Saturday, I share all the events of the past week with Doctor Hartland. She listens quietly, writing notes in her book as I tell her how mad I am that Toby won't even give me a chance to talk to him about what happened.

"What would you tell him if you saw him?" she asks.

I slump further into the chair, pulling my hood up over my head. "I would tell him how fucking pissed he's making me. What kind of best friend just disappears on you like that, especially after revealing something as important as *loving* you?"

"Look at it from his point of view: you were with someone else."

"But I'm not with that person anymore."

"True. Maybe now he's afraid of your response." She steeples her fingers before her face. "Besides being angry, what would you say to him?"

"That I'm in love with him too." I sigh. "I blame all of this on you."

"Why?"

"Because you told me to open myself up to new experiences, and that's all I have been thinking about. I keep telling myself to just go back to my no-dating rule, but then I hear your voice, and Toby telling me he loves me, and I just *know* I can't go back to that rule. Not now, not when it involves him. The thought of us not being together makes me feel ill."

Doctor Hartland smiles slightly. "Then you should talk to him."

"I would love to, if the asshole would ever return my damn messages."

After leaving Doctor Hartland's office, I head to a coffee shop where I'm meeting Shelby. She has a box of random stuff I left at their apartment over the course of the last few months: a charger, a book, and a hoodie.

When I arrive at the shop, Shelby is sitting in the back corner, partially hidden by some plants. She's sipping a latte from a mug that's painted to look like the ocean. Her hair is up in a ponytail, and she's barely wearing any makeup. It's rare to see her like this. The box of my stuff rests by her feet.

"Hey," I say, sliding into the seat across from her.

Her face brightens a bit at seeing me. "Hi. I ordered you a tea, I hope that's okay."

"Thank you." I wring my hands nervously. The idea of Shelby being mad at me upsets me. "I'm sorry," I say.

She waves me off. "Honestly, I figured it would come to this."

"What do you mean?" I sip from the mug of tea before me. She's even ordered my favorite kind, oolong.

"You're in love with Toby. We all saw it." She pulls her hair out of her ponytail and fixes it. "It's kind of blaringly obvious."

Shame, guilt, and so many more negative emotions fog my brain. "Please, tell me you don't hate me. You and Abel have been friends for a long time. The last thing I wanted to do was hurt him."

"I know. We can't help the way we feel about people, so no, I don't hate you. I mean, yeah, it sucks seeing Abel getting hurt again. But you're my friend too. I'm not gonna ditch you just because you guys broke up. I don't know how the rest of the band will feel, but I'm still by your side." She sips her coffee again. "Oh, you might want to avoid Zack for a while. He's *livid*."

Zack and Abel are best friends; it makes sense he would be the angriest. Abel's told me that Zack is like a brother to him. They would literally go to the ends of the earth for each other.

"Guess I have to go back to avoiding A/AA again."

"Zack is quick to get fired up and quick to forgive. You'll be back in A/AA in no time."

Doubtful, but I don't say anything about it. "Thanks, Shelbs." As much as I like the other members of Poisonous Winter, losing them wouldn't gut me half as much as losing Shelby as a friend.

"What are you going to do about Toby?"

"I want to tell him how I feel, but I haven't seen him since the night of the dance."

"He's still avoiding you?"

"Seems like it."

"Do you want me to call him and pretend you got into some accident? I'm a really good actress."

"Of course your brain goes straight to the most dramatic scenario. If you see him, can you just tell him I'm looking for him?"

"Of course." She places a hand over mine on the table. "Promise me you're not beating yourself up over all this. You're not a shitty person, Jess."

"I feel like I am."

"One bad decision doesn't make you a bad person. You might have handled a very complicated situation poorly, but I don't even know what I would have done differently in your shoes. We're human, we make mistakes. You're so worried about how everyone else feels, remember to forgive yourself too."

"Thanks, Shelbs."

It'll take time, but hopefully one day I will get there.

Chapter 53

On Tuesday morning, I get a text from Toby to meet him at the duck pond before class.

"Shit," I say out loud to my empty dorm room. This is it. This could go either really fucking good or really fucking bad.

Why do movies never show how absolutely nerve-wracking it is to confess your feelings to someone else? People in movies always just decide it's time to say they love one another, and then in the next scene they're running through an airport. What about all the shit that comes before that? What about the equal parts feeling like you're going to throw up and feeling like you could take on John Cena in the ring? What about the tight pain in your chest and the fluttering in your stomach?

I feel mildly betrayed by all the rom-coms my mom and I watched over the years. This is my airport moment, and I'm fucking sick with nerves.

Don't overthink. I repeat what Shelby told me when we talked last night. *Just do.*

Breathe in.

Breathe out.

Sweating in places I didn't know exist, I open the door of my dorm room and step out into the hall.

I walk slowly to my favorite spot on campus. The morning breeze brings a chill to the air that stings my cheeks. Frost clings to the brown lawns, and people bustle to their early classes, looking groggy and carrying coffees.

Toby sits on a bench that faces the direction I'm coming from. He sits straighter when he sees me, but from this distance I can't tell if he's happy or not. He's wearing clothes that don't belong to him: a pair of brown pants and a burnt orange puffer jacket. They're probably Patrick's; they look like his style. Toby has on his signature black bucket hat, and for some reason, the sight of it makes me smile a little.

"Hey."

I sit on the bench next to him, balling my fists in the loose fabric of my gray sweats. The nerves are making my palms sweaty.

"Jay, I—"

"Can I talk first, please? I'm afraid that if I don't get this out now I'm going to burst."

He motions at me to go on. Where do I start? I look out across the pond, unable to look him in the eyes right now.

"I love you, T." I pause, trying to gather all my thoughts into something coherent to tell him how much he means to me. Since he's disappeared, nothing has been the same. I want to tell him that I dream about him every night, and every morning I look forward to seeing him sleeping across from me in his bed. But the only thing that comes out of my mouth is, "I'm in love with you. I have been for a long time."

"Jay."

Toby gently grips my chin, making me look at him. I've missed the hazel of his eyes and his citrusy smell. "I'm so sorry that I put distance between us and that I've been avoiding you. I'm so, *so* sorry." He crushes me to him, holding me in a hug that seems to glue the both of us back together. He holds me like that for a long time, with his face buried in my neck.

"I love you, Jay," he whispers in my ear before pulling back, but his arms stay around me. "I don't know exactly when I fell for you, but there it is. You are all I think about. Being away from you for so long has been hell on Earth."

"Promise me you won't do that again. You scared the shit out of me."

"I promise." He stares into me, and all I see is the affection he has for me in the depths of his eyes. I fall into them, getting lost. "Can I kiss you?"

"Yes, please."

We close the distance, breath mingling, noses brushing. I have no time to wonder if crossing this line with Toby will be strange. There's no time to process the fact that I am kissing my best friend. As soon as our lips meet, the world just aligns. I don't have to think or second-guess. There's only us and this kiss that feels so fucking *right*.

He tastes like coffee, and I push toward him, wanting to be closer to him, to taste him even more. I'm practically in his lap, and my body is vibrating from his touch. My fingers are pushed up under his hat, tangled in his dreads as I hold him to me, deepening this kiss that feels like the start of the rest of my life.

Chapter 54

Clouds are rolling in by the time Toby and I even think of moving from the bench. I'm freezing—probably not the ideal weather to be making out in—but I'm so fucking happy that it doesn't matter that my entire body has turned into a popsicle.

"My class was canceled, and you don't have class on Tuesdays, so what do you say to us staying in our dorm all day?" After being away from him for weeks, I need all the Toby time I can get.

"Sounds like a plan," he answers.

"I'm hungry." I pick up my head from where it's leaning on his shoulder. "I could go for pancakes with a shit ton of syrup."

He groans. "Same. Should we get breakfast before we commence our day of being potatoes?"

"Absolutely," I say around a yawn.

Toby reaches out, cupping my face in his hands and tracing his thumbs over the dark circles under my eyes.

"I haven't been sleeping well lately." Hoping that he would return, I have been staying up late into the night. After finally falling asleep, I toss and turn or my body jolts awake at the smallest noise.

"We'll take a nap after we eat, okay?"

Toby stands first, adjusting his bucket hat, which was knocked askew as we kissed. I admire the sharpness of his jaw, the slope of his nose, the way his mouth looks like it's moments away from bursting into a smile for no reason. His handsome face is awe-inspiring.

"What are you staring at?" he asks, smirk firmly in place.

I blush and glance away. It's too cringey to tell him that I think he's the most beautiful person in the world. It's better to just remain silent and maintain my reputation as my apathetic, sarcastic self, not the lovesick sap he's turned me into.

He shakes his head at me then holds out his hand. We intertwine our fingers as I stand. Together, we start walking toward the parking lot nearby, his hand wrapped tightly around mine as if he's afraid we're going to get separated. I couldn't bring myself to let go if I tried. His fingers are longer than mine, and there's a scar on the back of his hand from when he fell off his bike when he was eleven.

After a five-minute drive in Toby's car, we reach John and Sadie's 24-HR Breakfast Haven. The host leads us to a booth, and Toby slides in next to me. That little action reminds me that Toby and I are a *thing*. We're not just friends anymore; now we kiss and stuff. We're *boyfriends*.

Heat rises to my face and ears. *Is this a date? Is this our first date? I'm too exhausted! I don't want our first date to be when I'm tired and look like shit! It should be special!*

"Hey, Jay." Toby turns toward me in the booth, making me look at him. "Stop overthinking. Just order eggs and a coffee."

"I want pancakes."

Toby rolls his eyes. "Okay, then order pancakes."

"Is this our first date?"

He snorts. "Our first date is going to be a hell of a lot better than eating at a shitty diner."

I nod, satisfied.

The waiter comes, and I order coffee and the biggest stack of pancakes on the menu. Toby orders eggs, toast, and coffee.

After the waiter leaves, silence stretches between us. It's not awkward per se, I just don't do well with silence. It allows my mind to retreat into itself and wander.

How am I supposed to act with him now? Should I take his hand? What do we talk about now that we're dating?

"Stop overthinking. We're going to play a game so you don't work yourself into a panic attack."

"I hate that you know all my weird shit."

"Why do you think I fell for you? It was because of all your weird shit."

"And here I thought it was because I always let you win at video games."

"Hmm, that's reason number one."

I hit his shoulder. "What game are we playing?"

"Rock, paper, scissors. Best three out of five gets to pick where we go on our first date. The loser has to pay for the food today."

In the end, I lose, and Toby gloats over his victory even after our food comes. We eat while goofing around. I feel way better by the time I finish my coffee and pancakes.

After paying, I follow Toby outside. Now that there's no food to distract me, I keep yawning. All I want at this moment is my bed and a movie.

"Stop yawning!" he admonishes me as he yawns as well. "I haven't been sleeping very well either."

"You haven't?"

"I can't sleep without your snoring."

"Shut up! I do not snore!"

Toby howls with laughter.

I swear I hate him.

He wraps an arm around me as we head to his car. His mega-watt smile graces his face. Damn, how I have missed seeing it.

When we arrive back on campus, we walk hand in hand to our dorm, stopping just inside our room to stare at the two beds. We haven't discussed whether or not we're going to nap together. I want him to be in bed with me, but how do I ask? Instead, I go to the closet and pull out my *Game of Thrones* pajama pants. Behind me, Toby hangs up his jacket.

I head to the bathroom to wash my face and pee. When I return, Toby is in his own bed. Disheartened, I crawl into mine.

Though I have been sleeping alone since arriving at Westbrook—except when Amy's spent the night in our room or I stayed with Abel—the bed feels empty. Too empty. I hate it.

Time passes. I can't fall asleep.

"T?"

"Yeah?" He answers right away. It seems he can't sleep either.

"Can you—can you come over here?"

"Thank fuck," he whispers.

His bed squeaks as he shifts. Seconds later, my mattress dips as Toby crawls practically on top of me. The twin mattress is so small that by the time we settle, our limbs are so entangled it's nearly impossible to find where Toby ends and I begin. It's uncomfortable, but I'm so content that I don't dare move to find a more comfort-able position.

I fall asleep with a huge smile on my face and Toby's fingers playing with my hair.

Chapter 55

All that week, I attend class in a happy fog. Toby walks me to and from every building on campus when he can, never letting me leave without a swift kiss on my cheek. At night, we go to sleep in our own beds, but in the morning I wake up either snuggled with him under his covers or with him under mine.

"Jesse." My photography teacher's voice cuts through a happy daydream of Toby and my first date: he took me to a concert in Philly, and the night ended with kisses under the moonlight. The entire class stares at me as I snap out of the daydream.

My cheeks and ears heat with embarrassment. "Yeah?"

"Please stay after class for a few minutes," she says. Her voice is neutral, so I have no idea if what she has to discuss with me is good or bad. "The rest of you are dismissed for the day; take the extra fifteen minutes to study."

Everyone packs up and leaves. Wimbley sits on the desk in front of me. Her skirt gets caught on the chair, and she fiddles with it for a moment before looking at me.

"I'm sorry I wasn't able to let you rejoin the photography club."

"It's all right. Actually, my new classes are harder than the first semester, and I don't think I could keep up with my schoolwork plus the extra projects anyway."

She nods. "Understandable, but promise me you'll join next year. We need more kids like you in there."

SHADES OF US

"I promise. Is this what you wanted to talk to me about?"

"Not really. I entered your photos into the campus's Rising Star Showcase."

My brain short-circuits a bit. I just stare at Wimbley, and she stares right back, looking for some sort of reaction.

"I'm confused. I thought the showcase was only for sophomores and juniors."

"Usually, but you have such a good eye. Your photographs show so much emotion and intrigue, so I talked to the dean of the art department, and he's agreed to let you enter the showcase a year early if you'd like."

I still don't know what to say. "Why?" Honestly, I don't think my photos are *that* good.

Wimbley smiles. "You're talented, Jesse, and you should start showing that talent." She clears her throat. "You don't have to take part, but this is a great opportunity. A freshman has only entered twice before, and they have both gone on to do incredible things. You don't have to decide today, but please let me know by the end of class on Monday so I can give the dean a final answer."

"Um . . . okay." I'm still in disbelief and unable to form coherent sentences.

My parents, Toby, Alan . . . everyone around me has always told me that my photos are great, but never has an outsider—someone I truly respect, no less—told me that my photos are emotional and intriguing.

And to be the third freshman to ever take part in the showcase? I can hardly believe it! Gallery owners from all over the East Coast come to the showcase to pick out students' work to display and sell in their galleries; it's a community outreach program to bring fresh faces into the East Coast art scene. The showcase is a *huge* step forward in making a name for myself.

"I don't need to think about it. I want to do it."

"Great! I'll email you with the details later. Oh, this is so wonderful, Jesse!" She seems almost more excited than I am. Pride swells within me because she believes in my art enough to go out of her way to help get my photos seen.

"Thanks, Wimbley." I jump up and gather my backpack. "Thank you!"

Smiling wide, I run out of the classroom and hurry through the halls. I feel giddy, and I *need* to tell Toby about what's happened.

Thud!

I smack straight into a wall of solid chest and drop to the floor. When I hit the ground, I bite the inside of my mouth so hard it starts bleeding. Gentle hands scoop me up into a sitting position before I can come to my senses.

I'm so fucking embarrassed and wish I could pull my beanie over my eyes. Slowly, I look up: ripped jeans, studded jacket, long black hair. Abel. We haven't talked in weeks, and the first thing I do is run straight into him.

Awesome.

"Did you hurt yourself?" he asks.

"Only my pride." The outside of my cheek is tender, but I don't think there will be a bruise. The inside is starting to swell.

Abel pulls me to my feet. Now that we're both standing, everything is awkward again. Our breakup has caused a strain in our friend group—besides Shelby, I haven't seen much of the PW crew since the night of the dance. I miss our hangouts and having Abel as a friend.

"Where are you going in such a hurry?"

"To find Toby. I just got some great news, and I want to share it with him."

Abel's face shifts, shutting down. "Oh. Don't let me keep you. Bye."

He walks off before I can say anything. Despite wanting the air between us to be clear already, I let him go. I don't know what to say besides, "I'm sorry. Let's be friends." He's made it clear that he doesn't want that . . . at least not yet.

Not letting my run-in with Abel dampen my mood, I continue on my path to the science building where Toby is taking chemistry.

I arrive thirty minutes before his class lets out, so I sink to the floor in the hall outside the room, pulling out my earbuds and the book I'm supposed to be reading for my art history class. But it's so boring that I can't make it past the second chapter.

The next thirty minutes are spent staring blankly at the pages and humming along to my music. Finally, the class lets out. I don't pull my earbuds out but do look up as students begin to enter the hall. Toby comes out, walking backward and talking to two of his basketball buddies.

He's animated, hands flailing like they do when he talks about something that excites him. He's wearing my gray-and-black hoodie, and I am *very* enamored of that fact. Honestly, if he stole my entire wardrobe, I wouldn't be mad about it.

One of his friends nudges him and nods at me. Toby turns, his big smile getting wider when his eyes meet mine. I pull my earbuds out and stand.

"Sorry, guess I won't be eating lunch with you guys," he tells them.

"You're ditching us?"

"One hundred percent. My dude is picking me up, and I would rather eat lunch with him."

"We can eat lunch together," I reassure his friends. "I have something to tell Toby. I didn't mean to interrupt you."

"He was going to invite you anyway," James says.

"I really was."

James and Drew walk ahead of us as we head to the cafeteria. Toby and I walk hand in hand, and I'm trying very hard not to show how pleased I am with this situation. When will our newfound relationship stop being so novel to me? I get all stupid and happy at the dumbest things, like the way Toby rubs the back of my hand with his thumb. The feeling of it is starting to become an addiction.

"So, what's up?"

There's no suppressing my smile as I tell Toby about the showcase. He lets out a loud whoop that has everyone on the sidewalk looking at us.

"I'm so happy for you, Jay!" He leans over and kisses me. My smile grows to the point where it's starting to hurt my cheeks. "I'm so proud of you!"

"I want to tell the others, but they still hate me."

"Try reaching out. You won't know where you stand with the crew if you don't try. Text them and tell them that you have something to celebrate and you want to share it with them. I'm sure they'll still be happy for you, even if they are still mad."

I sigh heavily. "I hate when you sound so smart."

"You must hate me a lot then."

"Only seventy-five percent of the time," I say, and then I pull out my phone and enter the group chat with all our friends. No one has been active on it since the night Abel and I broke up.

I have some awesum news that I want 2 share!

Can ALL of you meet me @ Aldo's @ 6?

I intentionally emphasize all so Abel knows that he is included too.

"God, your spelling," Toby complains when his phone beeps with the incoming message. "Can't you text like a normal person?"

"Texting was made for shorthand, and not all of us use proper grammar and correct spelling like you."

"You should. I spend hours deciphering your texts."

"That's bullshit—you always reply within ten minutes."

Toby laughs and ruffles my hair. "Whatever. I find your texts charming, even if the English major part of my brain wants to correct them."

"The things we do for love."

My phone dings with replies from the crew.

Shelbs: DUH! I'll be there!

Ames: Are u buying?

Zack: I'll go if Abe goes.

Sebastian: M & I will def be there

Abel: Maybe.

The "maybe" causes a knot to form in my throat, but at least it isn't a flat-out no.

Chapter 56

Abel and Zack didn't show up to my celebration at Aldo's. Part of me is still disappointed when I wake the next day, but I'm not surprised. It's going to take time, but the longer we go without talking, the more I overthink. I even texted him last night after coming back from dinner.

I kno what I did was fkd up.

I'm so sry.

I hope one day U can forgive me + We can B frens again

He didn't reply, and I didn't really expect him to.

Of course, Toby reassures me that I just need to give Abel his space and not freak out so much, which is easier said than done.

"All right, that's it, Jay." Toby lies across my legs reading while I scroll through social media, but somehow, even though I'm trying my best to keep my expression neutral, he knows I'm worrying about Abel again. "We're going out." He sits up and gently smacks my leg. "Go get dressed."

I make a face at him. "You're very bossy."

"You want free ice cream or not?"

SHADES OF US

"I never said I wasn't going to do what you said." I stick my tongue out at him. "I just said you're bossy."

We get dressed quickly and head out to Toby's car. Besides getting ice cream, he doesn't tell me where else we are going. Despite hating surprises, I am actually at ease with letting Toby take the reins. I guess that goes to show how much I trust him or something.

>> <<

"Should I invite Kelly to come to the showcase?" I ask him as we head to the car after spending hours in the bookstore. Toby bought three bagsful of paperbacks. I think reading helps him regulate the same way music helps me.

He looks at me as he pulls out of the parking lot. "Do you want to invite her?"

"Yeah. I think . . . I think I want to try to have some sort of relationship with her."

"Then I think it's a good idea."

I pull out my phone and text Kelly. She replies quickly, saying she would love to come. Toby reaches over and squeezes my knee in a gentle, reassuring way as I read him the messages.

A feeling of contentment washes over me, like everything is *finally* starting to settle into place and I can breathe again.

After stopping at a gas station to grab drinks, my promised ice cream, and a bag of chips, Toby drives us out of town to the woods where we spent Halloween night roasting marshmallows with our friends. He somehow finds the exact same spot as that night. We hop out, and I finish my ice cream before we head down to the water. We stop at the edge of the small lake, and I lean into his side, wrapping my hands around the crook of his elbow.

"This is where I first realized I was attracted to you," he says.

My jaw drops. "Excuse me?"

"You heard what I said."

"That was Halloween. You were with Madison."

He turns to me and places his hands on the sides of my face. His hazel eyes never leave mine. "I don't know exactly when I started to see you like that . . . like this . . . but it was before that. Then that night, the realization hit me that I thought about you more than I should for someone whom I only considered a friend."

"Can I ask you something?" I take his hands from my face and hold them between us. He looks worried but nods, telling me to continue. "If Madison hadn't cheated on you, would we have ever gotten a chance to be together?"

He shrugs. "I don't know. Madison and I had our problems, but I loved her. We probably would have broken up over something else, but I didn't plan on breaking up with her." He pauses. "If Madison hadn't cheated on me, she would've had to break up with me, because I don't think I would have even with all our problems."

It hurts knowing that there could be a timeline where Toby and I might not have ended up together.

Toby nudges me a little. "Don't worry, Jay. Everything worked out the way it was supposed to. I've never been one to believe in fate or destiny or whatever, but I think we were meant to meet."

"I think so too."

Abel said it seems like there's a string between Toby and me that ties us together. He's right; the connection between us is magnetic. He's the sun with his own gravitational pull, and I'm caught in his orbit.

Even if Toby and I weren't fated to date, I'm still so glad I met him. He is my best friend, and that friendship—the trust I have with him, the way his love and the friendship of the PW crew has helped heal some of the damaged parts of my soul—means more to me than anything else in this world.

"I love you."

The words aren't just romantic when I say them now. They encompass how grateful I am for him, for his strength and his friendship, for being a great partner, and for being my sunshine when my brain gets too cloudy. They mean I love him platonically, romantically, and everything in between. I love him on every level that it's possible to love someone.

"I love you too, Jay."

His arms surround me, and he pulls me closer, kissing me deeply. Everything we have yet to say is in this kiss. I want give him everything I am and everything I have yet to become.

"Let's go back to the car," I whisper, tugging up the hem of his shirt, letting him feel exactly what I mean by this statement.

"Are you sure?" he asks. It's endearing, and the tentativeness in his voice just makes me want to prove to him how *sure* I am.

I pull him along after me and open the back door to his car. He slides in after me, and I kiss him again. This time it's rough, urgent, and filled with the need to touch him, to bring him pleasure.

"Shirt off," I half growl, half whisper.

"Now who's being bossy?" he says even as he begins wiggling out of his long-sleeved shirt.

I ignore his comment and bend my head over his nipple and lick. He grunts out an, "Oh, shit," as his fingers tangle in my hair.

Moving my way down his chest and abs, I explore the contours of his body with my teeth and tongue. He arches up into me.

"Jay."

A devilish grin curls on my lips when I reach the waistband of his jeans. "How quick do you think I can get these off you?"

"I don't have a timer. Just do it."

I begin undoing his zipper and pull his pants and boxers down to his knees.

Chapter 57

On the Sunday morning before the start of spring break, I wake up with huge bags under my eyes, feeling very, *very* exhausted. I'm tangled in Toby's limbs when my alarm goes off, but I have already been awake for over an hour. Toby somehow manages to sleep through the alarm. I'm so glad he was able to sleep like a baby; meanwhile, my anxiety kept me up for most of the night.

He finally wakes after the alarm goes off again ten minutes later. He smiles up at me with a sleepy, blurry expression. "You look like shit."

I snort and push one of the dreads out of his face. "Thank you so much. Get up. I need coffee if I'm going to survive this day."

"No. Can't we just skip the whole thing and play naked charades?" He wiggles his eyebrows. "I lose an article of clothing for every one I get wrong."

"You would try to lose on purpose." I laugh. "Where the hell do you even come up with these games?"

The night before, he had me playing a game where I was blindfolded, trying to find sticky notes he had stuck to his body. Sometimes I feel bad that Toby and I will never have sex in the traditional sense of the word, but he assures me that he doesn't need it. Apparently, he likes the challenge of finding other ways we can be intimate.

"They just come to me. It's a gift."

He rolls out of bed and heads to the bathroom. The shower starts a few seconds later, and I have half a mind to join him but decide against it. I don't want to be late, and Toby can be *very* distracting.

Instead, I pick up my phone and scroll through my socials while I wait for him to be done. Everyone—even people I haven't talked to since middle school—has commented on my nana's post, congratulating me for being entered into the showcase. It's embarrassing how much Nana has posted about the show since I told her the news. In the future, I need to ask her to keep her bragging to a minimum.

I groan when someone knocks on the door and start searching around for a pair of shorts. When I open the door, Nana is on the other side. It's eight in the morning, and she's already bright-eyed, bushy-tailed, and all made up.

"Jess-bug!"

"Nana, what are you doing here? I thought you weren't coming until later."

She frowns in a nonserious way. "Are you trying to kick me out?" She pushes past me and enters our dorm. "It's way too dark in here." Before I can protest, the curtains are flung open, and sunlight assaults my eyeballs. "Get dressed, Jess-bug. I want a tour of the campus."

I look down at my naked torso. "I still have to shower."

Nana clucks at me. "Still not fond of those."

She means my nipple rings. I got them when I was seventeen, and she hates them the most out of all my piercings.

"I like them."

"Where is Toby? I brought him some cookies."

"Did you bring me cookies?"

"Absolutely not." She produces two containers from the oversized bag she calls a purse. "Don't eat them all at once."

Toby emerges, dressed in shorts and a T-shirt. They're dirty and defeat the purpose of a shower, but still thank God. Usually he comes out in just a towel—sometimes fully naked—and Nana doesn't need to be seeing all that.

"Nana!" he greets her, kissing her cheek. "I thought I heard you."

"The whole campus can hear her," I chime in.

Nana tuts at me again. "Go take a shower."

Leaving Nana and Toby alone together makes me nervous. Sure, they were alone when Toby came with me to Nana's condo, but that was before we started dating. The stakes are different now. Nana could tell him all about when I was four and ran around the house naked, or that time I fell off a horse when I was seven and screamed that I broke my ass.

When I come out of the shower, Toby is showing Nana how to add to her Instagram stories.

"Don't make her better at social media, you're only giving her more power."

Toby laughs. "Now she can brag about you in live videos."

Nana looks like a kid who has just discovered a new favorite candy. "Oh, this is going to change everything."

"Toby, what have you done?"

"I just want her to like me."

After we give Nana a tour of campus, it's time for the Rising Star Showcase. I get even more nervous as we walk to the art building—the coffee and yogurt I had for breakfast are not sitting right in my stomach.

"I'm going to puke," I inform Toby and Nana.

Toby squeezes my hand. "You're going to be fine."

"Oh, I'm so proud of you, Jess-bug!"

The school's gallery has been taken over by displays of student artwork—everything from sculptures to paintings to photographs. My classmates are talented—more talented than I am. My pictures don't belong next to Donna Herkamen's collages and Roy Bell's paintings. They deserve this so much more than I do.

We find the five photos of mine that have been submitted: one of my parents, one of Shelby, and three of objects and people around the city that I was inspired by. Shelby and the others are gathered around my photos. They clap when they see me, causing people nearby to turn their heads. My ears burn with embarrassment.

Titus got sick, so Kelly and her family couldn't make it. I understand, but I really wanted her to see my work. It's stupid, but I have this weird desire for her to be proud of me. She said that she's planning to visit Plainsburg over the summer if I am okay with that. We made plans to meet in July.

"Here he is," Amy says loudly as I approach, "our artist!"

"Shh!" I run the last few steps and clamp a hand over their mouth.

"Congratulations," Abel says. I'm surprised he even came since things are still uneasy between us.

"Thanks."

He nods and heads toward the snack table, taking Zack along with him.

"Don't worry," Shelby says. "He's forgiven you."

SHADES OF US

I nod once. Hopefully, our friendship will mend itself in its own time.

I spend the next two hours circling the gallery again and again, pausing by my pictures to see if anyone is still looking at them. When I stop there for the umpteenth time, there is a woman standing before them. She's studying them with a critical eye, and I don't know why or how, but I just know that it's important for me to introduce myself to her.

"Hello?" My voice shakes with uncertainty.

She turns to me, adjusting her glasses. "You're the artist, right?"

"Jesse Lancaster." I stick out my hand, wishing it weren't so sweaty.

"Natalie Lewis. Barbara told me all about you, her promising freshman student."

"Barbara?"

"Right, I forgot she has you all call her Wimbley." She smiles at someone over my shoulder. "Speak of the devil. Barb!"

Behind me, Wimbley walks toward us with two glasses of watered-down punch from the snack table in her hands. "I'm so glad the two of you met. Nat, this is who I was talking about."

I'm very confused, but Wimbley is still talking, so I don't interrupt.

"Natalie is the owner of Marigold Studios over on 4th Street. She runs a mentorship over the summer for one lucky student, and I may have mentioned your name once or twice at dinner."

Holy shit!

Natalie smiles at me. "Barb has referred quite a few students to me since I opened my studio, but she seems to be most excited about your work." She turns back to my pictures. "I can see why. You have a very keen eye."

285

"Th-thank you."

"No final decisions have been made, but I'll be adding your name to the list, Jesse Lancaster."

"It's an honor just to be considered."

I chat with Natalie and Wimbley for a few minutes longer before they leave to go and look at other artwork.

As soon as I turn to look for Toby to tell him about the surreal experience that just transpired, I see him walking toward me.

"I saw what happened," he said. "I'm so proud of you, Jay."

His words of praise fill my heart to the brim—I'm actually afraid it might burst out of my chest.

"Come on," I say, dragging him toward the snack table. "Now that the nerves are gone, I'm fucking starving."

Chapter 58

"Our friends aren't as sneaky as they think they are," Amy says.

A few days after the showcase, I'm driving them in their car to a surprise birthday party our friends have planned for us. Our birthdays are only a few days apart; I'm March twelfth, and Amy's March sixteenth. We aren't supposed to know about the party, but I accidentally saw an email from the restaurant on Toby's phone confirming their reservation for the party room, and Amy spotted Shelby coming out of the bakery this morning with a huge cake box.

"We have to at least pretend to be surprised or Shelby will skin us alive."

"I've never been that great at acting."

"You're in the drama club," I remind them.

"Honestly, I just joined that for the hot guy who was recruiting members."

I pull into the parking lot of the pizza place, turn off my car, and turn to them. "Let me see your surprised face."

They pull an over-the-top expression that causes me to wince.

"Yikes. It might be better if you don't react at all."

"Rude!" They hit my arm.

We exit her car and head inside. Toby waits at the entrance with a goofy I'm-up-to-something grin. He takes our hands and leads us back to the party room.

"Surprise!" rings out as soon as he opens the door.

"Oh my gosh!" Amy says, robotically and yet overzealously. "Wow!"

Shelby is on them as soon as the words leave their mouth. She crosses the room and stands before Amy, a huge pout on her face. "You already knew!"

"Sorry, Shelbs."

"Whatever. Last time I plan a party for you!" Shelby plops down in a chair to pout.

"Did you know too?" Toby asks.

"Should I lie and say no?" I hug him, pecking his lips. "Sorry, T. I saw the email about reserving this room last week."

"Well, shit. I thought I was gonna get extra boyfriend points."

"Nope. You know I hate surprises."

"I wanted to throw a party for you and Amy since your birthdays are so close together, but you know Shelby, she had to make it a surprise."

"You meant for him to find that email!" Shelby cries, poking Toby in the chest. "Traitor."

He leans over and kisses her cheek, which seems to calm her a little.

The pizza arrives quickly. When it does, Shelby decides it's time to open presents. I get a new headset from Mahara and Sebastian. Shelby gives me a voucher for one day of us doing whatever I want, with the stipulation that she can't hijack the day or complain. Abel is second to last. He gives me a card about friendship and a gift card to a game store in town. It's more than I thought I was going to receive from him, so it makes me happy. Zack doesn't get me anything. I didn't expect him to. Pretty sure he's never going to forgive me for breaking his best friend's heart.

Unsure why, I pay attention when Abel hands Amy their gift. They unwrap it and let out a squeal. He has given them an album by one of their favorite K-pop groups, Shinee. I don't feel jealous that they got something personal while I got a card and a fifteen-dollar gift card, but I'm aware of it in a way I haven't been with the other presents Amy's received. It feels like it means something, but I don't what exactly.

Last up is Toby.

As Amy tears into their new album to see what photo card they got, I focus fully on Toby. He's smiling shyly and looks absolutely adorable in his nervousness.

"This is probably stupid," he says as he thrusts a small gray box at me. "I know you love pins, so I got these made specially for you."

I open the box to find two pins. One is a small black heart that's been broken. White stitches run through it, and it has the letter T next to it. The other is a purple heart with a bandage, and on the bandage is the letter J.

"T." Tears begin to well as I take out the black heart and fix it to my beanie. "How does it look?"

"Perfect. You tell me all the time that I heal you—"

"You do. Every single day."

He smiles at me softly. "I want you to know that you heal me too. I love you, Jay."

I kiss him like there's no tomorrow, and I feel like I can't breathe.

Which is ironic in a way, because now that I have Toby, I can actually, *finally* breathe again. The static in my brain is the quietest it has been since my parents died. Being with him is like opening all the windows on a rainy day and curling up to play video games. He comforts and relaxes me. I would never tell him this out loud, but this guy is my home. He is my everything.

I don't know if Toby and I will last forever. I don't know if we're going to get married someday, maybe adopt some kids and buy a house, but right now what we have is cosmic, light and content. It's beautiful and everything I could have ever hoped for. Right now, I love him more than anything, and I hope that love lasts a very, *very* long time.

Acknowledgments

Shades of Us started as inspiration from a song. Without the people who helped get the story where it is today, I would have been non-stop yelling into the void about the PW crew.

To Bob, who has had to listen to me talk to myself in our office since day one. I heart you.

A big thanks goes to the Wattpad readers who read this book when it was still titled *Everything Is Just Fine*. The comments left on there about Jesse and the crew made me smile every time I got one.

Thank you to Jesse, who appeared out of nowhere while listening to "Breathe Me" and spoke to the inner teenager in me who struggled to find their identity within the LGBTQIA+ community.

Next up, the Wattpad editorial team. *Shades of Us* would not be what it is without you all. You have my endless gratitude for shaping this book into its final boss form.

Lastly, thank you to the reader who took a chance on an unknown author and a book about a lonely misfit who just wants to be loved. I hope you adore Jesse as much as I do.

About the Author

D. L. found their passion for writing in eighth-grade English. Since then, they have dabbled in poetry, short stories, and writing novels. When D.L. isn't writing, they can be found browsing antique stores and oddities conventions or listening to their favorite songs on a loop. D.L. believes in magic, kindness, and happily ever after. *Shades of Us* is their first novel. D.L. lives and works in Albuquerque, NM.

Printed in the United States
by Baker & Taylor Publisher Services